The Believers

The Breeders Series: Book Two

KATIE FRENCH

Copyright

Dedication

To my children – Dream big, my darlings.

PREVIOUSLY ON THE BREEDERS

New Mexico. Year 2092. Male to female ratio: 9 to 1.

Sixteen-year-old Riley Meemick is in hiding. Girls of reproductive age are worth a lifetime's wages to the Breeders: the group of doctors using cruel experiments to bolster the dwindling human race. The Breeders control everything: the local warlords, the remaining factories, and the fuel. They have unchecked power in this lawless society and they're hunting for girls.

When her stepfather, Arn, never returns from a trip to town, their existence falters. Knowing she's his only chance at survival, Riley disguises herself as a boy and drives headlong into her worst nightmare. In town she finds Arn in lock-up on a false allegation of stealing. Clay, the Sheriff's number one man, arrives and forces the warden to release Riley and Arn. Yet, that night the Sheriff's men attack their homestead. When daylight comes and the dust settles, she finds Arn dead and her mother and auntie gone.

Alone and starving, things look bleak for Ethan and Riley until peace offerings appear: food from Clay. When Ethan is bitten by a coyote, only Clay can get the supplies to save him. Riley lets him in and realizes he knows where they're keeping Auntie and her mother. Hoping she can still keep her gender from him, she talks Clay into taking them back to town.

Back in town, Clay and Riley find her mother is gone, sold to the Breeders. Auntie charges her with finding her mother before the Breeders can run their terrible experiments. On the journey they are waylaid by Clay's friend Bennett, who drugs them and tries to sell them to savage natives known as the Riders. After a shootout that leaves their enemies dead, they make their way to an abandoned town. There, they find a lunatic gunman who attacks and shoots Riley.

Riley wakes in the Breeder's hospital, strapped to a bed. It appears Clay has sold her when he found out she was female. She's irate, but vows to find her mother. Betsy, the very strange and very pregnant tour guide, tells her that her mother was trapped here, but either escaped or was killed. Now Riley knows she must get out and fast. Her escape attempt leads her to the Breeder's most horrific experiment, a room full unconscious pregnant women used as human incubators. She is horrified to learn her mother is one of them. When she gets in a scuffle with a guard, they sentence her to the same fate. Just when she thinks she'll be a vegetable, Clay shows up with his father and Ethan in tow, to barter for her release.

Still suspicious of Clay, she rides with them to an abandoned house for the night. Riley tells Clay he must help her save her mother. Clay disagrees, arguing there's no way to break into the highly guarded hospital. She and Ethan go alone.

Ethan and Riley arrive at the hospital where a trap is set. Clay's mother, Dr. Nessa Vandewater, uses Riley as bait to draw her son back to the hospital so she can reconnect. Clay follows and Nessa gives him an ultimatum: stay with her and she'll allow Riley, Ethan and her mother to live. Clay refuses, knowing the deal is sour. He fights his father, the Sheriff, killing him. The final gun battle ensues. Clay dives into the fray, hoping to save Riley and her family. Riley, realizing her love for Clay, helps him fight off the guards. In the battle, they both are wounded, but they make it to the van alive.

Holed up at an abandoned church, Clay and Riley finally confess their feelings. Reunited as a group, they head back into the lawless frontier to save Auntie.

CHAPTER ONE

Five of us duck behind a boulder scorched by the day's heat as the approaching car's headlights pierce the night.

"Get down," Clay whispers, drawing up his revolver. The steeliness of his voice sends gooseflesh galloping over my arms.

I curl up, my knees tucked into my chest, my back dug into the boulder's hard surface. Beside me, Ethan scrunches down until he's a little bit of a thing, a wiry jackrabbit of a kid with his bony arms around his knees. When I lay my hand on his shoulder, he's trembling. Mama crouches on the other side of him, one hand wrapped around her pregnant belly, the other on Ethan's arm. Even though we've cropped her hair short and she wears men's clothing, it'll be easy to tell she's a woman. No man has a stomach that round unless he's got a belly full of tapeworm.

Rayburn, the Breeders' doctor who helped us escape, sits beside her, clutching one of Clay's revolvers to his chest. I roll my eyes. A gun in Rayburn's fist is like a handsaw in the hands of a toddler: just as useless as it is dangerous. I heft the rifle. The warm stock fits snugly in my palm like it was made for me. I'm a decent shot, even in the dark, but I've got five shells left—maybe. Five precious shells. I try not to think about what will happen when the bullets are gone.

Clay shifts beside me, his thigh brushing against mine. I know this low crouch hurts his wounded leg. All night he's walked beside me without complaint, but he's getting weaker. The speckle of sweat on his brow is unmistakable no matter how many times he wipes it away when he thinks I got my eyes on the horizon. He hasn't had time to heal, but how could he? We've been driving and starving for days. Then our truck ran out of gas yesterday. We knew it would happen. It didn't make it any less of a punch in the gut when it did.

The sound of a car motor reaches us, a wheezy, choking sound. Whatever approaches is not some new, souped-up Breeders' vehicle, but that doesn't mean they're friendly. Everyone on this road is our enemy the way I figure.

The chugging motor draws closer, the ground vibrating in anticipation. I press my back to the rock and look up at the sky, trying to slow the patter of my heart. I recognize a constellation amongst the splattered stars, but I can't remember the name. Cassiopeia? Andromeda? Six pinpricks of light in the shape of a W. My step-daddy, Arn, used to teach me stars' names, pointing with his calloused fingers, drawing lines to connect them. Now Arn's a few months dead and my memories of him are fading. I look away and push the sadness down deep.

Then the car is upon us, headlights streaking everything into long, black shadows. We all crouch together and wait. Breathe. Pray. The car rumbles past, tires bumping down the pitted road. One red taillight glows as they continue along their way. I blow out a breath and wonder where they're headed. Hopefully to a town not far from here. We need food and a car if we're ever going to get back to Auntie.

A hand on my chest draws me out of my thoughts. Clay's tensed arm presses me back to the boulder. I open my mouth to protest, but then I hear it. The squeal of brakes. The slam of doors. They've stopped. They're getting out.

Mama's hand tightens around my arm. Rayburn looks at me through his greasy black curls, fear etched on every feature. He pushes up his glasses, the revolver wobbling in his hand. In the moonlight, I find Clay's face. Beneath his cowboy hat, his brow is folded, his lips a tight line. He's calculating. How many shots to take them out? What angle? I can see the discharge of his gun in my mind's eye. Hopefully it won't come to that. We can't waste bullets.

Footsteps head our direction, boots scraping the pavement, slow and steady. Two sets. Two men. Each step toward us makes my heart lurch. With my back to the boulder, I can't see them and it's making me crazy. There's only one reason they'd have stopped: they spotted us.

I shift and Clay's hand tightens. "Stay down," he breathes in my ear. Then he stands.

What in God's name is he doing? I reach for him, my heart slamming in my chest. Is he trying to get himself killed?

"Ho there," he shouts. He levels his revolver. "That's close enough."

I rise up ever so slightly and peer over the boulder.

Two men stand in the middle of the busted two-lane highway.

2

The first is tall and skinny with a wide-brimmed hat and a shaggy beard. His bug-eyes and long neck make him look like a lizard in a trench coat. I can't make out the rest of his features, but his clothes are worn and holey. Maybe he's a rancher or a lower-class road gang member. The man beside him is a little better dressed in patched jeans and a sleeveless leather jacket. His head is bare and the moon reflects off the bald surface. He's wearing cracked glasses that make him look owl-like.

"Whoa, friend," owl man says, holding up his hands in a gesture of surrender. He's missing both pinkies. "That's quite a pistola you've got there. Give 'er a rest. We come in peace."

Clay shakes his head, his aim never wavering. "Ain't nobody come in peace these days. Turn round and get back in yer dirt wagon."

Lizard man chuckles behind his scraggly beard, his neck bobbing back and forth. He pushes back his hat and narrows his bug-eyes. "Well, now," he drawls slowly, "that ain't too neighborly. We jist stepped out to take a piss. We ain't got guns."

"You ain't got guns *showing*," Clay says. "Doesn't mean you ain't got guns. You can take a piss a couple miles down. Now get back in yer car or I'll stop asking nice." He thumbs down the safety with a click that cuts through the desert.

The two men stand stock-still, hands at their sides. Lizard man tilts his head slightly, considering Clay. "Ain't nobody had bullets in these parts for months. What you so worried about us seeing behind that boulder?" He narrows his eyes and takes a step forward. "I know you ain't alone." A smile curls on his mouth, slow and nasty.

Clay's jaw hardens. "I asked you nicely." He takes a step forward, aiming. "This is how I ask now."

The gun fires. The shot cracks through the night like a bomb. Mama gasps. The gunpowder spark lights up Clay's face: his eyes squinted, his jaw granite. Lizard man whirls sideways, left arm out like a sail. A spray of blood wets his partner's shirt. Lizard man staggers twice and falls to his knees, facing his friend. Bent over and clutching his wound, lizard man stares.

Then he starts howling.

"Clay," I whisper. Will he shoot them both? We need every bullet in that gun. He says nothing, just keeps aiming.

3

Lizard man half-runs, half-staggers back to the car. Blood plops on the pavement with a heavy, wet sound. His partner pushes up his round, blood-splattered glasses, fear crinkling his face. "You didn't havta!" he shouts as he turns to run. "You didn't havta shoot 'im."

Clay narrows his eyes, still aiming. "I don't havta shoot you either."

Owl man lets out a little squeal as he runs back to the car jumps into the driver side. The car engine chugs to life and they peal out in a spray of gravel. When the taillight is a little red dot in the distance, Clay slumps down beside me.

I place my hand on his arm, smiling, but once I see his face my smile fades. Sweat sprinkles his forehead and rolls down his neck. His face is pale, yet his cheeks blaze red. The revolver clatters to the dust as his arm sags against the boulder. The calm gunslinger act has cost him.

Leaning over to him, I wipe the sweat off his brow with my sleeve. "Clay," I whisper, "you did it. You scared 'em off." I press my hand to his cheek tenderly. I hate seeing him like this.

His hand cups mine, his sky-blue eyes shining in the moonlight. There's no smile on his face. "This time." Slowly, he reaches for his revolver and flicks out the chamber. Five bullets rest in their cylindrical beds. He frowns and snaps the barrel back with an awful click. Rayburn's revolver has six shells and I have five. I know what he's thinking. What happens when we run out of bullets? What happens to us?

My mama stands, drawing my eight-year-old brother, Ethan, up with her. Her cotton T-shirt flutters against the swell of her newly pregnant belly. "Can you walk?" she asks Clay softly. He nods, pushing up, hiding a wince of pain behind a small quirk of his mouth. As I help him stand and take a sip of water from our canteen, a chilly wind stirs. Clay's body shivers. Then he throws his arm around me and shuffles forward.

We walk on the shoulder of the road. North, toward home and whatever awaits.

CHAPTER TWO

In the moonlight Rayburn and Clay crouch over two pieces of road map laid out on a boulder and squint at the jagged lines carving up the paper.

"Our approximate location puts us, uh, right about here." Rayburn presses his index finger into a dimple on the map. Then he looks up, pushing his glasses up the bridge of his nose. "I think."

"How d'you know that?" Clay's eyes narrow as he flicks a glance at Rayburn. "And how we know you on the straight and narrow now and not leadin' us right back in Breeders' territory?" Clay's hand floats slowly toward the revolver at his hip.

Rayburn blanches, his pale face growing paler. "I, uh, I, uh…" His pimpled jowls jiggle as he watches Clay's hand near the pistol.

I step in. "He saved us, 'member? He saved *you*." I put my hand on Rayburn's hunched shoulder and he flinches at my touch. "Ray stitched you up. If it weren't for him, you wouldn't be walking."

Clay frowns. "I ain't walkin' so good." The distrust seems to fade as he mulls over what I said. He leans over the map again. "Where you say we was?"

Rayburn, swallowing hard, peers over the moonlit highway. The blacktop carves through the desert like a hard black line, marred here and there by missing pavement or a burnt-out car husk. He points at the road, his chubby face scrunched up. "This road runs north and south."

"I know that," Clay says, jabbing a finger at the North Star.

Rayburn nods, blinking hard. "Yes, well, we're heading, uh, north and we've walked approximately ten miles, so that puts us here." He pokes a finger into the folds of the map and the paper crinkles softly.

Clay pushes back his Stetson and peers down, frowning.

I know a pissing contest when I see one, so I stand up and brush the dust off my knees. Clay looks up at me. "Where you off to?" His frown fades as he gazes at me and the corners of his mouth lift slightly.

"You two don't need me to fight about where we're headed. We all know we head north 'til we find a town. No map needed for that." Both men frown at me. I sigh and gesture down the ridge. "I'll see about Mama and Ethan."

Clay nods, his good hand sliding up to stroke my calf. One gentle caress and he's back to arguing with Rayburn about the map.

I think about what where we've come from and where we're headed. With the Sheriff dead, there's no telling what happened to Auntie as his housekeeper. Clay's hell-bent on claiming his rightful place as leader of his pa's town, but all I want to do is get my family together under one roof. That and somehow keep Nessa Vandewater off our trail.

I walk down the little dirt incline to where Mama and Ethan sit side by side, their packs behind them to prop them up. Ethan's head rests on Mama's shoulder, her arm slung behind him. I sit across from them, draping my arms over my knees.

Mama smiles at me and runs a hand through her short dark hair. "Take a load off, honey lamb." She pats her lap. "You wanna rest your head?"

"Nah, thanks." I lift one of our plastic water jugs from where it rests against her pack. It feels dangerously light as it sloshes against my hand. I bite my lip and put it down. My throat is starting to feel like the desert floor, but I can hold out a little while longer.

When I set the jug down, I get a glimpse of Mama's bare feet peeking from under her pants. "Oh God, Mama!" I point at the open sores, red and weeping, where her shoes have rubbed the skin away. "Why didn't you say something?"

She shrugs, looking down at her destroyed feet. The skin on one heel looks like raw meat. She touches it gently with a finger. "Nothing to be done. Rayburn has some cream he said he'd give me when he gets done frettin' over that map." The burned half of her face lifts slightly, the rutted skin rippling like a wrinkled bed shirt.

"We coulda stopped," I say, digging in Rayburn's pack. I find the tin of cream, lift her right foot into my lap, and start applying. "I forget that you ain't been walking much."

She nods, but says nothing. Her right hand strays to the Breeder's ankh, the cross with the oval head branded on the inside of her wrist. Her thumb rubs the raised flesh and her face darkens.

Images flash through my mind before I can stop them: a hospital bed with wrist restraints, a red-haired guard sliding his fingers up my leg, Betsy's ringlet curls bouncing from side to side as she fixes me with her sad, puppy-dog look. Betsy. Picturing her face is another punch in the stomach. Did the Breeders kill her? Did they put her under and take her to the plan B room because she helped me? I shiver.

"Cold?" Mama asks, studying my face. She purses her chapped lips.

"Yeah." I shift my eyes to the moon and try, try, *try* not to think about the Breeders.

I finish her right foot and reach for her left. Ethan stirs and blinks at me through his dark bangs. "I'm hungry, Riley. What we got to eat?"

I hate this question. *Not much* always seems to be the answer. I shrug and try to think of something light to say. "Rayburn baked a sugar rum cake, but he's letting it cool on the window sill." I lift my eyes to my little brother. "I think Clay's got some ice cream under his Stetson, too."

"Shut up," Ethan says tiredly. Then his mouth quirks. "I got some chocolate in my pocket. Wanna see?"

I lean forward and muss his hair. "Don't even joke about chocolate less you really got some. I might get so crazy I eat you up instead." I lean forward, grabbing for him, my teeth gnashing wildly.

He pulls back, squealing. The broad smile on his face warms my heart.

I go back to doctoring Mama's feet. The joking helps lighten the mood, but doesn't fix how skinny Ethan is. The shirt Clay found him hangs so loose it's like a skeleton's wearing it. I dig a hunk of jerky out of the pack and toss it to him. He snatches the meat, frowns, and then sets to gnawing.

Rayburn and Clay shuffle over the ridge. Rayburn points at one half of the map and holds it out to Clay. Clay pushes it away, his face stern. When he turns to say something to Rayburn, he tumbles down in the dust, his legs folding under him, his bandaged hand out to brace himself. When he hits the ground, he cries out in pain.

"Clay!" I jump up and run to him. His jeans are covered with dust and there's a red spot blooming through the fabric on his thigh where I know his bullet wound to be. "You're bleeding."

He pushes my hand away. "I'm fine." Sweat glistens on his forehead and his face is white.

"Rayburn!" I say, feeling a nervous flutter in my chest. I point at Clay's leg. "He's bleeding."

Rayburn kneels down. "We, uh, we need to get your pants off."

Clay smirks. "Rayburn, you know you ain't my type." He waves a dismissive hand. "Leave me alone." He turns his gaze away, the pain tightening his features.

I shake my head, touching his leg delicately. Blood seeps through his pants. "Come on," I say, holding out my hand. "We gotta get your pants off. He's a doctor."

Clay frowns at my hand, but finally takes it. Throwing his arm over my shoulder, we limp to a clump of cacti, Rayburn following behind. Clay gives me a pained look and drops his jeans. Heat flares into my cheeks as my eyes stray past his blue boxer shorts. Then I see his leg and all heat drains out of me. The bullet wound Rayburn so carefully stitched back in the church has busted open.

Rayburn shuffles over and squints at the wound. "It isn't, uh, isn't healing." He looks up at me and then at Clay. "It'll get infected if it doesn't close up."

Infection out here means death. I grip Rayburn's arm hard. "What do we do?"

Rayburn runs a hand through his black curls. "I could suture it, but it'll only open up again. If he stayed off his leg for a week or so—"

"Not a chance on yer life," Clay says, palming sweat off his forehead.

Rayburn sighs. "Then," he blows out a breath, "the only chance is to cauterize."

I snap my head to Rayburn in horror. "You mean *burn* his leg?"

Rayburn nods gravely. "I don't like it anymore than you do." He begins twisting his hands together nervously.

"I'm fine," Clay says, reaching down to draw up his pants. I put a hand on his chest and feel the sweat seeping through his cotton shirt.

I stare into his beautiful face, flushed with strain. "I can't let you die."

His good hand reaches up to stroke my cheek. The softness of his gaze turns my world upside down. "Please," I whisper.

He gives me a quick nod. Then he looks at Rayburn. "We got any whiskey?"

Rayburn shakes his head.

"God damn." He unbuckles his pants. "Then let's get this over with."

***

8

We build a fire behind a butte, hoping that it hides our light from the road. I tend the fire, flicking glances at Clay from time to time. He sits beside the flames, his leg out, his eyes distant. He knows as well as I do that this is going to be awful; he's got his cold-as-steel gunslinger expression set hard on his face. How can he be made of stone when right now my limbs are brittle as tumbleweeds?

Mama and Ethan wait for us over the ridge. They don't need to see this. I wish I didn't, but I know I'm not leaving.

When the fire's hot, Rayburn and I stand nervously to the side, staring at Clay's wound.

"What do we use?" I whisper, worrying my hands.

Rayburn holds up the revolver and shrugs. In the firelight, his expression has never looked so uncertain. He leans into me. "This might not work, OK? Burning the surrounding tissues could r-r-result in a bigger wound and cell death..." He sniffs and thumbs back his glasses.

In this light, Rayburn looks fourteen, not the twenty-two I know him to be. I place my hand on his slumped shoulder. "You told me this is the only way. Is it?"

Rayburn looks up at me, the firelight dancing on his dirty glasses. He nods.

"Then we do this. We do it quick and we do it right." I squeeze his arm. "We do it for Clay."

He licks sweat off his upper lip, turns, and strides to the fire. Then he leans down and begins heating up the barrel of the gun.

Clay looks over at me as I sit down. "I'll need somethin' to bite down on." His voice is so even it sounds like we're talking about the weather.

I nod and pull out the belt Rayburn gave me. Slowly, I hand the folded leather to Clay. "You sure?" I ask, grabbing his hand. "You sure you can do this?"

He nods, his blue eyes flashing in the firelight. "No other choice, right?"

I shake my head. "Guess not."

"Then let's get it over with." He flexes the belt in his hands. "You hold my arms? I don't wanna accidentally clock Rayburn while he burns me." A smirk lights his face. "Or maybe I do."

"You can't clock Rayburn." I try a smile, but it feels false. Rayburn crouches by the fire and grips the revolver handle wrapped in a huge wad of cloth. The barrel glows a menacing red. He stands up and walks over, eying the barrel like it's a snake ready to spring.

Clay swallows hard and looks up at me. "You got me?" he says, a small tremor sneaking into his voice. His eyes are suddenly wet. Afraid.

"I got you," I say, taking his hand. Holding it like it's my only lifeline to him.

He pulls me in, his lips pressing into mine. The kiss burns through me like a fever, heating my insides. His lips yield softly and I taste his fear, but also his resolve. If this is what he has to do, he'll do it. Like he's always done.

We pull apart. I caress his cheek once. Rayburn kneels down and Clay shoves the belt between his teeth and bites down, then gives a quick nod.

I hear the sizzle of skin before the smell of burnt flesh hits my nose. I squeeze Clay's hands. His eyes lock into mine and we're together in this awful moment.

Then he starts to scream.

CHAPTER THREE

When Clay can walk again, we continue up the busted highway. Each mile feels like a hundred. Mama limps so bad I wince every time I glance at her. Clay's no better. His leg, though no longer bleeding, is swollen and blistered beneath his pants. He needs rest or he'll drop dead.

Toward dawn, as the light is graying, we find a dusty shell of metal that used to be a roadside restaurant. Beside it sits a little four-pump gas station and service shop. The diner's broken sign reads RESTAUR in big block letters that look like they lit up at one time. The rest of the word lies in broken chunks out front. As we shuffle up, Clay draws his gun. No telling who might be holed up inside. We slink cautiously to the front and peer in. All of the windows have long since blown out, but the metal roof is mostly intact. Tables— their Formica tops wrinkling and peeling back like apple skins—are strewn in the corners. Sand has blown in and completely covered one side and most of the floor. A rusty metal stool glints in the gray light filtering through the holey roof.

"Stay here," Clay whispers. He limps up the broken concrete steps and slips inside.

I wait with the rifle pressed to my breastbone, my heart pounding against it. The first rays of sun are turning the east pink. With the Breeders looking for us and the heat index into the hundreds, we can't travel during the day. If we don't get off the road, we're toast. This had better be the place.

"All clear," Clay says from the doorway. He takes off his hat and wipes his brow. "I'm gonna check the service station just to be sure. You all go ahead and get comfy." He nods toward the diner and then limps off.

I blow out a breath. "All right, folks. Looks like we're bedding down here for the day." I shoulder my rifle and wink at Ethan. "Let's hope we find some grub."

A search of the larder reveals nothing but a dried lizard carcass so long dead it's just a wrinkled husk, three empty cans, and some rotten shelving. The same story for the nearby gas station. Just drained gas cans, rusty tools, and heaps of trash.

So we sleep on empty bellies, folding our bodies under the broken tabletops with mounds of sand for our pillows. I look up at the underside of the table at a wad of gum hardened to a black nub. What did the people who stopped here long ago eat? Pies? Bacon? Across the room a washed-out sign pictures a frothy mug with the letters A&W on the front. I sound out the words ROOT BEER FLOATS $3.99. I'd give my right arm for a foamy mound of cream right now.

Clay limps in the door and slides in beside me. I lean over, prop my head up on my hand, and stare into his face.

"All clear?"

He nods, taking off his hat and tossing it aside. His brown hair is messed into adorable wet curls that lap at his forehead. He rubs his good hand over the scruff on his chin.

"Nothin' out there but dust and car husks." He sighs and sets his revolver down.

"Think we can repair any of 'em enough to get 'em running?" I ask, stifling a yawn.

He shakes his head and runs a hand through his hair. "Nah. They're all busted to hell. No wheels. No interior. Somebody picked 'em over a long time ago." He rolls over to face me. Suddenly I'm aware of how close our bodies are, of how his blue eyes scan my face hungrily.

"I could take first watch, but it'd be nice if I had some help stayin' awake." He reaches out, fingertips grazing my cheek, my bottom lip, before he runs a finger down into the hollow at the base of my neck. I shiver. "I can think of a few things that'll keep me from driftin' off." He slides his fingers down my neck and then slowly undoes the top button on my shirt.

"Clay," I say, nervously. He smiles and presses his lips to my jaw line. Heat rushes through me.

I should tell him to stop. Mama and Ethan snore lightly from the shadows a few feet away and who knows where Rayburn is. And, frankly, I'm nervous. I've only kissed two men in my life: Hatch, who forced me, and Clay. I have no idea what I'm doing. What if I'm bad at this? What if we go too far? But instead of stopping, my hand presses to his chest. The steady beat of his heart accelerates. It pounds for me. I lean in and run my nose along his jaw line.

His good hand reaches around my back and draws my body to

his. The other hand, the puffy bandaged thing I feel at my back, is more tentative. What if I hurt him? His cauterized leg is still red and angry, but maybe this will help distract him. The trickle of dawn light from the holey roof lights up small parts of him as he moves closer. This is Clay. Clay who saved me. Clay who nearly died for me. Clay who I love. He scoots over a few more inches until his chest touches mine. My body begins a rhythmic hum. My breath quickens and my scalp tingles. His scent is warm earth and male musk, and it makes me want him even more. His breathing pulses against my face and an aching in my gut moves lower.

His head shifts down and a brush of stubble grazes my cheek. Then his mouth finds mine.

He kisses me urgently, kisses me until I can't help but draw up to him. I arch my back and press myself against him, fit myself into his body. I slide my hands over his back, the muscles flexing. His good hand cups my neck, my back, slips around and rests on my thigh. I stifle a low moan in the back of my throat. I've never known wanting like this.

He shifts me toward him, the sand making a shushing sound as if it too knows our need to be silent. He tugs up my shirt, the pads of his fingers circling my waist, inching higher. The skin there flares with sensation. My body molds into his as if it has a will of its own, but somewhere, as if at the bottom of a well, my brain is blinking *warning, warning.* But, my body wants him. *Wants* him. I lean in until there's no space between us, just his body touching my body. He's panting now, groping for me. His mouth finds my neck, kisses the hollow of my throat.

Stop! my brain says. *You're under a table in the dirt and your mama and brother are a few feet away.*

But they're asleep, my body argues. Clay's hand brushes my bare rib cage and my body ignites. Soon he will undo the binding on my breasts, unwind me, and lay me bare.

Then you'll be undone, my brain says. *You can't do this.*

I turn away from the voice and press my lips to Clay's. My tongue finds his and he tastes like warm earth. He moans and pulls me tighter.

What if you get pregnant?

Pregnant. Pregnant like Mama, sick and vulnerable on the road. Pregnant like poor Betsy whose fate I'll never know. Pregnant like the

Breeders hoped to make me before I escaped. I picture myself hobbling down the road, my round belly pulling me down like a lead weight, my legs giving out. How could Clay want me then? I'd be nothing but a liability. Pregnant is the last thing I wanna be.

Clay's lips find mine, but I pull back. My body fights me every inch, the low throb in my groin turning into an ache.

"Come on," he breathes, his lips grazing the skin of my neck. "Don't you trust me?"

Trust him? Sure I trust him, but not with *this*. I draw my arms up and cross them over my chest. His hands fumble a moment more, then slip off. He blows out a frustrated breath and rolls over on his back.

I sit up. Through the hole in the ceiling, dawn light brushes the sky. I look over at the shadow that is Clay. Even if I could explain why I pulled away, I can't tell him here. Not with my mama and Ethan sleeping nearby. With my heart thudding and my body aching, I stand up, fix my shirt, and shuffle to the open diner doorway.

I step outside through the doorless entryway and peer around. The sun's already a huge round ball, cresting over the ridge. It'll be hotter than Hades in an hour. I walk around the side of the little breadbox restaurant, trying to get out of sight of the road. I pass a window sign that reads 50s DINER. GOOD GRUB. GOOD TIMES. Too bad the good grub and good times are long gone. I kick an empty aluminum can and it skitters away. We have about three days worth of rationed food, four days of water. I lift my eyes to the horizon. How can I keep my family alive? That's the question I ask myself every single day.

I tromp down a little hill and into the hardpan where I'm hidden from the road. The dusty plain is quiet. In the east, a slash of orange is creeping over the horizon. The buttes and scrub brush will soon be awash with golden glow and the land will come alive. I rub my hands over my arms. My shirt has gone threadbare in the last few weeks. My boots are even worse; wiggling toes peak through holes in both boots. But I've got bigger problems. Like water. I lick my chapped lips and wish we could stumble on a vast blue lake. I'd dive in and swim around like a fish. I'd drink until the lake disappeared.

A little lizard skids past me on the path. If he can find water, we can. My eyes trace over the knobby cactus, the scraggy scrub grass, the rocks warming to orange with the first rays of day. To my right is a prickly pear; its flat oval leaves are covered in giant spines, but on top is what I want. I take my hunting knife from my pocket and cut a slice off the bulbous pink fruit growing from the top. I pluck the fruit from the ground, careful of the spines, and slice into it. As the juice dribbles into my palm, my stomach seizes. I press it to my mouth. Sweet and gritty, I suck and suck until it's a husk. It's not much, but it soothes my dry throat. I chuck the shriveled remains over my shoulder and reach for more. Ethan and Mama will love these.

Something behind me stirs. Someone or some*thing* is shuffling along the ridge behind me. Whatever it is, it's big and coming fast.

I whirl around, gripping my hunting knife. I think of the rifle I left back in the diner. Stupid. No time. I lock my eyes on the ridge and wait.

A figure lumbers into view, a dark shadow moving fast. It drops to its knees beside a rock. The sound of retching finds me. Mama.

When I reach her, she's bent over two rocks, spitting the last of her measly lunch onto the ground. I bend down and rub her back. "You okay?"

She nods, a trail of spit arcing from her mouth. One hand clutches the rock she's kneeling beside. The other circles her swollen belly. She spits once again and tries to rise. Her legs are so weak they almost buckle. I put my hands under her arm and help her up. When she turns to me, her eyes are sunken and wet, dark bags below them like bruises. Her gaunt, burned face forces a smile. "We gotta get back inside."

"Okay." I let her lean on me for support and we shuffle back to the diner. She pulls to a stop inside the diner's little entrance—a six-foot square area with double doors on both sides. The front doors are glassless, but the doors leading into the diner are intact and dusty as hell. The sides of the entrance have half-walls that can hide us from the road if we scrunch down. We do this now, our backs resting against the chipped paint. Near the floor someone's penned the words "DOMINE, LIBERA NOS AB ORCO."

On the floor beside Mama, a broken corkboard rests, brittle bits of paper still flutter from tacks. She plucks one off and the paper crumbles between her fingers. "Let's not go in just yet," she whispers, eying the dim diner through the dusty glass doors. "I wanna make sure I won't be sick again."

I hug my knees to my chest, frowning. "Is it the baby?" Her

stomach rounds out of her shirt and she rests a hand there. She looks too far along to only be a month or so pregnant. The words of Nessa Vandewater, Clay's mother, ring in my head. *There were some mutations to the fetuses.*

My mama rubs her stomach. "Probably something I ate. I told Rayburn those cans looked bulgy." She presses a hand to her forehead, her face contorting. Then she offers me another pained smile. "My good girl." She tilts her head giving me that proud mama smile. "Thanks for your help."

"Anything," I say, working my finger through a hole at the hem of my T-shirt. I watch my mother for a while as if my vigilance could keep away whatever is tearing her up inside.

That baby. She'll never say it, but I have a feeling whatever is inside her can only do her harm.

She looks out the glassless front door, glowing orange with the rays of dawn. "Can't sleep?"

I shake my head.

"We got a long walk tonight."

I nod.

She folds her burned hands together, the bumps and ridges of her skin like the road a few feet from where we sit. "Sometimes when I can't sleep I think of happy times. Like when you were seven and Arn took you to see the wild horses foaling in the back pasture at our house in Santa Fe. Do you remember that?"

Somewhere in the dusty recesses of my brain I find an image of me riding on Arn's shoulders as he steps toward a mare and her newborn foal. The small brown horse folds wobbling legs beneath him and pushes up, unsteady. Then the image fades out. "Yeah, I remember some. Did Arn take me a lot of places when I was little?"

She nods, her face animating. "He'd sit you beside him in his workshop while he worked on car parts. He'd give you something to tinker with. You loved working with your daddy." She looks up at me, a frown creasing her face. Arn is not my daddy. But I loved him. Truly.

I sniff and pick at the dry caulk inside the windowless frame above my head. I miss Arn, but I know my mother aches for him. She never got to say goodbye and it eats her up. I suspect it's not just morning sickness that keeps her sleepless.

She swipes a hand at her eyes and stands, using the wall to help

16

her. "I'm feeling better, love. I think I'll go in and lay down. You should give sleep a try, too."

I nod, though I feel anything but sleepy. I watch her slip through the interior doors. When they shut, the dust caked to the glass blurs her into shapes. Then I can't see her at all.

A few minutes later the door creaks open. At first I think it's Mama coming out to be sick again, but then I see how tall the shadow is and my heart beats faster. Clay slips out and limps over. In the morning light, he's just as handsome as ever: tall, with his strong chin and wild dark hair.

I smile as he sits down beside me, his feet digging wells in the dust.

"So," he flicks his eyes up at me, "not very romantic under the table? I thought the decor in there was real homey." There's an unusual shyness on his face.

"Homey for rodents and snakes, you mean."

He nods, smirking. "Lately I been feelin' pretty rodent-like. Yesterday I got a craving for cheese."

I laugh. "That's funny. I had a craving for *anything*."

He chuckles and digs around the edge of the bandage on his injured hand. The bandage is fraying, the white gauze now the dirty brown like everything else. There's a long pause as we both look out toward the road and the orange light spilling over the desert.

"Are we okay?" he asks, breaking the silence. "I mean, you and me?"

There's uncertainty in his eyes. It's funny how things have changed. Before the hospital, it was me speculating on what he was thinking and what he might want. Me longing for him but never being able to have him. The tide has turned. I'm not sure how I feel about it.

I reach for his hand and lace my fingers through his. "We're together." I look up at him, my heart pounding, awash in a love that surges through me. "That's all I ever wanted." I drape my arms around his neck and he wraps his around my waist. Being this close sets my heart to galloping away.

Clay shrugs. "I just wanna make you happy." He looks out at the sand-swept highway and shakes his head. "As happy as I can, considerin'. I wish I could make this all go away."

I press my cheek to his chest. "We gotta get to a town and

Rayburn can barter for a truck and gas. Those meds of his are worth enough to get us home. In the meantime, you gotta trust that you and me are fine." I lift my head and look into his eyes. "Okay?"

His blue eyes look deeply into mine. "Okay."

Then he's kissing me. Kissing me, kissing me, kissing me. And his hands are under my shirt and my heart is tearing through my chest as his fingers inch upward.

I push away.

He drops his hands, his eyes on the ground. "Sorry," he mumbles. He pushes up and limps back through the door.

"Clay," I say, but I let him go. First watch it is. It'll give me time to torture myself about all the things I've done wrong.

***

In my dream I'm lying on the desert floor. I can't move. Above, vultures circle like pinwheels of death. The need to get away is fierce, but nothing I do makes my limbs work. I open my mouth to scream, but all that comes out is a gasp. One of the big black birds dives down, boring its beak into the flesh below my ribs.

The pain. It drags me out of my sleep. Yet, something hard still presses into my stomach.

A raspy voice breathes in my ear. "Make a noise, you filthy half-man, and I'll fill your belly with holes."

I snap up, awake and terrified. It's mid-day. I've fallen asleep during watch, my body slumped against the wall. A large man leans over me, grips my hair with one hand, and presses a gun into my stomach with the other. His eyes are huge, round and shiny like a doll's, but then I realize he's wearing goggles, the kind the drivers wear to keep dust out of their eyes. The rest of his face is shaded by some sort of straw hat. Half a dozen gold chains dangle from his neck. He looks like a clown or those fashion ladies I've seen on pages of old magazines.

I pull back, terror raging through me. He jabs the gun barrel hard into my ribs, huffing the air out of my lungs. I gasp.

"Don't move!" he whisper-shouts. Behind him three large men slip into the diner, guns drawn.

"Clay!" I claw upright, my fingers digging into the wall.

He hits me with a sharp backhand across the face. Blood floods

18

my mouth. I shake my head and keep screaming. "Ethan, Clay! They got guns!" Noise from inside. A scream. *Oh, God.*

He shoves a dirty hand over my mouth to silence me, banging my head back into the wall. I thrash back and forth, lose his hand and scream. "Mam—"

His hands go for my throat. He pins me to the wall, the window ledge digging into my skull. I claw at his giant hands, trying to breathe, trying to scream. He shoves me harder into the wall and the plaster crumbles around me. He's big: barrel chested, tree-trunk thighs, arms rippling beneath his T-shirt. We're in trouble.

Sounds of a scuffle inside. Clay slams into the diner door, skids through it, and lands in a heap. Slowly he staggers up. I tug at my captor's hands as he tightens his fingers around my throat. Stars flare in my vision.

"Clay!" I croak, as I pry at thick fingers.

Clay lurches my way, digging for the gun at his hip. His bandaged hand paws at the revolver until he remembers that he's wounded. He reaches down with his left, but it's a clumsy movement. The gun catches on the holster, spins out of his hands, and buries itself in a mess of bricks and trash just outside the diner. His eyes go wide. Fear and shame war on his face for an instant, then he dives through the doorframe for his gun. I turn and kick at my attacker, but my blows do nothing to slack the hands on my throat. I slam my foot into my attacker's crotch and his hands loosen a little.

Another man bursts out through the diner door. This guy's huge too, with veiny biceps. His clothes are outlandish and bright: red lace-up sneakers, puffy green pants, and a tank top that reads VERA BEACH in neon letters. Who are these people?

The tank-top man runs after Clay. They square off in the dust outside the diner, Clay making a fist with his good hand and tucking his bandaged one to his chest. Tank-top man smirks, showing his four remaining teeth, and then swings like a prizefighter.

A fist arcs toward Clay's jaw. Clay ducks. The swing slices the air an inch from his head, rippling his hair. Tank-top man flies forward, carried by his own momentum. Clay follows, up and around, with three quick jabs in Tank-top man's kidneys. Tank-top man drops to one knee.

Inside Ethan shrieks.

I snap my head toward the diner. My attacker, recovering from his kick in the privates, shoves me back. His eyes move to the fight between Tank-top man and Clay. He's momentarily distracted. I think of Ethan, close my eyes, and punch him as hard as I can in the face.

There's a loud crack. His head snaps back. My hand instantly throbs, but his hands are off my neck. I scramble for his gun, loose in his right hand. We fumble for steel. My hands claw across flesh and metal. He grits his teeth and growls, pushing rancid breath into my face. We play tug of war with his gun. His sombrero slips off and I can see his thin, black beard, a two-inch scar cutting through it. Clumps of hair are missing on his scalp revealing raw, red patches of flesh. Behind the goggles one round eye is cloudy. Something's wrong with him.

Still fighting for the gun, he digs his elbow in my chest. A knot of pain spreads across my breastbone, but my fingers find the gun grip. I yank hard, stagger back, and find a gun in my hands.

I wrap my finger around the trigger. My attacker watches me carefully. I thumb down the safety. There's no fear of death in his eyes. He thinks I'm afraid, that I won't do it. Next to me I hear Clay and Tank-top man begin another round.

I grit my teeth and pull the trigger.

A dry click. Nothing. No bullets.

Jesus Christ.

He smiles at me, revealing corn-yellow teeth.

I smile, pull back my arm, and hit him across the face with the gun. His face ripples to the right with the impact. Blood spews from his mouth. His eyes roll back. He lands with a loud *thunk* on the debris-filled pavement.

Yes, I think. Then, *Clay!*

I whirl around. He's slugging it out with Tank-top man: awful rocking punches that make me cringe. I run up as Clay stumbles on his bad leg and falls over a chunk of broken concrete. He lies on his back, bleeding, panting. His injured hand has bled through the bandaging and his right eye is swelling shut.

I jump between him and Tank-top man and aim the gun.

"Riley, no!" Clay yells, rolling over and scrambling for me.

I lock my elbows and aim the gun at Tank-top man's heart. "Back up, you sonovabitch!"

He steps forward, smiling. Along with his four teeth and there's a giant red sore eating up half his upper lip. His pupils are cloudy, the whites are yellowed. And he smells like rotten meat. There's definitely something wrong with him. With all of them.

"Drop the gun, Bender." Even his voice is thick, like his tongue is a dead thing in his mouth. He nods toward the gun. "We both know there's no lead in that shooter." He takes a step forward, cloudy eyes searching my face. His big hands reach out, dirty fingers curling toward me. I don't move.

"Do what he says," Clay whispers in my ear. The pain in his voice cuts me to the core. He wants to protect me, but if I drop the gun, Tank-top man will kill Clay.

He takes a step forward and now he's three feet away. My eyes lock on the sore on his lip, the raw rancid strawberry that mars his face. He smiles, puckers his mouth, and makes smoochy sounds. "You like what you see? I hear Benders got real soft skin." He narrows his clouded eyes. "Guess I get to find out."

I smile in mock amusement. "Not today, you motherless bastard." I pull the gun back like a tomahawk and whip it as hard as I can at his face.

The gun smashes his nose. His giant hands snap over his bloody beak and he screams.

"That'll be enough!" a male voice behind me shouts.

I whip around. There, in the doorway of the diner, stand the other two men. The smaller of the two holds Ethan and Rayburn by their forearms. Their wrists are bound with rope. Rayburn has a giant welt on his forehead. Ethan looks okay. The other man has my pregnant mama pulled tight to his chest. Pressed up against her throat is a long, rusty blade. Her eyes go wide as the dull blade dimples her skin.

"Stop!" I yell. Behind me, Clay clutches my arm as I lurch forward. "Please." I use all my willpower to lower my voice. "You don't have to."

My attacker steps up, his hand holding his bruising cheek. He finds his sombrero, brushes the dirt off it, and fixes it back on his head. Coupled with the dusty goggles that magnify his eyes threefold, the hat makes him look ridiculous. I'd laugh if I weren't so sure he was about to kill me. His gray eyes zero in on me for a moment.

"We don't need all this violence," he says. "Either you all come with us or we slice every male on the spot. We take her," he nods to my mama, "and you, gut the others, and leave 'em for the dogs."

I start to speak, but Clay's hand cinches around my arm. "We go," he says through gritted teeth. He wants to fight just as bad as I do. I know he's the rational one and I should listen, but to go with these cavemen? I shoot him a glance, but he's watching the leader with his penetrating gaze.

My attacker nods and his man removes the knife edge from Mama's throat. She sags a little.

Tank-top man limps over, holding his bleeding nose. He wrenches my hands together. Clay shouts in protest, but his hands are being bound by the other man. I hate the feel of twine on my wrists. I hate seeing Ethan's eyes as they lead him off.

"Where are you taking us?" I ask and get a sharp push from behind. I stumble forward onto the road. A dusty white van is parked a ways back on the shoulder.

Shoving my mother before him like a stubborn mule, my attacker looks at me with soulless eyes.

"To the Citadel. The Messiah has been waiting for you."

CHAPTER FOUR

They shove us in a large white van with worn tires and a few rusty side panels, but, surprisingly, it's not as beat-up as every other vehicle on the road. In the back, the seats have been removed, leaving a large open swatch of scratchy black carpet. We're herded in, the back doors slamming behind us. I sit with my back to the van's side, Clay to my right and Ethan to my left. Rayburn and Mama are on the other side of the van, sitting cross-legged, bound hands on their laps.

Mama looks up, anguish darkening her face. She's thinking the same as me: we're prisoners, we're unarmed, and we're helpless. This is how we end up dead. She offers me her reassuring smile. I think she's beautiful, but I try to see her as these men do: a middle-aged, pregnant burn victim. I drop my head and sigh. It doesn't matter what she looks like. She's a woman. Most men would give anything to own a woman or to have one to trade to the Breeders.

They've assumed I'm a Bender, the half-male half-female mutations that are born now instead of girls, but it doesn't do me much good, seeing as how Tank-top man seems to have a taste for Benders. I picture his giant hands on me and feel the strong desire to crush something. His windpipe, hopefully.

The leader opens the driver's door. He turns to Tank-top man. "Stephen, you're up front." Then he speaks to the two men standing at his door. "Lavan, Kemuel, you're in the back. Stay alert."

The other two take their places: backs against the front seats, facing us. Lavan glares at us, the knife in his hand. Kemuel sits next to him, hands around his knees. He may be the only one who doesn't come from a family of giants. He's slender, about fourteen with the wisp of a mustache sprouting on his lip, curly black hair, and heavy eyebrows. His delicate features and long lashes make him almost pretty. Maybe he's a Bender, though his compadres don't seem to act like it. His clothes are more subdued, holey pants, a white T-shirt, and only a single silver chain dangling from his neck. He's the one who I'd go after to plead our case, the only one who might have some pity on his face as he looks at Clay's bruised cheek. I try to meet his eyes as the leader starts the van and bumps us onto the road, but Kemuel keeps his eyes on the holes of his pants.

Clay's eyes are locked on his knees, too. I can almost taste the shame rolling off him. He fumbled the gun. If I hadn't seen it, I wouldn't believe it. He's never missed a shot since I've met him, though he's never been this hurt either. I know how he's seething inside, wanting to crush these men. I watch his hands squeeze into fists in his lap. I want to touch him, soothe out the wrinkles on his forehead, but I'm not a fool.

"Riley," Ethan whispers as soon as the road noise picks up. "What's gonna happen?" His leg brushes mine as he leans in closer. I can feel him tremble even over the vibrations in the road.

I whisper, "Don't worry." Hollow words. We're all worried. No, terrified.

"Shut up," Lavan says. He glares at me with his clouded left eye.

"Who's the Messiah?" I ask, jutting my chin out. "Why's he been waiting for us?"

Lavan pushes back his beat-up ball cap and narrows his less swollen eye. "Shut," he leans forward and raises his knife, "up."

I scowl and let my head bang against the van as the broken road vibrates us back and forth. If they wanted us dead, they would've killed us, which means one thing: they need us alive.

***

Twenty minutes of driving through desert and we come to the remains of a town. We cruise past crumbled buildings and see two-thirds of a concrete warehouse, bone white and roofless, on the left. A house with loose siding waving like long fingers sags on the right. We pass a burned-out car husk. My eyes follow it until I see the bleached skull lying in the passenger seat. I flick my eyes to the horizon and try to control the awful dread crawling around my stomach.

We turn down a long, dusty road that dips into a hollow valley. The road winds around to a building half a mile long. The giant rectangle looks like it used to be one of those large shopping areas, a... mall. Some shop names still cling above the entrances though many have fallen away: DILLARD'S, something that just reads J. PEN, and MACY. At first glance the mall might seem like another dead building, but there are signs of life. To the west, in a cracked parking lot, several black rectangles angle toward the sun.

Clay sees my eyes and nods. "Solar panels," he says.

"Shut up," Lavan says. He flashes what's left of his teeth in a nasty sneer.

We pull up to another aging white van. A guard stands beside it with a semi-automatic rifle in his massive arms. One of his nostrils is crusted and oozing yellow pus down his cheek. These people are sick. Are we breathing in their disease right now? I feel every breath expand in my chest as I taste the air.

The van slides to a stop and the leader leans out. "New recruits," he says, thumbing behind him.

I can't see his face, but I can hear the smile in his voice. My skin prickles. Ethan leans his shoulder into mine. I grab his bound hands.

The guard leans in and looks at us. His face quirks up in a knowing smile. "Nice haul, Andrew. Haven't had fresh blood in a while." He pats the top of the van with a *thunk, thunk* to indicate we're good to go.

Fresh blood. I hope he's kidding.

We trundle past the white van and pull up to one of the mall's loading docks. The van backs up to an elevated opening covered by flaps of black plastic. Andrew jumps out of the driver's seat, comes around, and opens the van's back doors. He climbs inside, his sombrero brushing the ceiling. "Don't go thinking you're gonna run." He nods toward the guard at the front. "That gun he's got. Real bullets."

I snort. He draws his knife out and points it at me again. "You're looking for trouble and you're gonna find it. Mark my Gods' loving words."

I narrow my eyes, but Clay's foot slides out and taps my knee. He wants me to shut up. I bite my tongue and taste the bitterness of self-control.

The back door swings open and the heat from the blacktop rolls in. A smell too, something... dead. Andrew and Kemuel shove us forward toward the doors. Rayburn stumbles, banging into the door with a loud *thunk*, and falls out onto the pavement. Andrew laughs.

I whirl around, anger pulsing at the back of my throat. "Hey!" I shout. "Leave him alone!"

Andrew tromps through the interior of the van, shaking it. He holds the knife edge an inch from my face. "You want I should pick on you instead?"

"Go right ahead." My heart pumps with anger, pushing the fear down. Mama shoots me a terrified look, but I don't care if he hits me.

Anything to keep the fear at bay.

"Andrew," Stephen calls nasally through his broken nose. "No time to dally."

Andrew frowns, puts the knife in his belt, and shoves me forward. When I jump out of the van, I help Rayburn collect his glasses. "Keep your head down," I whisper. "He already doesn't like me. He doesn't have to hate you, too."

Rayburn nods, tears in his eyes. He slips on the scratched glasses, making his wet eyes shine. The rest of my family piles out of the van.

We walk toward the mall. Around the loading dock symbols are painted on the walls in a rusty brown. I recognize a few crosses, a Star of David, and then some other religious symbols I can't recognize. The symbols closest to the door aren't brown. They're blood red. As we walk toward the stairs leading up, I see a pile of what looks like charred sticks. That's when the smell hits me—that burnt animal smell. Not sticks, bones. A white rib bone curves from a four-foot-high pile. I lurch back and press my bound hands to my nose. My heart slams into my chest. Ethan looks into my face for reassurance, so I bite down on my tongue and give him a nod.

Bloodied symbols and animal sacrifices. Dear God.

The four men push us up a chipped concrete staircase and through the long black flaps hanging over the entrance. Through the loading dock is a big warehouse, scattered with metal shelves holding old tools, grinders, pieces of machinery, car parts.

"Move," Stephen says behind me. Andrew pushes my skeletal mother forward and rage bubbles in my brain. Clay shoots me a look and I try to bottle my anger. For now.

We wind through the warehouse and push through a set of double doors. A rancid stink smacks me in the face as grunts and squeals echo down the hallway. In another large room, a horde of pigs runs toward the metal sheeting fence and presses their snouts against it. I stare in awe as their pink and gray noses bob up and down, smelling us. Andrew bangs his knife handle against the grating as we walk by. The herd goes careening back into the warehouse with a chorus of squeals. There are dozens in there, hundreds maybe. I see the source of the stink in a soupy mess all over the floor.

As we are ushered by the pigs, Stephen grabs Kemuel by the neck and points toward the pen. "I know what you're doing this afternoon, baby boy." His braying laugh echoes through the concrete space. Kemuel shrugs him off, shoulders hunched, head down. I keep my eyes on him. *How can we talk, Kemuel?* I think. He might be our one chance at escape.

We come to two heavy metal doors and enter what was once a mall. I expect darkness, but instead overhead lights flicker in several parts of the hallway. Not a lot of light, but enough to keep us from stumbling. The only electric light I've seen was at the Breeders' hospital. A sick feeling crawls over me as I think about that place again. My eyes flick down to my sleeve where the pink, puckered ankh brand is burned into my flesh. Are these people in league with the Breeders?

Broken-down storefronts spread out left and right. The glass windows are mostly covered with strips of cloth stitched together, but one of the curtains has fallen open. Inside two people sit Indian-style, clothed in bright, gaudy fabrics, outlandish hats, jewelry. Next to them, a storefront that reads ICING has a metal grating pulled down over the entrance. As we pass, a little face peeks out at me. A child? I swing my head back to get another look. Brown curls fall around his face as he presses his nose through the grating. I crane my neck to see and Andrew shoves me hard. I stumble, bang my knee into a wooden bench, and spill onto the floor.

"Hands off," Clay growls.

Andrew smirks at him, yanks me up, and shoves me forward.

We round the corner and come into a giant open space. Faded plastic tables and chairs are set up to seat groups of six and eight. Above us, the ceiling looks like it was once a giant glass dome, but now is open air. This room is hot, but not stifling. They must be running fans or using the mall's ventilation system with all that solar power they're soaking up.

My eyes fall on a large structure in the middle of the food court. Dozens of carved horses on poles are ringed around a platform. Though the paint's chipped off in places and the glass bulbs are broken, I can't help but stare. The horses look so lifelike, their marble eyes flashing, the tufted crests curling from their foreheads like royal steeds in story books. The carousel is a spot of beauty in a place that seems to hold so much darkness.

"Come on," Andrew says, pushing me forward. "The Messiah's waiting."

***

27

We sit in plastic chairs in the Messiah's antechamber. The room is sparse with some plastic leafy plant angling in one corner and nothing else. There's no electricity here, just a few sputtering candles, creating a shimmering darkness that makes my skin crawl. The other men have left us except Andrew, who stands guard outside the door.

I stare at the solid metal door that separates us from the Messiah. We've been waiting for at least a half an hour. My mind has run every horrible scenario and come up with some amazingly disturbing possibilities: a mutated fetus baby as big as a man, a Christ-man missionary gone deranged, Nessa Vandewater and her guards. I can't take it anymore. I stand up and start pacing.

"This is crazy. We should rush the door and take Andrew. He doesn't even have a gun." I say, stopping in front of the door and eying it.

"Honey, please sit down," Mama says. She's paler than normal and blue crescent bruises have cropped up under her eyes. Looking at her only makes the desire to slam my body through the door stronger.

Clay's eyes follow me as I begin stalking around the tiny room. "Riley, do as yer ma says."

I whirl on him. "Wow. You sound just like Arn. And yet, *neither* one of you is my daddy."

He cringes. Beside him, Ethan's head sags. Bringing up my dead stepfather is not a great way to make a point. I throw myself into the plastic chair and blow out a frustrated breath.

"So, what *do* we do?" I ask, tugging against the twine around my wrists. Unfortunately, Andrew seems to be the best knot-maker in New Mexico.

Clay scans the room. "Wait and see. We got no weapons."

"Yes, an-and they have knives," Rayburn stutters. He scratches his chin against his shoulder and blinks at me through his smeary glasses.

"What if they want to eat us?" I ask.

"Riley!" Mama scolds, looking at Ethan. He blinks up, eyes wide.

I nod at my brother. "He may be eight, but he's seen a helluva lot in the last few weeks. I think he oughta know what we're up against."

My mama shakes her head. "They're not cannibals."

"B-b-but those bones," Rayburn says with a shudder.

"That's not helping." Mama gives Rayburn the same disapproving stare she usually saves for me.

"Speculatin' is about as good as castratin' a mare," Clay says, rolling his shoulders back. He scans the room, meeting our eyes. "I'll get you out. I'll find a way."

His brass-balls confidence is one of the things I love about him, but deep in my heart, I can't believe him. He's barely healed from being shot up, his right hand is a mangled mess of hamburger, and his last attempt at drawing from the hip was a disaster. I won't say it, but I can't count on Clay to get us out of this mess. This time it'll be all up to me.

The inner door draws open. We all turn, jaws dropped. Through the dim light, a woman dressed in a white robe steps out.

Ethan gasps. We all do. She's nearly old as Auntie with long gray hair brushed to a sheen flowing down her back. Her feet are bare. One pale hand sweeps toward the door and her sleeve ruffles in the breeze.

But what my eyes are really drawn to is the pregnant belly rounding out of her gown.

"Come," she says, her gray eyes narrowing. "The Messiah will see you now."

CHAPTER FIVE

We all stare, unable to move. The pregnant woman waves us in.

"Get up. You do *not* want to keep the Messiah waiting." When she frowns her face looks like beaten leather.

Clay stands and we all follow. He limps to the doorway and lines up in front of the pregnant woman. "We're ready," he says in his man-in-charge voice.

She leads us into a room where candles glow on every flat surface. The air is stale and smells of burning sage. It takes all my willpower not to choke on it. The room reminds me of a market store for oddities. Every nook and cranny is chalk full of trinkets: stacks of yellowing books, crinkled scrolls, and religious relics. At least twelve crucifixes litter the area, including the seven-foot-tall wooden cross that dominates the far wall. Strange items lurk on a shelf to the right: a jar with a bulbous animal fetus floating in yellow liquid, a golden statue of a woman with six arms, and a shrunken head in a shadow box. On the other wall, dozens of paper calendars are pinned, overlapping one another. They've been marked and circled in something that looks like dried blood. The door clicks behind us and the hairs on my arms stand up. I lean into Ethan until I can feel his elbow at my hip. I'd throw my arm around him if my hands weren't bound.

The Messiah steps out of the shadows. The flames highlight his features: the long brown hair, the matching beard, the white gown that drapes over him like a silk curtain, showing off every muscle. Facial sores peek through a coating of make-up—a scab below his ear the size of a quarter, a red blister below his left eye. He stands in front of us, his chin up, his eyes closed, his lips moving in some sort of prayer. Finally he spreads his arms wide, his sleeves fluttering.

"My friends," he says, his eyes still closed, "the Gods spoke to me about your coming. It has come to pass as the Heavens revealed to me. Welcome."

He opens his eyes. They're yellow and cloudy like sandblasted glass. Can he see at all? Yet the edges of his mouth are curled into a small, contented smile.

Every bit of this shouts *crazy person*. His act makes me wanna sprint out the door. The door that Andrew is now slipping back through with his knife in his hand. I step in front of Ethan and tighten my body.

"Please, Andrew, sever their bonds. I want the Gods' guests to be comfortable." His gaze floats somewhere near the ceiling like he doesn't need to see us, like he's seeing us in his *mind*. He waves Andrew in our direction and then floats off into the dark shadows of the room. Meanwhile, Andrew stalks over with his knife raised.

I watch tensely as he saws through Mama's bonds, then Ethan's, then Rayburn's. He hesitates at Clay, but then, looking down at Clay's bandaged hand, cuts through his ropes. Clay rubs his wrists and glowers, and there's a fire in his eyes, the kind that would usually go before flashing steel and a loud bang.

Finally, Andrew gets to me. He flicks a look back to the Messiah. "You sure you want 'em all freed?"

The shadowed figure waves a hand. "Yes, yes. It has been decided. They will not harm us." He turns back to whatever he's doing.

Andrew leans into me and slips his knife between my wrist and the rough twine. "Remember what you did to my face?" he whispers, sawing. His breath stinks like an outhouse on a hundred-degree day.

My chest heaves as he works the blade back and forth, but I meet his eyes and smile. "I sure do."

"And you thought there wouldn't be payback?" He smirks.

There's a sharp pain at my wrist. Blood springs up in a red line and trickles into my sleeve. It's not a bad cut, but any cut can spell death when medicine is scarce. I flash my teeth at him, but he's already wiping the blade on his pants and walking away.

Bastard.

As we're standing around, rubbing our wrists, the Messiah floats back to us, his arms wide, reminding me of a crane with wings outstretched. "Sit," he commands, swinging one arm toward a row of food court chairs. We settle ourselves into the plastic bucket seats. Ethan leans close to me.

I look around the dark room for weapons. Andrew's knife is the only one, as far as I can tell. If I could catch him by surprise—

"Which one of you is the girl who escaped the Breeders?" the Messiah asks, turning.

I freeze, suddenly aware of every hair on my head. My hand goes instinctively to the ankh brand on my wrist.

"And which one of you is the man who murdered his own

father?" The Messiah lets his cloudy eyes float in our direction, skimming over the tops of our heads.

I swallow hard and look down at Clay. His jaw is ramrod straight and he is clenching his fists in his lap. The Messiah glides to a stop in front of Clay, his gown billowing around his legs.

"It's you, isn't it?" he says, pointing a loosely cupped hand at Clay's chest. "Much like Krishna killed his uncle Kansa." The Messiah gestures to a statue of a blue man sitting with his hands turned upward. "We murder out of fear or we murder for power. Which was it that caused you to slay your kin?" The Messiah points his expressionless face in Clay's direction, but does not look at him.

Clay says nothing, just sits with this fist jammed in his lap.

The Messiah floats over to stand in front of Mama. His cupped hand hovers over her swollen belly. Finally, he presses his hand onto her stomach. His thin lips move, but no sound comes out. His face darkens.

"Kalli," he says, and the pregnant woman shuffles over. He reaches out for her hand and places her palm on my mother's stomach as well. She frowns and shakes her head.

"What?" I say, leaning forward. "What are you doing?"

The Messiah turns my way, his eyes floating in my general direction. "A hospital-grown fetus. An aberration. We do not believe in the experiments those doctors perform on the Gods' children."

"Neither do we, but they really didn't give us a vote before they put one in her," I say.

"What's wrong with Mama?" Ethan whispers to me.

The Messiah turns his head toward Ethan. I don't know if he naturally looks like the Jesus-man or if he's dressed that way for effect. Either way he's creeping me out.

"Your mother is infected with one of their fetuses. The baby will grow exponentially in the coming months. They gestate much faster than normal."

I look down at Mama's distended stomach. We all knew she looked too pregnant.

"What'll happen to her?" I ask, my pulse throbbing into my head.

The Messiah tilts his face to the ceiling. "Only the Gods may know. Here we can ease her pain. Our midwives are blessed."

"How can you have women here?" I ask, looking over at the pregnant woman who stands next to him, her hand on his sleeve.

The Messiah bobs his head up and down as if he has been expecting my question. "The Gods have carved out a place for us in this citadel. This land is holy. The Breeders may not enter. The Gods have granted us fertility in exchange for obedience to their commandments. The diseases of the world do not affect the Gods' people."

In the flickering candlelight, his face is calm and assured. *These* lunatics are the chosen people? The giant and cruel Andrew? And Stephen, who seems to like raping Benders? Really? I shake my head. "That doesn't make sense."

"How dare you contradict the Messiah," Kalli hisses, lurching forward, her gray hair crowding her face like a storybook witch. "He is the Word. He is *not* to be contradicted."

"Gentle, Kalli," he says, placing his hands on her shoulders. "They will learn our ways soon enough."

He turns and floats toward the back of his room where the shadows grow darker. Soon I can only hear the swish of his fabric. "Tonight you will rest. Tomorrow you will be inducted into the fold."

We stand to shuffle out, but his voice calls to us again.

"No harm can come to the Gods' people. Should you disobey the commandments while you are here and put any one of my sheep in danger, the Gods' wrath will fall down upon you like the seven plagues of Israel. There will be weeping and gnashing of teeth."

He says it so calmly, a proclamation of death. They may be the Gods' people, but I got a feeling we've stumbled into hell.

***

I sit on my mattress, arms around my knees, and watch Mama try to get comfortable beside me. They've locked us in one of the shops in the women's wing of the mall and ushered Clay, Ethan, and Rayburn down another hallway. Panic rippled in my chest as I watched Clay and Ethan walk away. I know Clay will protect my brother, but in his weakened state I worry about all of them. Every layer we unpeel of this onion is more rotten than the last.

Our room appears to be a store that once sold face creams and perfumes. There's a faded poster of an attractive woman with sunglasses pouting at the camera. I can't read the caption below, but I get the impression that whatever she's selling is meant to make women feel attractive to men. The room is bare except for a few things: the yellowed mattress my mama and I will share, broken hangers, small plastic hooks, crumbling cardboard boxes, and the plastic dinner tray with the food we've already scarfed down. Before he left, Andrew pulled down the metal grate at the store's entrance. He locked it, smirking, and said the Messiah doesn't want us to hurt ourselves by wandering around. I've already tried the back door and found it locked too. I think of the open ceiling, but it's twelve feet up with nothing to stand on, and there's no way I can get Mama up and over in her state.

Mama's hand slips over my elbow. "You need to sleep, love." She rolls over slowly and props her head up on her hand. "You can't solve all our problems tonight."

I drop my head to my knees and dig my chin into the hole that has worn through my pants. "I just don't get this place. What're these crazies playing at? The Gods' chosen people? Breeders can't come here because this is holy ground? Sounds flakier than lizard skin."

Mama ponders this a minute, her burned face crinkling as she thinks. "Maybe they have faith that lets them believe it's true. Sometimes faith is enough for people to act in a way that protects them from harm."

I bite my lip and stew on this. "Did you ever believe anything like that? I mean," I say, shifting on the saggy mattress, "did you ever have faith in something bigger?" I spread my hands out across the disheveled storefront.

Mama pushes herself up. It hurts me to see how hard it is for her to move. It hurts me to hear what the Messiah had to say about the baby that saps a little more of her strength each day.

"Riley," she says, taking my hand, "I believe in my children. You're the future I see. In you, there grows something better than what's out there." She gestures out toward the world. I lean into her, pressing my shoulder against her boney one. She rests her cheek on my head. "I don't know if there's a God. I hope there is, but if He's there, I don't know why He would choose to let some of His children suffer and protect others. I think that's just convenient thinking on their part," she says, gesturing toward the mall's interior.

She quiets and stares off into the distance. "I used to believe there was someone out there watching out for us. How could we have survived this long without being captured? Then when Arn was killed," she drops her head, swallowing hard, "it felt like something was severed inside me. I didn't even get to bury him. I was so *angry*. I wanted someone to be angry at. Other than the Sheriff, God was an easy choice." She takes my hand, turning her burned face to mine. "One morning, when Auntie and I were the Sheriff's prisoners, I asked the guard to take me to the outhouse. As I walked over the concrete, I saw dawn's first light. The heat hadn't yet settled over the land. It was so peaceful." She looks up and a sad smile lights on her face. "A morning star shone bright as any diamond in the west. Arn loved morning stars. He used to…" she sniffs back a tear. "He used to point them out to me." A tear traces down her cheek and she brushes it away. "The minute I saw that star, Riley, I swear to you I felt Arn's love pouring down on me." She lifts my hand to her lips and kisses it. "I think he's still up there loving me. Love like we had, like the love I have for you and Ethan, is too big to die with this body. My love will exist somewhere even if I don't."

"Don't talk like that," I whisper, resting my chin on her shoulder. She holds me like she did when I was small. Suddenly I feel like sobbing. "You're always gonna be around."

Mama says nothing, just strokes me. Finally, she sighs. "I hate that you always have to worry about me. I should be the one protecting you, not the other way round."

"I don't mind." I swallow down the tears and lay back on the mattress.

"I do," she says, with a faraway look in her eye.

"I'm gonna go to bed," I say, trying to control my voice. She doesn't question me, just lies down beside me. Her hand finds mine and we fall asleep connected, just like we were long ago.

***

I wake to shaking. Movement. Something's happening, though my brain is foggy from sleep. I roll over and see the dark, empty room, the bare mattress. Where am I? The mall. The mattress is shaking and something warm is puddling under my elbow. I roll over.

Mama sits, her face white, hands trembling. Beneath her the mattress is stained red. She lifts frightened eyes to mine. She's sitting in blood. Her blood.

"Mama!" I crawl to her side and hover, frightened.

She looks up at me. "Riley," she says, her hands shaking, "something's wrong."

CHAPTER SIX

"Help!" I shake the grate, the metal rattling in its casing. It echoes down the hall. Let them all hear. Then they'll come. I shake it until my arms throb. "Help us!"

The grate across from me pushes up and a puffy-eyed, salt-and-pepper-haired woman climbs out. "Shhh!" she scolds, putting a finger to her lips. "We're trying to sleep."

I stick my arm through the bars and wave her toward me. "Please, unlock the grate. My mother is bleeding. She needs someone... a doctor."

The woman frowns and tightens her blanket around her shoulders as if the thin fabric could ward off the crazy I'm infected with. Another woman with smooth, brown skin and short black hair approaches the grate. She clutches a tattered blanket to her chest. Even straight from sleep she's wearing half a dozen gold bracelets on her wrists. "What's going on?" she asks, groggily.

"My mother. She's bleeding!" I gesture back into the store. Both women stare at me like I'm a wild animal gone nuts in her cage. "Go!" I shoo them away. "Get help." I don't wait to see if they'll listen. I turn back and run to my mama.

She's sitting stock-still, her eyes on her knees. Beneath her, a red blossom spreads on the mattress. How much blood am I looking at? I kneel before her. "What do I do?"

She raises her eyes to me slowly. Her face has gone past white to a pale green. "I ... I don't know. Something's wrong with the baby." She shakes her head slowly. "Maybe it's for the best."

Behind me the grate rattles up. Guards rush in, rumpled, sleepy, and annoyed.

"You gotta get a doctor." I stand up and tug on the arm of a man I've never seen before. He brushes me aside and goes for Mama. Behind him another man pushes a rickety wheelchair. They lift her. In the giant man's arms, she looks like a child. They lower her into the chair and she winces. I clutch my face.

"I'm fine, Riley," she says, waving a weak hand at me. Her head sags forward as they wheel her back to the grate. She's a terrible liar.

I trot behind them, but a hand presses against my shoulder. The guard shakes his head.

"I'm going," I say, pushing his hand aside.

He shoves me back. I stumble into the store as he lowers and locks the grate.

"I'm going with her!" I scream. I was supposed to protect her. I promised myself when we got her out of the Breeders' hospital that I wouldn't leave her side, and here we are, separated again. How could I have failed her so soon?

I rattle the grate. Rattle it as they wheel her away. Rattle it as she turns and looks over her shoulder at me. Rattle, rattle, rattle until the women glare at me and go back into their stores.

I slip down against the grate as a cold dread steals over me. I press my sweaty forehead to the metal until it hurts, until it's a piercing spike in my head, until it's a quiet throb matching the pain in my heart.

***

I wake to someone shaking me. I snap upright and the hallway lights blind me momentarily. It's morning. I've fallen asleep against the metal grate. My neck aches, but not more than my chest as I remember my mama being wheeled away, bleeding.

I scramble to my feet and notice who's been doing the shaking. On the other side of the security grate, a girl blinks at me. She's petite, with wide, curious eyes, and a cute, puckered mouth that spreads into a smile. Her hair is a mess of curls circling her head like a golden halo. Jeweled bangles run up both her skinny arms.

She tilts her head to the side and grins at me. "Riley?" she asks. Her voice is quiet, squeaky like a child's, but her manner is much older. I wonder how old she is. Eleven, maybe?

"Yeah," I say, rubbing the kink in my neck. "Who're you?"

She holds up a food tray with a glass of water, a bowl of soupy grain, and two strips of cooked bacon. "Breakfast patrol," she says, beaming. "Can I come in?"

"You'd be the first person to ask." I gesture inside.

She sets her tray on the floor and works at the lock. Behind her, one of my neighbors walks past and glares in my direction.

"Thanks for your neighborly kindness last night!" I yell at her, unable to contain my anger. What's happening to my mama right now?

The girl opens the grate, slides it up and walks in carrying the tray. Surprisingly she leaves the grate up. I stare at the opening, thinking, planning. If I bolt now—

"They have your mom," she says, setting the tray beside me on the floor. "They say if you run you'll never see her again." She looks up at me with her wide, gray eyes, framed with long golden lashes. "Sorry."

I sit on the floor beside the breakfast tray. The food sends my stomach cart wheeling, but I wait. I look over at the girl. "Do you know what happened to my mama?"

The girl shrugs. "She's with the Middies."

"The Middies?"

"Yeah, the ladies the Messiah anoints to care for the sick. Stupid old birds won't let me in there." She leans forward, whispering. "I peeked in, though," her eyes flick to the hall, "when they weren't looking."

I nod and lean forward. "What'd you see?"

She leans closer, her eyes going wide. "She was lying on a bed."

"And?"

"And she had her eyes closed," she whispers.

I pull back. "Is that it?"

"Yeah. Sorry. I wanted it to be way cooler than it was." She takes a piece of bacon off my tray and chomps it. "I'm sure they'll fix her up proper. The Middies might be ugly, but they know how to heal."

Feeling a little more assured, I lift the warm bowl in my hands and spoon a bite into my mouth. The soupy porridge slides over my tongue. "When can I see her?" I need to find out what's going on with Ethan and Clay too, but one thing at a time.

The girl tilts her head, curls bouncing. "Maybe later. But first I get to give you the tour." She grins, pieces of chewed bacon peeking behind her teeth.

"Great," I say with as much enthusiasm as I can muster. I look back at the open grate. I can't chance a run for it. Not when they have Mama and the rest of my family locked up.

She pulls a bright red scrap of paper from her pocket and begins folding it while I eat. I've never seen paper that bright. Where do they get all these amazing relics from? I watch her thin fingers for a moment. "Hey, how come they let you come in here? Don't they worry I'll take you hostage or something?"

She runs her thumb and fingernail along a crisp paper crease, her bracelets jangling. "My dad told them you won't."

"How does he know I won't?"

She bends her fold into a triangle, which she spreads and folds again. "He's the Messiah."

"Your dad's the Messiah. Wow." I lean back and eat my one slice of bacon. Damn, it's good. I wish the girl hadn't eaten the other one. "What's that like?"

She shrugs as she folds. "He's real busy all the time. You know, getting prophecies and talking to the Gods or whatever." Finally, she stops folding and lifts her creation to me. An angular red bird has emerged from her single sheet of paper.

I touch the tip of its bill. "How'd you do that?"

She hands it to me and I examine its careful folds. "I can show you later." She stands. "Are you done?" She points to my tray.

I nod and pat my happy stomach. A full meal. When was the last time I had one of those? Probably in the Breeders' hospital. I cringe at the thought. "What's your name?"

"Mage," she says, tucking the paper bird into a large pocket in the front of her oversized jumper. "What do you want to see first?"

"My mother," I say and she shakes her head. "Okay, how about the boys' wing?"

She considers this. "It should be safe now during the daytime."

I shoot her a look. "What d'you mean?"

Her eyes go wide. Quickly she wipes the shock from her face. "You probably want to see your friends, huh?" she asks, leading me out.

I nod, ducking under the grate and into the hallway with her. Nearly all of the grates are open now. A woman walks by, pushing a cart laden with food trays. Two others walk in front of us with large bins of dirty clothes on their hips. So many women, and they're all free. If I didn't get the impression that this place was sitting on a big, nasty secret, I might want to stick around.

Mage leads me past the rows of stores that make up these women's homes. I pass by a smaller store with worn pink carpet and faded plastic posters with pictures of glittering jewelry, advertising, "BUY ONE, GET ONE FREE." Small hexagonal-shaped racks that look like they can spin line the walls. Between them, a group of toddlers sits cross-legged on the carpet while an elderly woman claps and sings them a song. As we pass, their little voices repeat her refrain. "In the Gods' sight we lie. Show us, fathers, your reply. Open the eyes of a heart most true. Show us, fathers, what to do. "

Mage thumbs back at the store. "That's Little Tree. Kids stay there until about five. Then they move up to lessons with Yusuf in the Willow Room." She leads me past a bigger room where older children lie on their bellies in small circles. They're writing on big canvas sheets with something that looks like bits of charcoal as a middle-aged man with a long gray ponytail walks around, monitoring their progress. He waves a hand to Mage.

"That's Yusuf," she says.

We turn a corner. In a large department store, I see where my soupy breakfast came from. Inside, where racks used to hold clothing and sporting goods, these people have set up a makeshift greenhouse. Plots of dirt run in staggered rows, covering nearly every surface. The ceiling's been cut away in big rectangular sections and sheets of sand-blasted plastic have been stretched across to let in the light while keeping out the sand and heat. Men and women with stooped backs and dirt-covered fingers water, weed, and tend each little green sprout.

"My papa was the one that got the water working." A tinge of pride coats Mage's voice. "That's when they made him Messiah."

"How's this possible?" I ask. An old woman with her back bowed like a candy cane plucks a tomato from a vine and drops it into a basket she wears at her hip.

Mage stuffs her hands in her pockets and rocks back and forth on her heels. "We use the juice from the solar panels to run power to sections of the mall, the water, the ventilation and the air conditioning. My papa says when they first came here two generations ago, it was super hot and dark. No toilets even," she whispers, making a face. "Then the Gods showed him how to make the power, and the people have lived blessedly ever since." She talks like she's repeating some rote message.

I fix her with a look. "The *Gods* told him how to hook up the power?"

She blinks at me and nods. "My papa's a prophet. He has the sight. He keeps us safe by following what they say."

"I didn't know God was an electrician."

41

She tilts her head, confused. "Come on," she says, turning. I take one last look at the little indoor farm nestled under old "FOR-SALE" banners. It's amazing, really.

After a few more stores, the floor plan opens up to the giant food court we walked through when we first entered. I peek in a restaurant cubby that's decorated with pictures of a black and white bear smiling and holding two thin sticks in its paw. Behind the counter, people are chopping, tending the stove, and stacking dishes.

Mage leans into the counter and presses her face to the display front glass. "They're making lunch." She peers in and makes a face. "Ham roast. Blah. Get ready for a lot of pork."

I shrug. "After what I've been eating? Are you kidding? Pork sounds amazing."

"Pigs will eat almost anything," she says, shuffling forward. She twirls around on one toe, a clumsy ballerina, and then stops and looks at me. "I hate pork. Pork makes you a dork." She hops on one foot across each tile as she says it.

"If you say so." What I don't say is, *You've never known starvation. You have no idea what it's like out there.*

"The carousel," Mage says, swinging around one of the outer poles. I stop to touch a horse's flared nostril, when footsteps thud toward me.

"Riley!"

It's Ethan, running at a full clip. He slams into me, his bony body nearly taking me out as he tightens his arms around my waist. I wrap my arms around him and press my face to his dark hair. Behind him Rayburn follows, pushing a greasy strand of black hair off his glasses. Clay limps between tables and chairs, his face breaking into a smile. He throws his arms around me. My heart thrums as I pick up his scent.

"Didn't sleep at all," he whispers into my hair. "I didn't know what they done to you."

"I'm okay," I say, pulling back, realizing I have an audience. People have stopped their business and turned.

"We heard 'bout yer ma," Clay says, clutching a chair to help support his weight. "D'you know how she's doin'?"

Ethan's hand finds mine. "Is she okay?"

I run a hand down his hair. "I don't know. Mage..." I pause. "Everyone this is Mage. Mage, this is Clay, Rayburn, and Ethan."

Ethan's hand slips from mine as he notices her. He stands up straighter, puffing out his chest.

Mage smiles as her eyes linger on my little brother. The flush in his cheeks is unmistakable. "We don't know anything about your mom," she says, "but I'm sure she's doing dandy. We'll go check when we're done." She blinks those golden lashes and the blush burns deeper through Ethan's cheeks.

I'm about to ask how long this tour will take when she grips my hand and pulls me close. "I have something to show you," she whispers, her eyes flitting around the noisy room. "Can you be quiet?" She looks at everyone's face. We all nod. "Follow me and act natural."

She leads us through the noisy cafeteria and down a hallway. A group of women walk by and Mage smiles, but the instant they're gone, her face becomes stony again. "This way." Instead of heading back to the sleeping halls, she heads right, down a dark hallway.

We walk together, Ethan at my side, Clay and Rayburn behind. Clay limps heavily. At the pace Mage is going, I know it hurts him. I bite my tongue. Nothing would embarrass him more than me asking to slow down so that he could rest his tore-up leg. I've got no idea what we're into and I don't wanna ask in case she changes her mind. She might be showing us a way out, trucks or even weapons, though I'm not sure why she'd do that. Either way, I wanna see what's on this side of the mall.

As we move farther from the warm, bustling food court, the dark hallway is eerie and quiet, sending nervous tingles up my arms. The hallway has the worst signs of decay I've seen so far in this camp. Large cracks run up the plaster walls. The carpet's been stripped away, leaving only pitted concrete. Our footsteps echo. It smells like mildew, stale air, and something else—something sulfuric and chemical.

Mage turns around, her features hollow in the dim light. "If anyone asks why we're down here, I'm going to tell them that I found you wandering off and I'm bringing you back. It's the only lie I can think of that they'll believe. Okay?"

"Mage, where are you tak—"

"Shhh." She presses her finger to her lips. "Just a little farther."

Clay's hand finds the small of my back. He's just as nervous as I am.

"Stop," Mage whispers and we do.

Dim outlines lurk in the corners. Ethan's hand finds mine. I hear the distinct sound of a struck match and the hiss of flame. Then light floods the darkness as Mage turns on a gas camping lantern she's lifted from a stool beside her.

A giant crevasse cuts across the ground where the floor used to be—a deep, black scar, ominous and ugly. We're only steps away. If Mage hadn't stopped us at that exact moment, we would've plunged to our deaths. I peer down. Crumbled bits of concrete run around the crevasse wall in a jagged slope like a makeshift spiral staircase. There's no visible bottom. The sulfuric smells waft from its depths so strong it makes my eyes water.

"What're we doing here?" I ask. Part of me wonders if she's going to shove us forward and be done with us. I grip Ethan's hand tighter.

Mage steps closer and the light spills into the hole. Still no bottom.

"This is the Temple of the Spirits. Or the hole as some call it. We aren't supposed to come near here or enter without the Messiah's permission. To do so means banishment. There will be no pardons." She repeats her memorized warning and then swings the lantern back to look at our faces. "Freaky, huh?" A smile finally breaks out on her face. "Like Alice's rabbit hole." She leans over. "Down, down, down."

"Who's Alice?" I ask, edging closer. A sick unease is crawling up my limbs. I don't like this place at all. "Why you showing us this if it's forbidden?"

"Cause no one else will come with me," she says, peering down, a strange wonder on her face. "I think there's something weird going on down there."

Goosebumps run up my arms as she says it. I step back and take Ethan's hand. "We should go."

"Yeah," she says, dimming the lantern light until its rays die. I stare into the blackness and pray my eyes adjust soon. I don't like being in the dark with my back to that awful pit.

"Well, back to the food court. Stay quiet now." Mage's voice trails away. Ethan, Clay, and Rayburn follow. I'm about to go when a small noise catches my attention. Some sort of low, humming sound. It's coming from the hole. I can't see the black void anymore, but I

44

stand stock-still and wait. Finally, I hear it again. A low, desperate moaning.

Human moaning.

CHAPTER SEVEN

I stand in the darkness, my heart thudding into my ears.

"Riley?"

It's Clay's voice. I'm about to answer him when a very large shadow appears out of the dark and grabs my arm.

"What're you doing back here?" a man asks, his voice thick with anger. His breath is more rancid than the sulfur smell wafting up from the pit.

I pull back. "I'm lost."

He shakes me and my head snaps back, a pain twanging in my neck. I pull away, but his hand is a vise.

I recognize him now, even in the dark: the bandaged nose framing two black eyes, the same red lace-up sneakers. Stephen draws me close, heat radiating off his chest. He's sporting a different tank-top. This one is an American Flag. "You listen to me," he growls. "If I find you back here again, I'll make things very unpleasant for your family. You want your brother on solar panel duty outside? I hear it's going to be 108 today."

I can't see his face, but I know he's smiling viciously. He loves this. I say nothing and will myself not to do something crazy. He tugs me forward, down the dark hallway, and into the light trickling in from the food court. Mage and the boys stand at one of the tables with worry on their faces.

Clay strides up, his eyes hardening as he looks at Stephen's hand on my arm. "Riley, you okay?"

"Fine," I say, glancing at Stephen. "I got lost."

"Keep this one in your sight at all times," Stephen says to Mage. Then he points a meaty finger back toward the buzzing food court. Mage leads us in and sits us at a table near the center. The sun bores down from the open ceiling. Glass windows above must have insulated this area from the heat and sun, but that glass is long gone. Tarps and canvas sheets shade the tables from direct light, but it's still hot. I don't mind it. Anything to get away from that creepy cavern.

Stephen slams a giant container of peas down on the table. "Shell them." Then he wanders to a booth and begins a conversation with a pretty blond girl.

I take a pea and pinch it between my fingers. Rubbing the crisp green pods between my hands is strangely soothing. I lean in. "We gotta figure out how to get the hell outta here." I think about saying something about what the moaning, but I don't want to scare Ethan. And really, I'm not sure what I heard.

Rayburn drops his eyes, his fingers trembling around a pod. He wasn't made for life outside of the hospital and frankly, he needs to toughen up. I open my mouth to say so when Clay interrupts me.

"I don't like this place any more'n you do." He pauses as one of the cooks shuffles by with a huge stack of bowls. "We'll bide our time and figure out what they plan to do with us. Then we make our move. But not before." He fumbles with a peapod, it slips out of his hand, and plops on the floor. He frowns at the cotton bandage on his hand. I look away from the pain on his face.

"What about Mama?" Ethan asks, tossing a dark curtain of hair out of his eyes.

"Mage said she'll come back later to take us to see her." I watch the slow burn creep up Ethan's neck at the mention of Mage. I want to tell him that a crush on the daughter of this commune's crazy leader is about as dumb as shaking hands with a rattler, but I don't. I look back to the peapods, green and slick between my dirty fingers, and pop one in my mouth.

"At least it, uh, it happened here," Rayburn says, squinting behind his glasses. He rubs a thick hand across his forehead and continues. "Your mom, I mean. At least if she's going to m-m-miscarry, she's here instead of... of on the road." He drops his eyes and shakes his head. "Not much I could've done."

I frown at him. "You think that's what happening? That she's...miscarrying?" I have no idea how I feel about this. That baby in her stomach is my brother or sister. But maybe not. I'm not even sure if the fetus has any of our genes. Nessa Vandewater's words echo in my head: *problems with the fetus*. I squeeze a peapod so hard the pea shoots out and skids across the floor.

Clay's hand finds mine. I stare into his sky-blue eyes, so kind, so understanding. I fight the urge to shuffle around the table, fall into his arms, and let him hold me. Instead I relish the brush of his fingers on mine until someone walks by and he pulls them away.

"So, we watch and wait," I say, trying to sound confident. I scan

48

the food court before I continue. Stephen is leaning over the counter, his fingers tracing down the girl's bare arm. I crouch forward. "But I want everyone's eyes and ears open. Watch for where they stash weapons, look for exit doors, back alleys, anything that might be important." They nod. I look up into the searing mid-morning sky. "I don't know how, but we're gonna get outta here."

***

After peapod duty is dish duty. After dish duty we serve lunch. When we're finally released to eat our bowls of pea soup, the sloppy green liquid is cold, but I don't care. We've been eating charred jackrabbit and lizard for weeks. A vegetable feels like a treat. I slurp the fresh green liquid until my bowl is empty and look around for more. Seconds are not offered and I don't ask. Andrew walks around with a clipboard, shuffling between tables, eying everyone's portion size. We're just five more hungry mouths to feed. Why is the Messiah so hell-bent on keeping us?

Mage appears as we're finishing lunch. She's got another folded paper animal in her hands, a frog this time, made out of paper the color of our pea soup. She sets it on our table, reaches out, and presses an index finger to the frog's backside. It springs forward at her touch. She giggles and bats golden eyelashes. Ethan drops his eyes. He's getting attached, just like he does with any animal we trap. The ending with Mage won't be so brutal, but it's still gonna cut him when we leave.

"So, you said you'd take us to see our mom?" I ask.

Mage nods, the blond coils of hair bobbing. "I got permission, but only you and him." She points at Ethan and me. "You two," she says, pointing to Rayburn and Clay, "are going to get your permanent job assignments." She shrugs her narrow shoulders, making her cotton jumper rise and fall. "Sorry," she says, pocketing her paper frog. "Best I could do."

"It's fine," I say, anxious. Mama. I am dying to see her and dreading it. I push up, needing to move my body. "Can we go?"

Ethan stands beside me. I wait for his hand to slip into mine, but they're locked at his sides. His eyes follow Mage.

I turn back to Clay and Rayburn. Clay hugs me, a sympathetic smile at the corners of his mouth. "Go," he says. "We'll be fine." He

49

looks at Rayburn, who stares blankly back. An elbow from Clay gets Rayburn unstuck.

"Yeah, uh, fine," Rayburn manages.

Mage leads us back down the hallways at a fast clip. No one speaks. I'm too nervous and Ethan is either love-struck or feeling the nerves too. Mage fiddles with the frog in her pocket. Her silence makes me worry.

At the end of the hallway is a large department store, with a wide rectangular entrance and glass display windows that have naked, limbless life-sized dolls piled like a plastic holocaust. A guard sits at the entrance on a metal stool, slumped over, one boot hooked around the stool leg. He's wearing a patched security guard uniform that must've come from the days when this mall still saw shoppers. He doesn't have a gun, but there's a seriously long knife hung at his belt. Does he use it to keep people out, or patients in? I run my hand over the ankh brand on my wrist. I vowed never to step foot in a hospital again.

"We're here to see the newcomer." Mage shoves both hands in her jumper pockets and smiles innocently up at the burly guard.

Rising to his full height of over six feet, the guard stands, his stool scraping on the concrete floor. "I heard no visitors." His voice is mumbled and phlegmy. When he opens his mouth again, I see a red sore like a smooshed raspberry on his tongue. There's another blistered patch of skin just above his wrist. My stomach lurches. Have we already been infected by whatever it is they carry? But then, why doesn't Mage seem infected? Why have all the women looked healthy?

Mage rocks back and forth, heel to toe, looking every bit a little schoolgirl. "My daddy says we can go in."

The guard's brow furrows. He scratches his crop of brown hair and shrugs. "Didn't hear nothing."

Mage tugs down a blond curl. "That's 'cause he didn't tell *you*. He told *me*. Can we go in now?"

The guard blinks, confused, but he shuffles aside and sits back on his stool, falling easily back into looking bored. Mage grabs my hand and I tug Ethan along. When we're out of earshot, she leans in to us.

"Perks of being the Messiah's daughter." She winks.

"He didn't tell you we could visit?"

She smirks and places a finger to her lips in a don't-tell gesture. I have found myself one powerful ally. Or maybe she just likes getting me into trouble.

She leads us around the gutted department store. The front has nothing but discarded racks and old display tables. The dirty, scratched linoleum sits bare and lifeless. Faded posters cling to the walls. My eyes trail across a large poster with two bored-looking girls in tight jeans and even tighter shirts. What would it have felt like to be a kid when this mall lived and breathed? When throngs of girls marched with plastic shopping bags slung over their wrists.

We turn the corner. Cots and mattresses line the floor. Patients lie on them. An elderly woman with rheumy eyes and skin like crinkled paper. A middle-aged man covered in large red sores writhes on the bed. A little boy with a splinted arm watches us with wide, wet eyes. Then he turns and buries his head into the yellowed mattress.

I search the beds, my heart starting to pound. What will Mama look like? Will she be awake? With sweaty palms I walk, eying each patient. A girl about my age lies so still on a cot I wonder if she's breathing.

Then I see Mama. My heart freezes to ice as I walk over, Ethan at my heels. She's lying on her side, turned away. Slowly I walk up, bend over, and place my hand on her frail arm.

She jumps and I yank my hand back. As she rolls toward us, I see her burned side first, the diminished ear, the rippled skin of her cheek. When I can see her fully, my heart sinks. I was expecting her to look better than I'd last seen her, but instead she's worse—nearly translucent skin, dark circles under her eyes, sharp cheekbones that look cut out of stone. Her trembling hand seeks out mine and she lifts a smile to her cracked lips.

"Darlings," she croaks.

I kneel by her cot and take both her hands in mine. Her knuckles protrude like walnuts beneath her skin. "How... are you feeling?" I swallow over the lump in my throat.

My mother nods and runs her tongue over her chapped lips. "Okay. How're you?" She reaches a hand out to Ethan. He's a statue beside me, his eyes the size of dinner plates. I place my hand on his arm. If only I could spare him this.

"We're...okay." I flick my eyes up toward the Middies who float around, checking temperatures and changing bandages. I thought they were supposed to fix her, not make her worse.

As if reading my mind, she answers. "I'm feeling better. They're giving me fluids and I need to rest. The time on the road was hard on me."

I study her face. How can she be feeling better? She looks like a corpse.

"The baby?" I manage, nodding to her stomach beneath the scratchy blanket.

She drops her eyes. "It seems to be faring fine despite my..." she pauses and swallows "difficulties." Is that bitterness in her voice? Did she ever feel this way with me? Like I was a burden?

"Mama," I say, leaning close, my elbows resting on the saggy cot, "we'll get you out. If these people are making you worse, we'll find a way to—"

She cuts me off with a shake of her head. "No, darling. We can't chance that right now. You stay and eat and rest up. Auntie can wait a little bit longer."

Auntie. There's the pang of worry again. With the Sheriff dead, who knows what's happening to her. Just one more problem to add to my heap. My mind returns to the human moaning I heard in that crevasse.

A Middie shuffles up, an aging woman in loose cotton pants and a tunic with only a single gold bracelet glittering on her wrist. Her face wrinkles into a look of displeasure as she scans our group.

"Really. That's enough. You're not supposed to be here anyway." She fixes a disapproving gaze at Mage who shrugs her narrow shoulders.

"Please," I say, facing the Middie, "is there anything you can do for my mother? She looks..." I can't finish. I clasp my hands together and will myself not to choke up.

The Middie turns her eyes to my fragile mama. "She needs rest. I assure you she has the best care here. Trust us." She places her hand on my back and leads me toward the door.

I whip around and crouch down to grab my mama's hand. Her eyes meet mine, and for a moment I think one or both of us might cry.

"I'll come back. Every day. I'll make sure they're doing what they need to do to get you better." My eyes flick down to her stomach. "Both of you."

My mama nods, her eyes wet. "Don't worry about me. Take care of Ethan and the others, but don't worry about me."

CHAPTER EIGHT

There's a special place in hell for whoever assigned me laundry duty. My fingers are wrinkled white raisins and my body aches from kneeling over the wash tub. The smelly undershirt I'm holding goes back into the sudsy tub and then I scrub it on the washboard. I've already nicked one knuckle on the board leaning out of the washbasin. Eying the jagged edge, I know it's just a matter of time before I rip open another.

Plunge and scrub. Plunge and scrub. Mage sits beside me twirling a wadded-up shirt through the soapy water in a figure eight. As the Messiah's daughter, her plunging and scrubbing are mostly for show. She chats with the other women stationed around us in this abandoned shop. It must've been a beauty parlor—some of the swivel chairs and mirrored vanities are still in place. Faded posters show women with big curly hairdos. On the back wall is a huge sign with the words REDKEN and some other faded print I can't read. I stare longingly at a cracked leather swivel chair that sits with its sisters along the wall. My knees throb from kneeling on the tile beside the washbasin. I look up at the woman in charge. Prema's frown looks like it's been etched out of rock. Her wrinkled brown skin and five-foot frame don't diminish her bulldog manner. She shoots me sharp glances whenever my plunging and scrubbing slow. I scowl and shove the shirt down with a splash of sudsy water. Maybe if I rub a hole in one of their precious shirts, she'll kick me out. A few more hours of this and I'll wish I was back in the diner starving to death.

Mage bounces over, another paper animal in her hands. I'm not sure what this one is supposed to be, but she flits it in front of me anyway, making it loop and dive as I wring out the shirt and stand.

"Thirty minutes 'til dinner," she sings, making her animal gallop over my shoulder with a "dumpty dum" song. "*Wook* at me," she says in a baby voice, dancing her animal in my face. "I'm *Wiley* and I'm *soo sewiuos*."

I plod over to the clotheslines strung along the back wall and spread my shirt out. Two of the metal clips molded out of old wire hangers fasten my shirt to the line. The watery *drip, drip, drip* is soothing. I stand, staring dumbly at the black REDKEN poster, and wonder what a "wax pomade" is while the blood returns to my legs.

"*Eh hem.*" Prema glares at me. Her wrinkly chin waddle, that reminds me of a wild turkey, trembles angrily. I push a huge, dramatic sigh out of my chest, lumber over, and grab another dirty shirt from the pile.

Death by starvation might not be that bad.

"Tell me about the outside," Mage says, resting her animal on my arm. "Tell me about," she drops her voice, "the Breeders."

She says their name like it's a curse word she's afraid a parent will overhear. Her eyes flick to Prema nervously and then lock on my face, hungry to know. I stare at the sudsy water. The bubble-filled froth clings around my wrist where the ankh brand rests. It'll be there forever, just like the memories of the Plan B room. The skeletal girls strapped to beds with computers keeping them alive.

I shake my head to rid it of the image. "The outside's a cruel place. You're better off in here."

Mage frowns, clearly not liking my answer. "But, there's so much to see. Old buildings. Mountains." She grips my arm and leans in close. "Are the Breeders really taller than the tallest man?"

"The worst Breeder is really a woman." Nessa Vandewater's face appears in my mind. Is she hunting us right now?

"Really?" Mage squeaks. Prema looks over at us. Mage lowers her voice again. "What does she look like?"

"What does it matter? You're never gonna meet her." At least I hope not.

Mage slumps back against the wall. "My papa says if the Breeders ever come here, we won't go with them. We should die before we let them take us." Her eyes stare into the distance, a sadness filling them.

I drop the shirt I'm washing and lean in to get her attention. "Hey," I whisper, "have the Breeders ever come here? Do they know we're here?"

Mage shakes her head. "Papa says we're protected. As long as we please the Gods', they'll keep us safe from the Breeders."

"Huh. That's good, I guess." I plunge my shirt into the wash while my mind mulls this over. I don't know if I believe the Gods are protecting them, but somehow they've managed to keep their women free this long. Still, this conversation helps confirm that we need to get on the road as soon as possible. I don't want to lead the Breeders here and jeopardize these women's safety. And I don't wanna be caught either.

I unfold a shirt covered in bright green stains. It smells rancid, like rotting death. Suddenly I'm transported back to the clinic in the abandoned town Clay, Ethan, and I found. All those dead bodies killed by an epidemic and stacked on top of each other until they moldered into a giant mound of festering flesh. I reel back, holding the shirt in front of me out like a rotten carcass.

Prema, kneeling at her own basin, looks alarmed. She gets up, lurches over, and snatches the shirt from my hands, a redness creeping into her brown cheeks that I don't understand.

"What is it?" I ask, watching as she balls the shirt up and shoves it deep into her own laundry basket. "What happened to that shirt?"

She shoots me a daggered stare and says nothing. Her rheumy eyes say *mind your own business*. Little does she know, that's impossible.

"Dinner time," Prema snaps. The other women finish hanging up their last items and shuffle off toward the aroma of pork wafting down the hallway. Prema points an arthritic finger at me. "Finish up." She nods at my half-full basket. "If I see you in line and later find that basket has clothes in it, it'll be a double load for you tomorrow, dust." She shuffles out, her long skirt *shushing* behind her.

"Can you hurry?" Mage asks. She bounces onto one of the cracked leather salon chairs and swings her feet. "I'm starving."

I roll my eyes. She doesn't know what starving means. "Why did she call me dust?"

Mage leans into one of the cracked vanity mirrors and stares at her teeth. "That's what we call all the outsiders. I guess 'cause people out there are so dusty."

"Oh." I walk to the basket where Prema stuffed the T-shirt and drag it out. The green stains look sulfuric in the light, nasty like someone puked up their intestines after eating nuclear waste. "Why did she get so mad when I pulled this out of the bin?" I say, holding the shirt up to Mage. "What happened to this?"

Anxiety floods Mage's face. "Put it away."

I tuck it back into the basket. "What's so secret? It's just a dirty shirt."

She hops off the swivel chair and shoots a look down the hallway, knitting her hands together. "Riley, there's some stuff you shouldn't ask about. Like that," she says, pointing to the basket.

"Seems like there's *a lot* I shouldn't ask about." I turn and fix her with a serious stare. "Are the people sick here? You need to tell me. If we've been infected... if my mother's been infected, or Ethan..." Anger surges through me. If they've brought us here just to kill us with their diseases...

Mage shakes her head. "It's not catching."

"So, there *is* something wrong with people." I step closer. "How do you know it's not catching?"

She folds her arms angrily over her flat chest. "I just know, okay. I'm not sick, am I?" She throws up her arms in an I-told-you-so gesture.

"You're the Messiah's daughter; maybe they gave you some... antidote."

She shakes her head. "None of the women are sick."

"So, it's just men?" I step back, taking this in. What about Clay, Rayburn? What about Ethan?

Mage takes out another slip of her colored paper and begins rashly folding creases, making angry triangles with her trembling fingers. "I don't know why you're digging. It's just gonna get us in trouble. My papa wouldn't like you knowing."

I step closer, placing my hand over hers, trying to still her frantically folding hands. "Mage." I wait until she looks up at me, her gray eyes lifting. "Whatever's going on, I need to know about it. I need to protect my family."

Mage drops her eyes. "It might be too late for that," she whispers.

I grip her arm. "What d'you mean?"

She stiffens, her eyes locked on my hand. I pull it off her arm, but the look on her face tells me I've played this all wrong. She stuffs both hands in her jumper pockets and won't look at me. "So, dinner?"

I frown. Another false move. It seems that's the only thing I'm good at lately.

***

We enter the food court after everyone else. The lines that normally curl around the stalls are thin with everyone already seated at the tables, eating. My stomach grumbles at the roasted meat smell, but the hollow pit that's normally there isn't so hollow anymore. Three square meals, even small ones, are miraculous. I have more energy, more stamina. What would it be like to stay here indefinitely? No days on the road. No Breeders chasing us down. No famine. My eyes fall on Stephen spooning a soupy grain into his mouth. No, this place isn't free. There's always a price to pay.

Mage flits off toward a group of kids her age sitting on a bench near the decaying play area. She doesn't even say good-bye. I've made her mad and it'll take some work to fix what I've broken. I'm thinking this all over when a hand cinches around my wrist and pulls me backward down a dark hallway.

I stumble back, unable to see my assailant. When I open my mouth to scream, another hand wraps around it. I swing back to plant an elbow.

"God, I love it when you're feisty."

Clay. I stop fighting and whirl around. In the dimness, his features are shadowed: his strong jaw flecked with a week's worth of stubble, his dark hair rippling over his forehead. A smile rises on his lips as I turn to him.

"I've missed you." I wrap my arms around his neck and tuck myself into him.

He stumbles back, bumping into the wall. His hands circle my back and rub up and down. My heart pounds. He cups my chin and kisses me. My body floods with fire. I press into him, locking my hands around his back. His hands are in my hair, on my face, pulling me closer. We kiss and kiss. I pull back, panting, smiling.

"I missed you," he says, his voice low and sexy.

"God, you have no idea how much I've wanted to talk to you," I say, staring into his blue eyes. "This place is so..."

"Messed up," he says, nodding. His forehead wrinkles. "There's something wrong with the men in the Brotherhood. They're all huge and they have these...sores."

I nod. "Mage hinted as much. Stay away from 'em much as you can. Try not to touch 'em or drink from their water."

He leans his head back on the wall. "I tried, but they all share a water bucket and we got no choice but to drink. It's so hot in that damn grow house, we can't go more'n a few minutes without needin' water." He shakes his head. "Whatever they got, it shouldn't affect you or Ethan. I think he's too young or somethin'. None of the other boys his age seem sick."

"Clay," I say, reaching up and touching his cheek, "if you say we go, then we go. I'm not okay with letting you get sick. We'll find a way."

He sighs heavily. "Yer ma can't travel yet, and I ain't much good on the road neither." He looks down at his bandaged hand and frowns.

"Is that what this is about? You don't need to protect us on the road. I can worry about that."

He pulls back. "That's just it. I don't want you to worry 'bout defendin' us. That's *my* job." He pounds his chest with his fist. "I was supposed to stop 'em from capturin' us, but I couldn't. I couldn't even keep hold of my goddamned gun." He tightens a fist on his good hand, the veins on his arm pulsing. "I dropped it."

I run my hands up over his shoulders. "You're hurt. There's nothing you coulda done."

"Do you know what my pa woulda done if I'd a dropped my gun like that on a raid?" His eyes are distant.

I shake my head.

"Beat my hide, that's what. Beat me 'til I couldn't walk the next day. Gunslinger never drops his weapon." He lowers his eyes. "Never."

"It wasn't your fault."

"One time," he says, looking out, his eyes hard blue stones, "I dropped my gun when my horse reared up. I let go to keep hold of the reigns so I didn't fall off and break my damn neck. You know what my pa did?"

I say nothing.

"There weren't another soul around, so it weren't like I needed it or nothing, but you know what he did?" Anger has flooded into his face, making his cheeks flare red.

I shake my head.

Clay balls his fist. "He got off his horse, brushed the dirt off my gun, and hit me right here with the butt," he lifts the hair and reveals a white scar cutting into his scalp. "Split my head like a melon and it bled like a sumbitch." Clay swallows, his chest heaving. "I 'member lookin' up, the blood pourin' in my eyes, and there weren't no apology on his face. He stuck out his chin and said, 'Never drop yer gun again.'" Clay stops and presses his eyes closed. When he looks at me, his face is full of pain, anger, and shame. "I was ten."

"Clay..." What should I say to that? *Your father was a goddamn monster? It's a good thing you killed him?* I place my hand on his arm and it trembles beneath my palm. "That wasn't your fault and neither was us getting captured. They overpowered us."

He looks up at me, his jaw locked tight. "They overpowered us because I'm weak."

"No." I take his hand, but he pulls it away.

"I don't wanna talk 'bout this," he snaps. Then he softens. "We should go 'fore they notice we're gone."

I nod, but feel like a cored apple, empty and centerless. Our moment alone and it turned into this? He strides up, kisses my cheek, and then he's gone, limping into the food court, and I'm left standing alone.

***

We sit together and eat, Rayburn, Clay, Ethan, and I. The din in the food court covers our silence. People chat at their tables, dishes bang, and children squeal as they tromp around the carousel, hopping from horse to horse or jump on the decaying foam fruit in the play area. My eyes lock on the faded plastic slide that must be a giant watermelon slice, though now it's dirty beige with bits of foam peeking out. The children slide down the bumpy surface, whooping. A little boy jumps off a big banana and lands with a thump. They're so carefree. I look at Ethan, whose sad eyes gaze into the distance and then at Clay, whose anger is still tucked in the corners of his frown. We'll never be careless like that.

"I think I, uh, know where they get their supplies," Rayburn says.

For a moment, I almost missed it over the din, but then I turn to him. "What'd you say?"

He blinks at me behind his smeared glasses. The acne on his chin looks better since we've been here, not as red and blotchy. With everyone's eyes on him, he seems to shrink. His stutter gets worse. "I, uh, I said that I think, uh, that I know where they get their s-s-supplies." He shrugs and then scoops a big bite of stringy pork into his mouth.

Clay swivels on him. "What took you so long? Spill. Where do they come from, 'cause I know they can't have snatched it all from inside this mall?"

Rayburn chews and swallows hard. "I'm pretty sure, uh, it all came from the Breeders."

My insides grow cold. "How?" I say, leaning in. "How could they have supplies from... there?" I can't say the word. My brand seems to tingle.

Rayburn shrugs his bony shoulders; his dirty white button-down hospital shirt hangs loose on his frame. It's amazing how much weight he's lost since we've been on the road. "The van we rode here in was, uh, an old model hospital supply van." He pauses, gulps, and looks around. "The solar panels are Breeders technology, I think. There are panels like that on the hospital roof."

I nod him on, prickles crawling up my skin. "They couldn't have done that on their own. Is that how they make girl babies? With Breeders' technology?"

Rayburn shrugs. He's downplaying his intelligence, blinking behind his smudged glasses. I've seen him do this a few times. He knows more than what he's saying. I lean forward to press him further when Clay speaks.

"So, what're you sayin'? They're in cahoots with the good docs back in Albuquerque? Are they gonna turn us back over to my... to my mother?" Clay rubs a nervous hand through his hair.

Rayburn shrugs again. "Can't tell that."

I grip the table with clawed fingers. "We gotta get out of here."

Clay nods. Beside me, Ethan sags. When I look over at him, his eyes have found Mage across the food court. She's flitting from table to table, showing off her paper animals, giving a few away. Her golden hair glows. Ethan watches her, his mouth twisted down. I don't say it, but I think, *Give it up, kid. We can't take her where we're going.*

***

After dinner we scrub plates until my already puckered fingers are raw. When we finish I'm so bone tired I can barely keep my eyes open. I ask Mage about seeing my mama again, but she shakes her head. She doesn't seem as mad as before, but the easy comfort we had has flown. I'll have to come up with a way to get her back on my side.

I'm about to ask for an early night and shuffle toward the girls' hall when a strange pounding begins. Drum beats echo from the high ceilings. The people begin gathering around the carousel. Ethan's hand finds my elbow and soon the four of us move as one; Clay stands behind me and Rayburn beside him.

"What is it?" Clay asks, his eyes on the two men before the carousel, pounding their palms on large drums. The *boom, boom, boom* seems to synch up with the thudding of my heart.

I shake my head. "No idea."

Prema shuffles by and I snag her arm. She swivels. Her look of surprise turns to a scowl like I'm a bug she's discovered in her tea.

"What's going on?" I shout over the drumming that echoes around the cavernous space.

She nods toward the front. "It's a Naming. Men on the right. Women on the left. Best get to your spots and zip your lips." She hobbles forward, her slippers scraping on the cement floor.

My eyes dart between my three boys. Sometimes I would give anything to be a man. "Guess I'll see y'all later." I try not to sound bitter.

Clay puts his hand on my shoulder. "We don't gotta do what she says. You stay with us."

I look around to see if this is possible, but already almost everyone has separated. As I turn, Stephen clomps in our direction. I shake my head. "Not worth making trouble. I'll hang with Mage. Go before the meathead blows a gasket." I nod to Stephen, who's trying to get around a clump of old ladies. I slip between a group of women and weave through the crowd toward the front. The heat intensifies with all this flesh, even though the sun has dropped and isn't baking us from above. The smell of hardworking women permeates the air: a salty musk, sprinkled with the tang of laundry soap or cooking oil. Soon, the sounds pick up, drums mostly and a strange chanting. Around me, women's lips move in unison as the drums pound, pound, *pound*. Will they lose themselves in the beat and start tearing things apart? It feels like we're inside a diseased heart. I search frantically for the boys. What if we have to run? What if I can't find them?

The noise stops. The Messiah slips up the steps of the carousel, his hand on Andrew's arm. He's wearing the same gossamer gown we saw him in earlier, his brown hair long and gleaming. A heavy necklace decorated with religious symbols dangles from his neck—a cross, a Star of David, a crescent moon and a star, a large gold bird of prey with wings outstretched. Next to him, Andrew looks like a study in opposites with his tidy pants and T-shirt, his short bowl haircut. His round goggles look silly on his serious face. He frowns as he helps the Messiah up the sagging steps, and then takes his place beside the prophet.

The Messiah's cloudy eyes scan his people. They stand, barely breathing, as he looks over the throng, almost a hundred faces all glued on him. He better have something good to say.

He holds up a hand and waves it over the crowd like he's calling for silence, though he already has it. Just before he drops his hand, I see a small tremor there, a tremor he's trying to hide. How bad is his health? What will happen if he takes a turn for the worse? Andrew will step up? He'd kick us out in a heartbeat. Or worse.

"Gods' people," he says, his voice booming through the silent food court. "The half moon is upon us. Tonight we ask the Gods for continued sight and celebrate the Naming."

There's a murmur of agreement from the crowd. Somewhere a baby lets out a cry. Then silence.

The Messiah pauses, his hand on Andrew's shoulder, his cloudy eyes locked on the crowd. "The Naming began with our forefathers who planted this seed and brought us to this holy land. Every moon we bring forth the male candidates, selected as our best and brightest, to join the throng of the Brotherhood. Tonight we celebrate brothers, Mordecai and Kemuel."

Two teenage boys are ushered forward. Kemuel is the boy from the van and behind him must be his brother, Mordecai. They look like twins, though not identical. Mordecai is broad-shouldered where Kemuel is narrow. Mordecai's hair is straighter and blonder than Kemuel's dark blond, curly mop. And Kemuel looks like he's about to throw up as they are led onto the carousel. Unlike the Messiah, when they step on the platform, it jostles and squeaks. The boys stand at attention, their arms locked at their sides. Kemuel's terrified eyes flick up as the Messiah brings out a tattered scroll. The boy is ready to bolt; his eyes look like a jackrabbit's in the hawk's shadow.

The Messiah holds up his crinkled parchment. On it are strings of text that look like they've been cut from other books and pasted on. He begins reading. "He who dwells in the shelter of the Most

High will abide in the shadow of the Almighties. It is He who has sent forth His Messenger with the guidance and the religion of Truth, so that we may prevail over all others, and none can bear witness to the Truth as the Gods do. So it has been in Jerusalem and Mecca, Harajuku and Sabarimala. So it is with the Citadel."

The Messiah stops and spreads his arms wide, looking every bit like a crucified Christ-man. Even the light from the open ceiling seems directed to illuminate his glory. It's no wonder these people follow him.

"Bring forth the holy water!" he shouts.

The drums pick up and the chanting renews around me. *Sight, sight, sight,* they chant. The hairs on my arms spring up. Kemuel's eyes go as wide as a trapped musk hog. He looks like the Messiah is about to gut him, but still he stands, trembling. Mordecai looks less afraid, but now there's fear in his eyes too. Behind me a woman begins quietly crying. What are they going to do to these boys?

Two giant men bring a silver bucket and hand it to the Messiah. He lifts a silver dipper and begins giving drinks to each of his men at the front. They nod, dip their heads, and drink from his ladle. Finally, he comes around to the two boys standing on the carousel.

The chanting drops away and the Messiah raises the bucket.

"I Name you, Mordecai and Kemuel, in the blood of the Gods: Jesus, Buddha, Mohamed, Yahweh, and countless others. With this holy baptism you are now men of the Gods and part of our Brotherhood."

He raises the full ladle to Mordecai who, with trembling hands, takes it and drinks. The Messiah nods, takes the ladle back, and refills it. He holds the full ladle out to Kemuel.

Kemuel stands motionless, his eyes wide with fright, trained on the ladle. He makes no move to take it. The Messiah holds it up, waiting. Someone behind me yells, "Drink, boy." The woman continues sobbing.

With trembling hands, Kemuel reaches for the ladle. He lifts it toward his mouth. Someone yells, "Go on." Kemuel's eyes dart around the crowd.

With a cry he tosses the ladle at the Messiah and bolts.

The Messiah wipes a hand down his water-doused face as

Kemuel's footsteps pound away. Slowly, he points a finger toward the boy.

"After him."

CHAPTER NINE

Men rush after the terrified boy. Behind me a woman shoves forward, keening wildly. The woman is the one I heard crying earlier—she must be Kemuel's mother. Now she's clutching her face and wailing. She uses her body as a battering ram, smashing people out of her way. One of the Middies pushes up behind her, grabs her elbow, and attempts to drag her back. The wailing woman shakes her off.

"Leave him be!" she wails. "Let him go!"

More shoving and pushing as men surge to grab her. Mordecai, who's been watching this open-mouthed, jumps down from the carousel and launches toward his mother. The Messiah's mouth moves, though no words reach us over this racket. It doesn't matter. I spot Clay's head above the crowd and he shoots me a frantic look. He struggles toward me, but gets pinned behind a wall of bodies. I slip around an elderly woman and a hand cinches around my wrist.

I turn. Stephen flashes me a nasty smile.

"Messiah said all dusts are to be put up for the night." His other hand clasps around my free arm. "Let's go, pretty."

I struggle, but his hands are big as baseball mitts and his grip is unbreakable. He scowls and drags me along. I crane my neck to catch a view of my boys. A wall of burly men is corralling them. Goddamn these people. If they hurt Ethan—

Stephen yanks me so hard my shoulder socket twangs with pain. He flashes a nasty smile, his bearded upper lip curling. He shoves me into the empty store that serves as my bedroom and slams the grate. I glare at him as he fumbles with the padlock.

"What's wrong with the water, Stephen?" I ask, now that he can't reach me.

He flashes me a startled look and then his eyes harden. "None of your business, dust."

"What'll they do to that boy?" I gaze out into the hallway. Women wander back down the hall, murmuring with hushed voices.

Stephen clicks the lock and stands. My eyes fall on the wide sore that has sprouted on his neck: red and goopy.

He points a massive finger at me. "What'll happen to that boy is what he deserves. We do what the Messiah decrees, or the Gods punish us. Kemuel put this whole community in danger. He'll be dealt with." He grips the grate, rattles it loudly, laughs, and strides away.

I walk over and curl up on the dirty mattress. The bloody stain, now dried to a brown rust, reminds me of Mama. I tuck my head to my knees as the emptiness seeps in. At least on the road we were together.

***

That night I dream of swirling sands that swallow me. Of clawing cactus clutching me with spiked limbs, piercing my skin. Of the Messiah with eyes like frosted glass staring at me, seeing through me. Lastly I dream of waking to find Mama in a pool of her own blood.

When I sit up, gasping, it's that image that stays with me.

"Bad dream," a voice behind me says.

I whirl around. The morning lights are on in the hallway. Mage sits Indian-style on the other side of the grate, working on a paper animal in her lap. Watching her deft fingers fly over the paper helps my pounding heart to slow.

"Where did you learn to do that?" I ask, slowly standing. My legs are boiled leather from yesterday's work.

Mage finally looks up. Her face is neither kind nor menacing. "My papa."

"You mean the Messiah." I walk to the grate. The bars between us rattle a little as I crouch down next to her. She shrugs and goes back to folding. In a moment she has a crinkly snake in her palm. She slips it through the bars and I take it.

"Thanks," I say. A peace offering perhaps? I put my hand on the bars. "You look fretful as a snared rabbit, as my Auntie would say. Did what happened last night bother you?"

She tucks her golden head down. "I liked him. He was in my class in the Willow Room."

I nod, weaving my fingers through the metal bars. "What'll they do to him?"

Mage grabs the grate, her fingers inches from mine. She stares into my eyes. "He'll be put out. They think I don't know what that means, but I do. It means he'll die. The coyotes will eat his guts."

It's hard to meet her wide gray eyes. I swallow. "Do they do that a lot?"

She shifts, one strap of her jumper sliding down her bare shoulder. "When they won't drink the holy water. When they break the rules. When someone starts causing trouble." She ticks each reason off on her fingers. "Breaking rules means you die, so pretty much everybody follows the rules." She lifts her eyes to mine. "Nobody wants to be put out."

"I came from out there," I say. "You can survive."

Mage shrugs again. "I don't want to think about it."

"Maybe I'll break a rule. Then they'll let me out of this hell hole." I mull this over for a moment. I'm sure they'd just find another way to punish us.

Mage frowns. "I said I don't want to talk about it."

"Fine." I drop down and sit on the frayed carpet next to the grate. I don't see a breakfast tray. "No bacon this morning?"

"You can come out and eat in the food court." She crawls on hands and knees to the lock and fiddles with it.

"Any chance I can see my mother today?" I ask. "You know how she's doing?"

Mage nods, not looking at me. "The same. They say she's resting. They won't let me in."

My heart sinks. I want her out. I want her with me. What's it going to take to make her well? Whatever it is, I'm going to figure it out. There's no way I'm losing her again.

I follow Mage into the food court. After we wait in line and get our trays—a pink slab of ham, four ripe strawberries (which I pop into my mouth instantly), and a weak tea that smells of mint—we find the boys. Ethan's eyebrows go up as Mage slides into the chair next to him. Clay reaches for my hand.

"How're you?" he asks, his eyes searching my face.

"Fine." I swallow my unease with a sip of tea.

Clay turns to Mage. "So, you're the Messiah's daughter?"

Mage nods, a big bite of greasy ham making her red lips shine.

Clay leans in on his elbows. His shirt's become as thin as paper, draping over his lean muscles. "Tell me," he says, zeroing in on her with his sky-blue eyes, "you ever heard of a woman named Nessa Vandewater? Or Marlin Tate?"

I clamp my hand onto Clay's and squeeze. This isn't the time for question and answer. I've only just regained Mage's trust. "Mage makes these great paper animals. Can you show us one?"

Clay frowns. "But I want to—"

My foot finds his shin with a swift kick. He shoots me a look, but stops talking.

Mage pulls a piece of bright blue paper out of her pocket. She begins folding. "It's called origami," she says, making a crease. "My papa learned it in some of the books he had brought here."

"The leader of the only free society in the west and he has time for paper folding?" Clay flicks his eyes to me, probably wondering if he'll get another kick.

Mage makes a complicated fold, her tongue poking out the corner of her mouth. Ethan's eyes follow her slender hands. He watches so intently that he startles a little when she finally flips her head up, a paper hawk pinched triumphantly between two fingers. "My papa's favorite."

We all smile and nod. Clay touches a finger to the bird, his eyes narrowing. "A bird of prey." Clay draws out the words like they mean something. I'm about to kick him again when his eyes snap up.

"Get down!" he yells, reaching for us.

A gunshot cracks through the food court.

Chaos.

Everyone's bolting, scrambling under tables, sprinting for the exits. A woman with a toddler hugged to her chest is crawling under a row of chairs, the child wailing. I grab for Ethan as my eyes search the crowd. Where did the gunshot come from? Then I see the shooter striding up, a gun clutched in his hand, his eyes wide with a crazed terror.

Kemuel.

His dark hair is a tangled mess. His clothes are tattered and one shin is a scabby. His thin face contorts into a look of rage, fear, and shock. He holds a handgun like he's never been allowed to before. However, that doesn't stop him from aiming it at anything that moves.

We slip under the table and huddle around the metal post as he stalks through the food court. I pull Ethan to me on one side, Mage on the other. Clay scoots up behind me, his body a taut wire. Rayburn balls up like a hedgehog.

Kemuel stalks through the play area, his gun out, arm extended. His cheeks puff in and out with panting breaths. A chair scrapes and he aims at it.

"Where is he?!" he screams, flecks of spit raining from his

mouth. "Where's the Messiah?"

No one answers. Somewhere a child wails. My eyes flick toward the exits. We're right in the center of the room. If we bolted, we'd be a target for sure.

"No?" Kemuel screams, veering our way. "The coward won't face me? Then give me his daughter." Beside me, Mage stiffens. I rub my hand up and down her bare shoulder. "Where's Mage?!"

Stephen stands, unfolding his bulk from under a table. He holds out his hands, smiling. "Kemuel, my boy, why don't you just put the gun down and we'll go talk to the Messiah. I'll get him to reinstate you, brother. Just put down the pistol."

Kemuel aims at Stephen, the gun barrel bobbing around. Silent tears trace down his pale cheeks. "You made me scrub out pig pens with my bare hands."

Stephen holds his hands up, still smiling, though it's fading fast. "Listen, little brother, it was all in good fun. We do that to all the boys before they're Named."

Kemuel wipes a sleeve across his eyes. "You rubbed it on my face. That wasn't *fun!*" Kemuel fires.

The gunshot cracks through the food court. Stephen's mouth drops open and he turns, but too late. The bullet burrows into his chest, spinning him, arms wide like a dancer. A spray of blood flies from his chest, then his back. He falls and lands hard and heavy. There's the slow patter of blood as it dribbles on to the concrete. One foot twitches. Then he is still.

I stare at his body, blinking. Dead. He has to be.

People scream. Someone bolts toward the exit. Kemuel moves like a man stuck in molasses. He shakes his head, murmuring, the gun loose in his hands. He stares at the man he just killed. Before we can bolt, he turns. His eyes land on Mage beside me.

"Go!" I scream, pushing them away. Kemuel runs at a full clip. Ethan scrambles forward, bumping into Rayburn, who's unrolling. I push Mage from behind, but she's stuck too. Tears stream down her face, her limbs move like noodles. I shove her. "Go! Now!"

A hand grabs my collar. I'm yanked back. A chair skitters and smacks into the concrete. Above me stands Kemuel. He aims the gun. The dark round barrel centers between my eyes, a hungry black void in the center. I throw my arms over my face.

He shoves me away. I wheel through space until my back and then my head bang against the concrete with twin thuds. Stars burst

71

in my vision. Above, the ceiling blurs.

The sound of a scuffle. I push myself up, my head swimming. He's got Mage by the arm. He hauls her upright and presses the gun to her temple.

The table flies forward as someone explodes from beneath it. Clay. He dives at Kemuel and tackles him. Mage falls back, skidding across the concrete. Clay lands on Kemuel, his hands around the boy's throat. Kemuel aims his gun at Clay's head.

"No!" I scream. I stagger toward them, hands out.

Clay slams his head into Kemuel's, their foreheads cracking with a sound like two eggs smashed in a bowl. The gun flops. Clay pins Kemuel to the concrete, teeth flashing, veins pulsing as he drops his forearm on the boy's neck.

The sound of thudding feet brings me out of my daze. Men latch onto Kemuel, pin him, and tie his hands. Another man grabs the gun. Clay staggers back and wipes blood out of his eyes, a bright red smear appearing across his forehead.

Behind the men, Andrew appears with the Messiah holding his arm. Mage runs to her father and jumps into his arms. Cradling her like a toddler, he strokes her golden curls as tears drip down his face. It's the first time I've ever seen the Messiah act like this…like a human being.

I stumble over to Clay. There's a cut on his forehead that isn't too deep, but he needs medical attention. I press my sleeve to his head, wrap my other arm around his neck, and draw him close.

"God," I whisper. "You know how to get a girl's blood pressure up."

"If that's all I gotta do…" He wraps his arms around me. I know people are watching, but at this moment I don't care.

We pull apart. The Messiah stands, waiting for us. I blush and drop Clay's hand.

"Clay," he says, "you saved my daughter's life. I owe you my heart. Please, come. Let me repay you." Mage is still wrapped around her father like a baby monkey.

Clay shakes his head. "It weren't nothing. I just hope she's okay."

The Messiah nods. "She will be. Please, you must come. Both of you." The Messiah gestures to Clay and me. "This way."

CHAPTER TEN

The Messiah's chambers swirl with incense that makes my head buzz. Clay and I sit on the couch in the candlelight, backs straight, ears alert. My eyes flit around the room as if by cataloging all the strange items I'll be able to figure out what this prophet has up his silk sleeve. To the right of our couch, paper calendars hang at odd angles. One calendar shows a pug-faced kitten in a shoe. Another has a watercolor painting of a sunset. Another shows a faded picture of a boy in a black cloak with round glasses and a wand. I peer closely at the black, numbered grids below the pictures. Each shows different months —January, July, April—and different days are circled violently with what looks like...blood? Many of those days are crossed out with a big black marker. What's the significance of those days? It might matter. Then again I don't even know what month we're in, let alone what day, and most of these calendars are decades old. Who can know the mind of a madman?

Every time I close my eyes I see Stephen twirling, arms out, the shocked expression spreading on his face just like the blood spreading on his chest. Dead. They covered him with a sheet and dragged him away. What'll happen to Kemuel? The boy was obviously sun-baked enough to think that he could take on a whole compound with one gun. Makes me wonder where he got that gun. Haven't seen any inside, but they gotta be stored somewhere.

I clench my hands together and look at Clay. "What d'you think he wants?"

Clay takes my hand and gives it a squeeze. "Probably just to congratulate us for helping Mage or somethin'. Don't worry," he says, flashing a put-on smile. "I got this under control."

It's the first time I've seen a smile on his face since we were taken. Saving Mage must have puffed him up some. At least all that awfulness did some good.

The door swings open and we both stiffen. The Messiah floats in with Andrew in tow. The prophet sweeps around, candles flickering. Andrew stands in the back, watching every move through his large, goggled eyes.

"Well, well, well. Our saviors," the Messiah says, sweeping an arm grandly. "Thank you so much for joining me. We have much to discuss."

I nod and Clay says, "Happy to help. Mage is a great kiddo."

The Messiah nods. "My daughter is one of the greatest joys of my life." But, no joy floods his face when he says this. Maybe they're different here, but when Mama talks about us, her eyes glow like a campfire. The Messiah's are dark as day-old ash.

He clasps his hands and continues. "I've been meaning to speak to you two for some time now, but the Gods have kept me busy these days." He lifts his face to the ceiling, smiling as if his Gods watch us. He gestures to a side table. "Please, have some refreshments."

I stare at the bounty: cheeses; big, plump fruits; a large jug of purple wine. My stomach lurches with want, but I don't trust the offering. Clay gets up and makes himself a heaping plate. I scowl at him when he sits down. *What?* he mouths.

The Messiah pours a glass of wine and sits in a plush chair across from us. He turns his cloudy eyes in my direction. "Riley, do tell me about your time in the Breeders hospital. Did they perform any of their experiments on you?"

I wrap my hand over my sleeve where the ankh brand rests. The images flash before my eyes before I can stop them: the lifeless women strapped to beds, Betsy on her final push in the delivery room, Clay's father bleeding out on the tile.

I shake my head. "Rather not."

"I see." The Messiah's voice is caked with disappointment. He turns to Clay. "Your father was the self-appointed Sheriff of a town north of here. Is this correct?" He runs a finger around his wine glass, though he hasn't taken a sip. Clay's finished half of his. I'd kick him, but there's no table to hide behind this time.

Clay's body goes stiff at the mention of his father. "Yes sir. My pa took care of the town, but was…overzealous in his practices." He clears his throat. "We didn't see eye to eye on how he run things."

"I gathered as much, since you killed him." The Messiah leans back, tenting his hands.

"How d'you know so much about us?" I ask, leaning on my elbows. "You got someone inside the hospital? A spy?"

Clay sputters on his wine and shoots me a worried look. I ignore it. There's no more time for beating around the bush.

The Messiah's expression doesn't change. He strokes his trim beard thoughtfully. "You don't believe the Gods told me? You don't believe in prophetic sight?"

I shrug, picking my next words carefully. "The Gods never showed me nothing."

"Are you sure?" he says, leaning in suddenly. "Are you sure you've never seen something from *above*?"

"I sure don't think so. And I don't know anyone who has."

The Messiah stands, his face animating. "What about you?" he asks Clay, putting a hand on his shoulder. "Have you heard from *them*? Do they give you sight?"

Clay shakes his head. "Sorry."

"I told you, sir," Andrew says, stepping up. "They're nothing but filthy nonbelievers. They don't have the Sight. Let's put 'em back in the dust where they belong." He leers at us through his goggles, his eyes bulging under the lenses.

"I don't believe it!" the Messiah shrieks, his arms flying up. "One of you." He points an accusatory finger. "One of you has it. I was told." He whirls around. "Andrew, get the sacrifice. We settle this now."

"Sir." Andrew places a tentative hand on the Messiah's sleeve, but draws it back when he sees the anger on his leader's face. He turns toward the door and leaves.

"What's goin' on?" Clay tries to stand.

The Messiah puts his hand out. "Please," his voice is calmer, his eyes not so frenzied. "No harm will come to you, but I need you to do something for me. Just be patient."

"I think we're done here." I stand. "Thanks for the cheese."

The Messiah strides to the door and blocks it. "Neither of you may leave or your families lives may be in danger."

Goosebumps run up my arms. "You're gonna hurt them?"

He shakes his head, his brown hair whipping behind. "Not I."

"I don't underst—"

Andrew slides back through the door with a small, squealing animal in his palm—a pink piglet, barely old enough to open its eyes. It thrashes its legs and makes a noise like a crying infant. Nothing about this feels right.

"What's that for?" I ask, pointing at the little pig, my finger beginning to tremble. "What're you gonna do?"

Its little pink ears shake as it bucks in Andrew's hand. The Messiah draws a knife from his belt and begins muttering. That distant, frenzied look is on his face. He raises the knife. "Sight, Sight,

Sight," he murmurs.

"Don't!" I cry.

He plunges the knife into the bucking animal's throat. The piglet lets out an awful, tortured squeal and then it's limp. The only sound is its blood pattering on the floor.

"Why did you…" I whisper, falling back to the couch. I've killed to survive, but never a baby and never with such awful joy. The Messiah's expression is one of pure rapture. My stomach churns.

The Messiah cups his hand under the dead piglet's sliced neck and begins collecting blood. He's still murmuring something about "the gift of Sight, the gift of Sight."

Clay pushes up, but Andrew draws his knife and points it at Clay. "Sit down."

Clay sits, his hands fisted. He looks at me.

What the hell have we gotten into?

The Messiah strides forward, his hands dripping in pig blood. I shy away, but his fingers wipe the blood on my eyelids. I lurch back, the warm wetness slipping along the creases of my eyes. "Stop!"

But he doesn't stop. Still chanting, his eyes roll back until only the whites show. He does the same to Clay, smearing blood on his eyelids. Clay grits his teeth, both hands dug into the couch cushions.

"Are you satisfied now, you psychopath?" Clay asks, flashing a gunslinger look that means only trouble to the one receiving it. "No goddamned gift of Sight. Now let us outta here or we got trouble."

But the Messiah's still murmuring. He goes back to the piglet in Andrew's hand and begins cutting. I can't look. I drop my head and try not to gag. The smell of blood is everywhere. When will this nightmare end?

When I look up again, the Messiah is chewing on something, his chin dripping with blood. He's eating the piglet's eyes. Through it all Andrew watches us, knife extended like his only desire is making sure we don't move.

Bile rises in my throat. The smell of blood is everywhere.

When the Messiah swallows and wipes the blood on his sleeve, he turns to us. The frenzied look is gone, replaced with the hopefulness of a child. "Well?" he asks like we've received a package and he can't wait to see what's inside. "What do you see?"

I shake my head, feeling sick. "A dead pig and a couple of sickos."

"Yes, yes." He dismisses it with a wave of his hand. "But do you *see* anything? From above?"

I grit my teeth. "I see pig blood on your beard."

He scowls and turns to Clay. "What about you?"

"Tell yer man to get his pig-gutter out of my goddamn face before I use it on 'im." The veins in Clay's neck throb. "Now."

Andrew steps forward. His sneer is back. He'd love to gut us. "Listen, dust—"

The Messiah puts a hand to Andrew's chest. The prophet's hope has flown and now a sadness has crept into his features. "I don't understand," he mutters, turning to looking at the books strewn on his desk. "One of you has the Sight. It was foretold to me."

"Sorry to disappoint," I say. "Can we get out of here?"

"Let me put 'em out." Andrew smiles nastily. "If they don't have the sight, we don't need 'em."

The Messiah shakes his head as he clutches some of the papers on his desk, smearing them with pig blood. "No," he says. "No, they stay. Something will come clear to me. I just need... time." He turns and gives us one more pleading look as if we're somehow choosing not to have his precious "Sight." Then he turns back to his papers and holds them up to his face, smelling them.

"Come on," Andrew says, tossing us each a towel. We wipe off the blood, but I can still smell it. "Back to your rooms."

We turn to go, but the Messiah whirls around. "Wait!" He holds both hands out. "Maybe it's because you're still outsiders." He rubs a hand through his beard. "We must induct you. You'll become Believers and then you'll have the Sight. Then you'll be able to stop the plagues."

"Stop the plagues?" I ask, but he continues like he hasn't heard me.

"We'll have the ceremony tonight." He turns toward Andrew.

"No!" I shout. "We are *not* joining you." I cross my arms over my chest. "No."

The Messiah's face falls. Andrew draws his knife again. "We could tie 'em up and force 'em to drink."

"No, no," the Messiah murmurs, shaking his head. "They have to be willing converts. No one can become a Believer unless their heart is open." He turns to us, bloody palms out in a pleading gesture. "There are so many benefits to being one of us."

"Our hearts are not open," I say, thinking of the little pig heart that was beating a few minutes ago.

The Messiah blows out a breath. "You'll stay until I'm satisfied neither of you has the Sight. We can't take chances on the gifts the Gods have provided."

Andrew opens the door and gestures us through. As we turn to leave, I think about the so-called gifts the Gods have provided. My eyes fall on the gutted body of the piglet lying discarded on the Messiah's floor. Was it a gift? Are we gifts to be consumed?

In the hallway outside, Mage is waiting for me, playing hopscotch on a board she has drawn with chalk onto the worn carpet. She looks up, teetering on one foot, hops down the rest of the squares, and lands in front of me. "Hi, Riley." She looks at Andrew. "Want me to take her back?"

He shakes his head. "This one is...dangerous."

"I can handle it." She shuffles over, takes me by a wrist.

"But—" Andrew says.

"You're not allowed in the women's hallway at night." Mage hops on the carpet like it's still a hopscotch board. Andrew tries to protest again, but she leads me away like she can't hear.

I glance over my shoulder at Clay. I need to talk to him about what just happened, but Andrew is already shepherding him back to the men's hall. Goddamn this place for always separating us just when I need him most.

Mage, still hopping, turns and looks over her shoulder. "Andrew is a bad apple," she whispers. "You should stay away from him."

"I'm trying." My emotions are a stew of fear, confusion, and anger. I wipe at my eyes, still sticky though the blood is gone. "What's the 'Sight'?"

She stops hopping. "What do you mean?"

"Your dad said either Clay or I have 'the Sight'." I step over a hole worn into the carpet. "What is it?"

Mage stuffs her hands in her jumper pockets and falls in step beside me. "My papa's worried that we're being punished for our sins."

I frown. "The Gods are punishing you?"

She nods. We pass under a triangle of overhead light and she peers up into it, the beam illuminating her angelic face. "He thinks that if we don't fix whatever we've done, we're all going to die. Do you know that during the ten plagues of Egypt God killed all the first-born children?" She lolls her tongue out of her mouth and begins fake gagging. Then she stops, her face suddenly serious. "My papa is dying. He thinks I don't know, but I do."

"I'm sorry." I don't know what else to say. Plagues? Punishment from the Gods? Something's wrong with these people, but I'm not sure how much the Gods have to do with it. I *am* sure I'm not the one to save them.

I glance at her as we walk under another cone of light. Somehow she can look six and sixteen in the span of ten minutes. "I know how you feel about your dad," I say. "My mama's not doing so hot either."

She nods, kicking at a loose piece of carpeting.

While she's so chatty, I try again. "Why do men and women sleep in separate hallways with their grates locked? What are people afraid of?" I peer through the grate of a dark shop as we walk past and goose bumps break out on my arms. I think about the moaning echoing up from the crack. Maybe it wasn't human.

Mage plods along and doesn't meet my eyes. "You ask too many questions. You're gonna get in trouble, bubble." She stops and turns to me. "I don't want you to end up like Kemuel."

Goose bumps again. I wrap my arms around my torso. "There's too many secrets around here, Mage. I don't like it. No one will give me a straight answer."

Mage nods like she isn't the one I'm talking about. "Just keep Ethan away from the Brotherhood as much as you can."

"What about Clay?"

"Oh him," she says, pulling a curl down and tucking it into her mouth. "It's too late for him."

I whirl on her, my breath suddenly staggering in my chest, but she's jogged ahead and is standing at my open doorway. I can tell by her face that she won't answer any more of my questions.

Too late for Clay?

I crouch under the grate and she closes it behind me.

"More to protect you than to keep you in," she says, spinning the padlock. "Only me and Stephen know..." her face drops, "*knew* the combination."

She shuffles to bed and I curl up on my mattress. I fall asleep and dream of pig's blood.

***

A rattling, loud and insistent, pulls me out of my dreams. Always with the rattling. No one wants to let me rest. I swim up out of sleep and blink towards the light streaming in from the hallway.

Three figures stand at my grate. Mage, Clay, and Ethan. Where's Rayburn?

"What is it?" I say, pulling up, my hands gripping the metal grate. My little brother's face is ashen. Fear burns away all the sleep.

Tears pool in Ethan's eyes. "Riley, come quick. It's Mama."

CHAPTER ELEVEN

Our feet slap on the concrete as we sprint to the infirmary. People stare and pull their children out of the way, but I don't care. A cold sweat runs down my back, dampening my shirt. What's happening to my mother?

My mind races as we take a corner and the department store-turned-infirmary comes into view. A million scenarios run through my head of what's happening to her—none of them good. She was better, resting up, and getting fluids. There's no reason she should've taken a turn for the worse. My chest is heaving and my mouth is dry. I just need to see that's she's all right.

The guard on the stool outside the infirmary entrance jumps up and holds out a hand. "Visiting hours are—"

"I don't care," I pant, skidding to a stop. "Where's my mother?"

He crosses his big arms over his chest and shakes his head. Flakes of dandruff float onto the shoulders of his sleeveless cotton shirt. "You don't have clearance."

"They're with me," Mage says, shooting around him. "Come on." She waves us into the store.

We run. The guard moves to block our path, but I duck around him and skitter into the store after Mage. When I look back, the guard's throwing his hands up in frustration as Clay and Ethan race around him too. He picks up a walkie-talkie and presses it to his mouth. He'll have back-up soon. We don't have much time.

Startled Middies fire dirty looks in our direction as the four of us jog past the rows of beds. I search each mattress for my mama, but we don't find her. Mage waves me to the back.

The sign above the little hallway says "FITTING ROOMS." A Middie with large, sagging breasts and loose jowls sits on a bench outside, fiddling with something. She looks up as we stop in front of her.

"What's this?" she says, standing. Her voice is high-pitched, but coarse. She narrows her eyes.

"Where's their mom?" Mage says, pointing at me. "A Middie told me she wasn't doing good. They came to see her."

She frowns and glances toward the little hallway with fitting rooms behind her. "She's in there. Had to isolate her from the other patients. She was moaning and carrying on."

Mama would never cry out in pain, not unless it was unbearable.

"What's wrong with her?" I ask.

The Middie won't meet my eyes. I don't have time for games. Guards will be here any minute to drag us out. I run into the dim hallway with wooden slatted doors on either side. Which room? The old Middie lumbers in, cussing at me. Then I hear moaning. Mama.

The moan is throaty and awful. I run toward the sound, the light growing dimmer. There, in the largest of the changing rooms, my mama lays on the musty carpet. Her eyes are squeezed shut and her face contorts with pain. She's withered even more than last time: her cheekbones rise sharply beneath her paper-thin skin, collar bones poke out of her shirt, and her hands look skeletal. The only big thing about her is her stomach, the round lump the size of a melon under her gown. How has it grown that big already? We've only been here a few days.

"Where's Mama?" Ethan asks over my shoulder. I can tell he's close to tears.

I look at Ethan. He's seen a lot, but only when I couldn't spare him. I look at Clay. "Can you get Ethan outta here? He doesn't need to see this."

Clay nods and takes Ethan's hand. "Come on, little bro."

Ethan yanks his hand away. "No! I'm not a baby."

Clay looks at me and I shake my head. He heaves a big sigh and hefts Ethan up onto his shoulder. Ethan drums his fists on Clay's back and begins to wail. I pretend I can't hear. I have to focus on my mother. She looks horrifying. I kneel beside her, my hands trembling as I reach for hers. "Mama," I say, trying to rouse her. "Mama."

"She's sedated."

I whirl around. The old Middie stands behind me, looking down. Her eyes are sapped of anger, and her expression has gone doughy and soft. Somehow her pity makes me feel worse.

"What's wrong with her?" I turn back and my eye catches movement. Is she awake? Something shifts under her gown where the baby grows. I stare, filling with dread. Slowly, hand trembling, I pull up her gown.

At first there's nothing, but then… movement on her belly, the baby rolling, stretching the skin there.

I stumble back, slamming into the slatted door with a crash. In the doorway, I grip the wood and try to breathe. That fetus has only been growing for a month and a half. How can it be that big and that... mobile? Images of alien creatures, monsters with fangs and claws, flash through my head. The room tilts as I clutch the door.

"It's the fetus," the Middie says, watching me from a few feet away.

"What d'you mean?" I ask, hanging onto the door. My legs feel unhinged.

She steps around me and kneels beside my mama, her knees popping at the effort. She places one wrinkled hand on her abdomen. "The fetus is one of the Breeders' mutations. A genetic hybrid meant to mature at double, even triple, the rate of a normal human fetus. They wanted to produce humans faster. Imagine a baby gestating in three months. The problem is the babies become parasitic in order to speed up their growth." She pulls her hand away as the baby rolls. "Not natural," she mumbles, shaking her head.

I stare at my mother's stomach and the baby rolls again. "Para...sitic?" I clutch the door. "What does that mean? What is it doing to her?"

"It's taking everything, nearly every nutrient she eats, and using it to accelerate its growth. She may survive until gestation. After that..." The Middie shakes her head, her jowls swinging softly. Like she's given up. Like she's already buried my mama.

I grab her arm and she stiffens, the thin flex of sinewy muscle and bone beneath my hand. "There has to be something you can do. Can't you...cut it out?"

She shakes her head. "No, I'm afraid we can't—"

"Can't or *won't*?" I tighten my grip on her arm.

"*Can't,*" she enunciates. "The placenta has already begun to attach itself to neighboring organs. It's like a cancer, directing blood flow to itself, suffocating your mother's kidney, her liver, her spleen... In the hospital they could sustain her body with I.V.s and medication. Here, well, we don't have that kind of ability. She has about a month."

My head is spinning. The world tilts and I can't see straight. What is she saying? Mama can't be saved? She'll be sucked dry, swallowed up by that *thing* in her stomach? I place my hands on my knees and try to breathe, try not to be sick.

"We've been able to help before," says a quiet voice at the end of the hall.

I lift my head, tears swimming in my vision. Mage is the small shadow, clutching at her jumper. She takes another step forward and says it again. "We've helped before."

The Middie folds her arms over her chest, her billowy cotton top fluttering. "Once, and it was a mandate from the Messiah. The Gods had deemed that she live."

"Why can't God deem that my mother live?" I ask, struggling to stand. "Why not her?"

"It's very difficult and expensive. The cost of the drugs alone could feed us for weeks. With the food shortage—"

"I don't care." I turn and clutch Mage's jumper in my fists. "Can you ask him? Can you ask your father to save my mother?"

Mage shrugs. "I can try."

***

Mage and I stand outside the Messiah's chambers. She's so close I can feel the heat baking off her pale skin. Her hands fumble in her jumper's large front pockets while we wait. Her anxiety doesn't help settle my nerves. I try not to visualize my mother in that fitting room, pale and lifeless. Like she's a corpse. Like she's already dead.

"I hope he's not mad," Mage says under her breath. She draws a curl down and bites it between her tiny white teeth.

"How come you're helping me?" I ask, staring into Mage's big gray eyes. I wonder where her mother is. She's never mentioned her.

She shrugs, her unconscious habit. "If I tell you, do you promise not to tell anyone?"

Goose bumps break out over my arms. "Tell me."

She leans in until her face is nearly touching mine. "When you go, I want you to take me with you."

I'm shocked. I open my mouth to question this and a door slides open. Andrew waits on the other side. He's frowning, already angry as a stepped-on scorpion when he sees us. The dread in my stomach expands like a cancer, like the baby eating my mother from the inside out.

"Come in," he snaps.

Mage and I enter and the door shuts, taking the hallway light with it and leaving the dim candle light behind. It takes a moment for my eyes to adjust. We bump through the antechamber and Andrew opens another door. Instantly, the overpowering smell of incense reaches my nose, making me feel lightheaded. We enter and again the door seals shut behind us. I stuff my trembling hands into fists at my side. *Mama,* I think. *Whatever it takes.*

"Where's my darling daughter?" the Messiah says, turning. He's still dressed in his flowing off-white robe, his long hair unbound behind him. Mage presses herself into his arms. The hug is thin; the Messiah's face never changes as he embraces his only daughter. Mage pulls back, sheepish and shy. Her gray eyes are especially wide now, like a field mouse, taking in every movement. Maybe if I'm still, he won't notice me.

"Riley." He rolls my name on his tongue like a delicacy.

I nod sharply, forgetting he probably can't see me. I cough the anxiety out of my throat. "Here. Here, sir." My voice warbles. So much for showing no emotion.

Andrew starts tidying up the piles of paper on the Messiah's desk. He stacks the Messiah's strange documents, the little words cut from many books and glued onto the large parchment pages, crinkling delicately. How can a man with little to no sight left manage to manipulate paper like that?

Andrew breaks the silence, coming up behind the Messiah. "They're here to ask you to save the girl's mother. I strongly advise against it."

"Hey!" I shout before I realize what I'm doing. I drop my voice. "Why would you say that? She's dying."

Andrew glares at me coldly. "People die. The medicine that would save her can help feed us for weeks. We're rationing as it is. I can't spare anything else to help a dus—"

"Silence," the Messiah says calmly. He turns his head toward me. "The baby? It drains her, yes?"

"Yes." The image of her sunken body appears before my eyes, making my knees weak.

"And we can stop it, yes?" he says, whirling toward Andrew.

Andrew's knuckles turn white as he grips the paper he's holding. "Yes," he says slowly.

"Then we should do so." The Messiah draws Mage to him with one arm.

Both Andrew and I stare open-mouthed. It was so easy. I thought after I turned down his offer to be converted he'd throw it in my face. I blow out a breath. "Thank y—"

"On one condition." He leans toward me, one hand on Mage's blond curls.

Of course. I narrow my eyes. "What's the condition?"

He strokes Mage's hair. There's another large sore on the back of his hand, a wide red swatch of skin missing.

"You must join us."

My heart's hammering again. It's the exact opposite of what every fiber in my being wants to do. "We don't have the Sight."

He shrugs as if he doesn't believe me.

"What if we say no?"

"Then we cannot help you." He turns his cloudy eyes away and stares off into the distance.

"Fine," I say, nearly choking on the words.

We'll get my mama fixed and then get the hell out. What does it matter if I break my word to these freaks? The only person I'll miss is Mage and she'll be fine without us. I turn to go.

"One more thing," he says.

I whirl around.

He's staring at me. Really staring at me as if his blind eyes could see through me into the depths of my heart. Does he know I plan on hitting the high trail the second she's well?

He lets Mage go and strides up. When he's a foot away, the smell that was disguised by the sickeningly sweet incense reaches me. The smell of rot, the same smell of the soiled T-shirt I found. As if some part of him is dying.

"You must allow Clay to join the Brotherhood. He will take the oath this evening. He will replace Stephen." He narrows his clouded eyes. His lips, behind his tidy beard, tighten in anticipation.

A lead weight slowly circles my heart and begins squeezing. It means Clay drinking that water, Clay becoming whatever they are.

"I can't." I step back, bumping into the wall. "That's too much to ask."

"But he wants to join, yes?" the Messiah asks. His blind eyes somehow find me again, bore through me.

"No," I say, clutching the wall.

The Messiah nods slowly. "He *wants* to join us."

It can't be true. Clay doesn't want to be what they are. Sweat prickles on my skin and the urge to vomit returns. The incense is too sweet, and yet I still smell the rot coming off the Messiah, like meat left out in the sun.

I drop my head. "If he wants to join, I can't stop him. I'm not his master."

The Messiah nods, folding his sore-covered hands. "And you will tell him you approve of the position? That you want him to join, yes?"

I raise my eyes and glare at the Messiah. "How can I? It's a damned lie."

"Then your mother dies!" he shouts. It's terrifying, the echo reverberating around the tiny room. My head is spinning. I can't think. I have to get out.

"Okay!" I shout, burying my face in my hands. "Just save her." Tears prick at my eyes, but I don't allow them. My body feels numb, dead.

"Good," I hear the Messiah say. Then Mage's hand is in mine, leading me out. The incense smell falls away and the light from the hallway lets me know we're through. I open my eyes.

Mage still holds my hand. "It's okay. You did what you had to do."

"That's not true," I manage. "All I've done is sacrifice one person I love for another."

CHAPTER TWELVE

The crowd murmurs as they march Clay toward the carousel. His blue eyes scan the crowd for me, seeking reassurance. I have none to offer. For once I'm grateful for this crowd of surging, smelly bodies. Here I can hide my shame.

After I agreed, the Messiah sent word to have the Middies use whatever expensive drug they needed to slow the growth of the fetus and save my mother. But only after Clay swears allegiance and joins. I can't feel happy about saving my mother. All I can feel is shame.

I'm such a coward.

I look up now, unable to stop myself. There stands the boy I love in clothes I've never seen him wear before: a bold yellow shirt and pants, both so tight they show off his muscular arms and thighs. He's a duplicate, a member of their Brotherhood. The thought sends a spike through my heart. He's one of them now. Not one of us.

They stand in a line, arms taut, chins jutted. The other men's eyes are locked forward, but Clay's eyes rove around the crowd. I duck behind a woman with a huge head of curly black hair. I hide and hate myself. Hate every ounce of me.

The drums and the chanting are the same as the night Kemuel and Mordecai were named. No woman wails, though. At least not out loud. My cries are silent, but just as pained. The Messiah raises his arm and everyone goes silent. Above, a bird flutters into a nest high in the metal rafters. I let my eyes settle on it as the Messiah begins speaking.

The Messiah sweeps toward Clay, his arms outstretched, his gown fluttering back to his elbows. "Tonight we have gathered for the sacred purpose of inducting Clay Tate into the Brotherhood." The Messiah fumbles a bit for Clay, but finds him and then wraps his large hands around Clay's shoulders. "This young man saved my daughter. He offered his life for one I hold dear. That night the Gods spoke to me, revealing that this man of courage would bring peace and stability back to our people. My heart is glad because I know Clay will do great works here, among the people." At this the Messiah drops his head as if overwhelmed with emotion. I remember his stiff hug with Mage last night, the way his calculating eyes seemed to bore through me even in that dim light. It's all an act: the emotion, the fancy words and dress. He's like one of those people on Betsy's TV shows, acting. Manipulating. Those tears when Mage was in danger were probably fake too. And we're swearing an oath to him tonight.

He holds a silver bowl up to Clay. "I Name you, Clay, in the blood of the Gods: Jesus, Buddha, Mohamed, Yahweh, and countless others. With this holy baptism you are now a man of the Gods and part of our Brotherhood."

The Messiah holds the bowl out and the water dances, its reflection lighting Clay's face. He shakes his head almost imperceptibly, but then he's reaching out, taking the bowl and lifting it to his lips.

Stop! I think. *Don't drink it!*

I say nothing. I'm lower than dust. I'm a slug who should be ground out of existence.

Clay swallows a big gulp of water. I watch, feeling like someone is slowly strangling me. The Messiah lifts the empty bowl over his head, smiling, displaying its empty contents for all to see. The crowd cheers.

A wretched, awful squealing cuts through the human voices. At first I worry it's coming from my own throat, but no. A few men drag in two hogs by ropes slung around their necks. The fat hogs lash their heads from side-to-side. Every heart-wrenching squeal reveals their long yellow teeth. Their hooves clatter on the concrete as they scramble to get away from the frenzied human crowd. The people chant and sway as the men drag the pigs to the front. I lift up on tiptoes to peer around the woman in front of me just in time to see a man with a knife step toward the hogs. He presses the blade under the animal's thick neck. I squeeze my eyes shut.

A squeal. A muffled thud. A cheer goes up from the crowd. The other pig is screaming bloody murder. A sickness lurches in my stomach. They take so much joy in killing. Why are they doing this?

I look up in time to see him slit the other pig's throat. Blood splatters on the floor and the second pig falls heavily on the concrete. Another cheer. Their bodies now rest in a large pool of blood. The stink of death clots the air. The people chant. I feel like throwing up. Then I see the Brotherhood step up with knives. I look away.

Finally, the tang of smoke fills the air and I look up. They've constructed a fire on the concrete next to the butchered hogs. They throw bloody legs and hunks of flesh on the fire and the smell of charred meat replaces the smell of smoke. The flames add a devilish glow to the crowd's frenzied faces. Clay stands near the front, his face frozen, his hands locked behind his back. He winces as they throw the pig's heads on the open flame. They aren't even going to eat the meat; they're letting it burn to ash. For their Gods.

With the stink of burnt animal thickening the air, the crowd begins to disperse. I turn to slink away, but then I see the Brotherhood stalking toward the dark hallway. The man in front begins fumbling with a gas lantern. Clay scans the crowd for me once more and then follows them.

I stop the girl with the wild black hair in front of me. "Where are they going?" I point at the Brotherhood.

She looks me up and down, frowning. "Down into the depths to finish the ceremony." She swings away.

I step in front of her and she scowls. "What happens down there?" In my mind I hear the human moaning.

The girl shrugs, her gold earrings tinkling. "Don't know. Women aren't allowed, only the Brotherhood." She steps around me and walks away.

The rest of the women and children have mostly cleared the food court. I watch as Clay steps into shadow and out of my line of sight. I can't let him go down there alone. What if they do something to him? Leave him down there or kill him? I've already given him to the wolves; I'll be damned if I'll let them feast.

I pretend to walk with the other women and then duck into the bathroom hallway. I wait several long minutes in the dark until the voices and footsteps subside. When the food court is silent except for the soft calls of birds up in the rafters, I peel out of the hallway. The open space feels haunted now. I stalk past the bloody mess and the charred pig bones. The pigs' screams echo in my head. The shops that once looked warm and inviting are eerily still. As I tiptoe past the carousel, horses sneer at me with flashing teeth and flared nostrils. Clutching my hands into fists, I stride forward toward the fissure.

In the darkness near the open mouth of the cavity, my courage evaporates. The smell is strong tonight: raw egg, rotting earth, and a chemical tang that makes my nose sting. The Brotherhood are gone, their lanterns too. How can I possibly enter the cave with no light?

The first steep pitch will send me plummeting to my death.

An idea pierces my mind. The emergency lanterns they keep in the back of the food stations. During dish duty a cook pointed the little electric lantern out to me. *"If the power goes out, it's pitch black back here,"* he'd said. *"Only use the lantern to get out into the light. We don't have many batteries to replace them once they're gone, so it's only for emergencies."*

I run back to the food court and slip into the first food station I find. Fumbling in the dark, my hands find the back wall, the sink, and then the tiny emergency lantern. I pray the battery holds out as I thumb the switch. The bulb blinks to life.

I sprint back to the fissure and crouch at its lip. The light does nothing to cut the terror as I stare into the hole. In the silence, my heart drums in my ears. I picture Clay's face as he drank their holy water. God only knows what's happening down there, but he won't go through it alone. I take my first step onto the incline, the darkness swallowing me as I descend.

The sloping broken concrete makes for poor footing, but I get the hang of it after a few steps. Peering over the edge sends my stomach cart wheeling, so I focus on each step. I pass steel beams and half of a busted neon sign with wires curling out like thin bones. About halfway down, a smashed kiosk rests in pieces on its side.

The blackness seems to go on forever. I hold my breath and listen for any sound of the men. They'd be ahead of me, but how far? If they catch me, they'll... what? Attack me? Drag me back to my cell? What more can they do to me? I've already given them the man I love.

My boots find solid ground, or at least a patch of level land that seems to stretch as far as my little lamp will illuminate. The chemical smell is even stronger and the air feels moist, like a wet hand on my face. I shiver and raise my lantern. The crevasse stretches out into a tunnel that leads into more darkness. I take a deep breath, shoving my fear down deep. With one hand on the rough stone wall to anchor myself, I step in.

A brown streak dives at my face. I duck and let out a muffled shriek. The bat veers away, its black wings slicing through the air above me. I stand for a moment and try to keep my heart in my chest. The wall under my palm and my small circle of electric light are all that's keeping me from turning and bolting back up the incline.

Twenty feet in, the cavern forks into two paths. I peer down each with my little lantern. As far as I can tell they're identical, the tunnels about fifteen feet in diameter. I can't tell if this is a man-made or natural cavern. The rock here sparkles with minerals that reflect my lantern light. It would be beautiful if I weren't so afraid.

I stand at the fork and listen. Silence. Then, to the right, I hear movement. It's a quiet sound, like an animal scuffling along. My arms tingle as I strain toward the shuffling noise. What's coming? Some sort of animal? A man? Fear pounds in my chest. Is it the Brotherhood or something else? I turn to run.

Voices echo from the path to my left. The men. I sprint toward the sound, away from whatever is lurking in the other tunnel.

When I'm close enough to make out individual voices, I flick off my light. I can't see my hand in front of my face. With my heart pounding and one hand on the wall, I walk toward the sound of their whooping.

From the cavern in front of me, there's a grunt and a yell. Someone shouts. Another laughs. It's all sounding very male and macho. I picture men beating their chests, flexing. Slowly my eyes pick up light. I see the faintest outline of a rock here, the sheen off the wall there. Ahead, the light trickles back from burning torches that flicker with orange firelight. I shuffle forward, breathless.

I peak around the corner and spot them. The space opens up to the size of a school gymnasium. The ground slopes down into a vast underground lake. The men are splashing in it, rubbing their bodies down. One man with a round, paunchy belly floats on his back, his glistening stomach cresting the water like a whale's hump. He, like everyone else, is buck naked. Three dozen oversized men in nothing but their birthday suits. Heat rises into my cheeks as I watch.

One man stands near me in the flickering light, flexing his bugling biceps. They look like veiny tumors as he raises and lowers his fist. Is this why they're so huge? The water? Will Clay...look like that?

Clay stands at the lake's edge, waded in up to his knees. I blush at the sight of his naked backside but can't help but admire how beautiful he is in the firelight: his sculpted calves, his strong back. The scar on his thigh from where Rayburn cauterized his wound has nearly healed. As he takes tentative steps into the water, someone runs up behind him. I almost cry out a warning but slap my hand on my mouth as the naked man slams his palms into Clay's back. Clay flies forward and hits the water with a giant splash. When he pushes up, soaked and sputtering, the man doubles over with laughter. The others pick it up, braying like a bunch of idiots. Clay stares, water dripping from his hair into his eyes. When the man walks over to him and helps him up, a slow smile spreads on Clay's face.

I press my back to the cold cavern wall, chilled inside. He's one of them. Something severs inside me, like a line has snapped and whatever it held is now drifting into space. I wrap my arms around my body and fight off a tremor. My cowardice put this awful pit in my gut and I deserve it. I watch the men for a while, feeling sick. They hoot and holler and splash, drinking large mouthfuls of lake water. Clay drinks too. I can't take it anymore. I turn away.

Suddenly male voices are closer...and moving my way. I snap up, eyes and ears alert, heart pounding. They're coming.

I scramble up, banging my knee. I grab the lantern, but it's too late to turn it on. The faint light from their torches will have to be enough. Twice I trip on rocks that send me sprawling. I taste blood in my mouth and feel a trickle down my leg. When their calls are farther away, I chance the lantern, trying to block the light with my body. Somehow I manage to scramble up all those steps. When I reach the top of the incline and stand on the main floor, I flick off my light and listen. The men's voices draw closer and now they sound different, more... animal. The growls and hoots behind me would make me think monster instead of man. My heart rabbits in my chest.

A howl echoes up from the depths behind me and my blood turns cold. I run to the cafeteria.

When I get to the end of the hallway that opens into the food court, I slip around the corner and peek back. Behind me, vast dark shadows spill out of the fissure like the dead clawing out of a grave. The men look...wrong. Their eyes are like hollow moons, round and violent. Almost... animal. Their postures are stooped, like predators on the prowl. Like they want only two things: to fight or feast.

And they're coming right for me.

CHAPTER THIRTEEN

I dive into the food court. My scraped knee smashes hard on the tile, sending a jolt of pain up my leg, but I keep going. Behind me muffled growls fill the silence like a pack of wolves. What did that water do to the men? What did it do to Clay? I'm both terrified and horribly worried. Is he one of the shadows in the pack?

On hands and knees I scramble to the first restaurant, clamber over the chipped stone counter top, and slide down to the other side. Back pressed against the serving counter, I clap my hands over my mouth to muffle my breathing. The light is so dim all I can see is the stack of green plastic serving trays and chipped mugs on the shelf in front of me. I hug my knees to my chest and try to stay calm. In my mind's eyes I see them stalking into the food court. I'm picturing werewolves, monsters. They're just men, so why are they acting like animals?

Footsteps tap on the concrete as they come closer. More growls. Gooseflesh prickles up my arms as I listen to them prowling around. I can't breathe. My flesh crawls as I picture them slinking over the counter to get me. I stare past the counter to the open space above my head and wait.

Long minutes pass. Minutes like centuries. My heartbeat won't slow. My fingernails dig wells into the flesh on my legs.

Finally, when all is quiet, I force my trembling legs upward.

I crouch and peek over the counter. Moonlight paints the food court in light and shadow. It's empty. I stand, my heart pattering. Somewhere deep in the mall I hear thumping. I know now is the time to dash from cover and run to my store, but the fear keeps me here. I press sweating palms to the cool stone counter and lift myself over. With my feet on solid ground, I turn to run.

A shadow bursts out of the darkness and barrels for me. Before I can stop it, a muffled scream escapes my throat. Someone tackles me. Arms pin mine as we scramble on the concrete. My head bangs against the wooden counter and pain flares up my spine. My attacker smells like lake water and chemicals. His clothes cling to his damp body. His wet hair drips on to my face. It's Clay. Yet his face doesn't light up when he sees me. His eyes hold that animal intensity. It's as if ... as if he doesn't know me.

"What happened to you?" I ask, worry creeping into my voice. There's a flicker of something in his eyes. He growls low in his throat and flashes his teeth. He presses his weight on top of me and with his good hand he begins violently tugging at my pants.

"Clay, stop!" I slap his cheek as tears pool in my eyes. I push on his chest. He's huge, immovable. He tugs off my shirt. Only the binding on my breasts covers me.

I close my eyes and bury myself inside my guilt. "Clay, please stop."

His body freezes above me. I open my eyes. His hand is still a vise on my bicep, but I see confusion in his eyes. He sits back. "*Whatshappening?*" It comes out as one slurred word. He sounds drugged.

I sit up and scramble back, clutching my knees to my chest. "What did they give you?" I ask, wiping away the tears.

Clay places his hands on his head. "I'm *sssorry*," he slurs. He crawls away from me. "Go."

"Clay."

"Go!" He lifts fear-filled eyes to mine. "Before I do *sssomething* awful."

I reach for him, but he pulls back, mumbling. I yank up my pants and tug my shirt back on. When I glance up, Clay is gone.

***

I wake in the morning with two scraped knees and bruises up and down my body. Yet it's my heart that feels the most battered. What did these maniacs do to Clay? Is it too late to stop it? I refuse to believe he's corrupted. When Mage appears at my grate in the morning, I take her hand and pull her forward.

"Where are we going?" she asks, scrambling behind me.

I plow through the morning crowds. Women stare at my bloodstained knees. I'm sure my hair is a matted mess. I don't care. I have one mission.

"We're going to see your father."

Signs of the Brotherhood's rampage last night litter the hallway: trashcans turned over, fingernail marks dug into the plaster, a glass window broken into shards. The people go about mending the mess like it's no big deal. This is why they lock themselves in at night. There really are monsters lurking in this community—their own husbands and fathers. What is in that water that causes them to act this way? Why in the world do they drink it?

We reach the Messiah's chamber. Andrew blocks the door, his arms crossed over his chest.

"We came to see the Messiah," I blurt.

Andrew's buggy eyes look tired behind his goggles. "He's sleeping. No visitors."

"I *need* to see him. Now."

Andrew's thin hair swishes around his head as he shakes it. "Do you know how much I care about your demands, dust?" he asks, looking down his nose at me.

I glare at him.

"Thanks to you and your mother we're on tighter ration restrictions." He folds his hands together and his knuckles pop. "Thanks to you, our people go hungry."

"I've gone hungry my *whole life*," I say through my teeth.

"You think you have us all figured out," he says with a wry smile. "Spoiled little community. The Gods' blessed people." He twiddles his fingers in the air, then he jabs one at me. "You have *no* idea what we have to sacrifice."

"So, you sacrifice my boyfriend? Is that it? Make him one of your monsters." I'm seething, hands clenching and unclenching. If I can't take my rage out on the Messiah, Andrew will do.

Andrew scoffs. "Your boyfriend? We've never had a more willing convert. Once he saw what we could do for him, he was first in line." Andrew licks his rotten teeth and smiles. "Any idea where he slept last night?"

My jaw drops and he laughs. "Guess he needed more than what you were providing." His eyes run up and down my body. "Can't blame him."

I charge at him. "You're a liar!"

Mage grabs my arms. "Stop, Riley. They'll put you out."

I point at Andrew's face. "Tell the Messiah Clay's out. He's done!"

Andrew laughs. "Why don't you ask Clay if he's done?"

Mage drags me away, but I head left, sprinting down the men's hallway before she can stop me. She calls my name, but I don't want to be told why I can't. I made this happen and I'm gonna stop it.

The walls here look like they did in the women's quarters: banged up, scratched. A fist-sized hole has been smashed into the plaster beside me. A brown clumpy liquid is splattered on the wall beside a former smoothie shop. It's a wonder these men don't tear this place apart and kill everyone in it. Why would they turn themselves into savage beasts if it meant destroying, pillaging, raping? I pull up to Clay's store. Heart pounding, I peer in. Two lumps lay on the floor under blankets. Is Clay one of them? I stoop under the half-open grate and tiptoe in, barely breathing.

In the first pile, a big bearded man sleeps. His eyes are shut and there's a cut on his cheek. The hand clutched at his chest is swollen—it looks broken. When I lean closer, he stirs. I pull back. He snorts and rolls over.

The next mound of blankets has a mop of shaggy brown hair poking out from the tattered sheet. Slowly, I draw it back.

Clay's face isn't scarred, but I can see he's ripped the bandage off his injured hand. I haven't seen the bullet hole in his palm since I helped wrap it after we escaped the Breeders. The raw pink skin puckers around the hole that cuts straight through his palm. Rayburn thinks that eventually he'll get some motion back in his fingers. The hole may even close up, leaving a divot. But it'll never fire a gun. What must it feel like to lose part of you forever?

I caress the tender skin around his palm and he stirs. "Clay," I whisper, leaning down until my lips brush his ear. He still smells like lake water and chemicals, but his own scent lies beneath it. He moans and rolls over. I place a hand on his chest—it's hot. "Clay."

His eyes flutter open. They take a moment to dilate and find me. He winces as he comes to. He attempts a pained smile and reaches up to touch my face. Fear stirs in me. I can't keep the image of him shoving me to the ground out of my head. But, *my* Clay would never have done that to me.

"Oh God," he whispers, pinching his eyes closed. "A mule kicked my head. Least that's what it feels like."

I brush hair out of his eyes. "You had a rough night."

He blinks. "Did I? Jesus, I don't remember. Not after goin' into that cave." He puts a hand to his forehead and looks up at me. "Were you…there? What happened?"

I lift my eyes to the ceiling. Above the empty metal grid, black electrical cords dangle like venomous snakes. I stroke his hair. "You weren't yourself."

"I feel like horse shit." He tries to sit up, winces, and slumps back into his blanket, a puff of stale dust spewing up behind him. "God."

Male voices in the hallway. I grip Clay's hand and lean close. "Listen, Clay, whatever they did to you last night, it made you do bad things."

He frowns. "What bad things?" His eyes search mine.

"Nothing." I look away. "You seemed... drugged. If you keep going with them, you'll get in too deep. You'll be one of them," I raise my eyes to his, "not one of us."

He places his hand on my cheek. "What do you mean?"

I lean into his touch. "You have to stop."

He shifts his eyes away.

"Clay, seriously."

"Riley, it's just, when I drink their water..." he leans back and sighs. "It's the only time I feel strong again, like I did before I was shot up. I feel like a man."

"It's not worth it," I say, taking his injured hand.

"I know." He looks down at his hand, the piece of himself he's lost forever.

***

When I finally make it to the laundry room, Prema meets me at the door. Her mouth is twisted into a wrinkled knot like I'm something sour she's just spit out of her mouth. She crosses her arms over her sagging breasts and glares at me.

"I'm sorr—"

Her arthritic knuckles slice through the air. "You're out."

"What?" Behind her, Mage twirls around in one of the cracked leather salon chairs and gives me an apologetic look.

Prema's face, on the other hand, could be made of stone. "You're surly, lazy, and late."

"What?"

She cut's me off. "You're fired. We don't want you."

I take a step back, looking around. "So...what do I do?"

She swings her arm toward the door, almost whacking me with it. "Go. Andrew will take you to your new job."

My insides go cold as I turn. There, propped against the entryway, arms crossed, stands Andrew. When our eyes meet he gives me a nasty smile. He hooks a finger, beckoning me toward him. "Got a job for you." He smiles even bigger.

I tromp over to him, scowling. He pushes on my shoulder. "Move."

We walk, Andrew behind me. My body is a rigid pole, my eyes and ears alert to his movements. The impulse to whirl and begin punching sits solidly in my belly, but I know that'll come to no good. Instead I picture horrible ends to his life. Death by vultures seems a good place to start.

When we get to a set of boarded-up exterior doors, I swivel and shoot him a questioning look.

"You've pulled garage duty. Gonna be pretty hot today, I hear." He steps closer to me. I stumble back and my shoulder blades bump into the wall. He's got me pinned. I glance down the vacant hallway. No one. My heart thrums. He smiles.

When I duck under him and shove through the boarded-up doors, he laughs and calls out, "Enjoy your day."

The heat hits me like a wall. Must be a hundred degrees with the sun cresting in the mid-morning sky. I jog down the concrete walkway that opens up into the blacktop parking lot. It's been, what? A week? More? A long time since I've been outside. A large part of me wants to take off running, but I can't leave my family and without vehicles or water we're dead. Beyond the parking lot, a few outbuildings sit, some repaired, some fallen down into a jumble of bricks. Past that a sea of sand and cactus stretches forever. No wonder Kemuel came back.

"Riley." Rayburn jogs awkwardly toward me, a smile on his round face, his dwindling paunch jiggling. I smile as he stops before me, panting with his hands on his knees.

"Rayburn, what're you doing out here?" I ask, looking around. Across the shimmering parking lot, a garage sits with three large doors thrown open. Inside, men in gray coveralls work on vehicles. Cars without tires are up on hoists; two trucks sit on pads. One man climbs out from a car-sized hole in the floor and wipes his greasy hands on a rag.

I have two thoughts: *Arn would've loved this*, and, *how can we steal a truck and get the hell out?*

"Heard you're assigned with me today." Rayburn blinks at me behind smeary glasses. He smiles, his eyes turning into two upside-down moons.

"Yeah, I guess. Show me where to go." I walk with him across the parking lot. The heat rolls across the blacktop in waves. I glance at Rayburn. I've been so busy I haven't noticed his sunburned cheeks and grime-encrusted fingernails. He hasn't even mentioned garage duty.

We clomp toward the garage and already I'm dripping with sweat.

"Heard you got fired," Rayburn scratches at a fresh cluster of tiny pimples on his cheek. "Sorry."

"My own fault," I say, kicking at a hunk of pavement.

"Did you see Clay," he asks, eyes on the pavement, "last night?"

"Yeah." I look at him. "Did you hear anything?"

"I saw the men coming back," he says, shrugging, already sounding uncomfortable. "They didn't look, uh, look right. They were acting like animals."

"Yeah, they did." I glance up, thinking of Clay's vacant eyes. I lower my voice. "Rayburn, I think those men were drugged. They went to this underground lake and swam in the water. I think it's the same water they used to induct the Brotherhood. The rest of us drink clean water, but for some reason the Brotherhood drink this contaminated water. They were guzzling the stuff last night. Maybe if they have a lot of it they turn—"

"*You* went down *there?*" He stares at me.

I put my hand on his elbow. "It's okay. No one saw me."

He frowns. "Contaminated water could, uh, could explain a l-l-lot. The chemical smell in the crevasse. Their sores." He points to the corner of his mouth and looks at me.

"Why? What ever-loving good would it do to poison their own kin?" Gooseflesh pricks over my arms. I knew these people were up to something. Now it's confirmed by Rayburn, who, despite his blinking eyes and weak chin, knows way more than he lets on.

Rayburn steps over a huge pothole. "The men came back last night in what seemed to be a, uh, testosterone rage coupled with a hallucinogen or deliriant. Maybe the water acts as a male hormone replacement. Maybe it makes them v-v-virile enough to generate female children. But it's also got to be polluted with other chemicals, either added on purpose or just happen to be there, that make them, uh, crazy."

"You sure water can do that?"

"Why else would they poison themselves?" He squints into the sun, thinking. "It would depend on what the water was contaminated with, but yes, uh, it would be possible. If the Messiah were playing amateur chemist with limited knowledge, he might have found a cocktail that allows them to reproduce. He probably also hasn't b-b-een able to stop the side effects. Tampering with the underground lake makes sense. It's s-s-separated from their main water source and he can take his, uh, his men down there and use them like human guinea pigs."

Prickles run along my skin, both hot and cold simultaneously. "Will it kill them?"

Rayburn nods. "You don't see many of the Brotherhood over forty. They, uh, probably don't live that long."

I shuffle to a stop. A few men in the garage look up at us. We don't have much time.

"What do we do?" I ask.

Rayburn eyes open far too large. "You have to get Clay out, and fast."

CHAPTER FOURTEEN

The garage is hotter than hell's kitchen and my greased-up coveralls are soaked through after thirty minutes, but I have to admit garage duty is a heap better than laundry. The four garage monkeys (as they call themselves) are young and fun and talk so nasty to each other Prema would curl up and die if she ever heard them. A slender guy they call Crank shows me how to use an air compressor and sets me to work checking tires for leaks. I fill the heavy rubber tires, sink them into a huge paint-stained tub of water, and watch for bubbles. Then I plop the wet tires on the concrete and mark the leak with a red marker. The big red X drawn on the tire tread gives me more satisfaction than scrubbing dirty panties ever did. Crank shows me how to patch tires using a grinder, gooey cement, and a tire patch. They're impressed by my prior knowledge and how quickly I pick up what they show me. I look at my grease-stained fingers and smile. If Andrew and Prema thought they were punishing me with garage duty, boy, did they ever get it wrong.

Lunch consists of ham slices that we eat sitting on stacks of old tires. The warm rubber is soft on my backside and the guys' banter makes me laugh. They sing a bawdy song about girls from the city with big titties and, though I blush, it's kind of nice not to be treated differently for once. These men are so different than the meathead Brotherhood members. Maybe the Brotherhood is revered for their strength and ruthlessness, but I'd take a grease monkey over them any day of the weak.

Donut, the twenty-something guy with a bald patch on the crown of his head and a mouth that would embarrass my cussing Auntie, puts me to work stripping wires and sorting through bins of parts. I sift through air filters, rusted lug nuts, and spark plugs. I clean threaded cylinders until they shine. Afterward, Crank gives me a tour of a car engine. I'm amazed at how much they know about fixing and piecing together vehicles. Lance, a long, lanky guy with a hawk-beak nose and wide-set eyes, shows me how to use a mechanical jack. By dinnertime, I'm almost sad to leave the sweltering garage.

Rayburn and I walk slowly back toward the mall. The garage

monkeys have locked the garage down tight. If we ever wanted to break in for supplies, we're going to have to either get one of those guys on our side or steal the keys. I watched intently as Crank dropped them into his pants' pocket. Maybe we can get him to see reason if we—

"Good work today." Rayburn smiles at me. There's a dimple in his left cheek that I've never noticed before. Then again, I don't see Rayburn smile very often.

"It's a good job." I glance back toward the garage. "Those guys are the nicest here."

Rayburn nods. "They're not Brotherhood, just regular guys." He pauses, stepping carefully over a chunk of missing concrete where the parking lot has fallen away in gray chunks. "Like me."

"Rayburn, you're not a regular guy," I say, elbowing him in the ribs. He huffs at the blow and rubs where I've jabbed him. "You're some kind of bona fide genius. You've got more stored in that noggin than I'll ever know."

He blushes, his sunburned cheeks reddening even more. "I'm not a genius. I just had good teachers and access to a vast library of books, as well as computer databases chocked f-f-full of information." A small smile touches his lips as he remembers.

"You had computers?" I ask, kicking at a hunk of concrete that goes skittering across the faded yellow parking lines. The mall looms close.

"We had computers," he says nodding. "The information was, uh, was monitored of course. But, yes, we had a database of knowledge on medical procedures and other things too. Electronics. Environmental Science." He laces his fingers together in front of his greasy jump suit. "I loved sitting immersed in all that information. I'd read until my eyes felt like they'd, uh, fall out of my head." He pushes up his glasses, his look distant.

"Must've been nice to get to see all that." I think about us growing up with one or two books we found lying around, half molded, how I still can't read great.

Rayburn stops. His face is solemn, the crease in his sunburned brow deepening. "That hospital was as much a p-p-prison for me as it was for you."

Heat burns up my neck. I cross my arms over my chest and stare down at the scraggly desert plant pushing its way up through the busted concrete. "Didn't see any chains around your ankles when you were walking around the halls. You had access to door codes, trucks." I flick angry eyes up at him. "I hardly think your life and those girls in plan B was the same."

"No," he says, shaking his head. "Not the s-s-same, but you think I could just leave? What do you think Dr. Vandewater would've, uh, done with me? *Will* do to me if she finds me?"

I shrug. "Invite you back?"

"Ha!" he laughs humorlessly. "She would flay me and then stake me in the desert for the coyotes to slowly p-p-pick apart."

For a moment we're quiet. Then I reach out and pat him once on the back. "Thanks for coming on this crazy adventure."

Rayburn nods. "Thanks for being p-p-patient with me."

We cross the last bit of parking lot together and slip under the shade of the fading awning. Rayburn pulls the boarded-up door open for me. Inside the mall, the air feels deliciously cold. The beaded sweat on my body cools and I strip off the coverall down to my T-shirt and pants. With Rayburn beside me, we head toward the buzz of dinner.

I look around for Ethan and Clay and find my little brother waving and hopping up and down. I tug Rayburn's shirt and head toward his table.

Ethan steps back and someone in a wheelchair sits beside him. Mama! She turns and her burned face toward me and smiles.

She's dressed in one of those white patient's gowns, still far too thin with protruding cheekbones and hollows under her eyes, but she looks okay. Alive at least. She smiles at me. "Darling." She reaches up and cups my cheek. I feel like crying.

"Mama. You're out." I press my face into her hand.

She nods slowly. "For the moment. The Middies thought it would be good for me to get some fresh air and see my lovelies." She touches a grease stain on my arm and asks, "What've you been up to, Riley?"

I blush and Rayburn answers for me. "She's a, uh, grease monkey now." He smiles awkwardly. "That is to say, er, she's working in the garage with me."

"She got fired." Ethan leans forward, hands on Mama's wheelchair arm. I shoot him a look, but he's beaming at Mama and not even looking at me.

"I got fired because I was late from tending to Clay." I look around the bustling food court. "Where is he?" I crane my neck.

The smile drops off Ethan's face. He points reluctantly.

I follow his finger to a wide table at the front. The Brotherhood sit, massive elbow to massive elbow, laughing and banging their fists on the table at jokes I cannot hear. And in the middle sits Clay.

Anger surges through me as he laughs at something his table mate says. When his eyes meet mine, the smile falls off his face.

"Don't be too hard on him, darling," Mama says, touching my hand.

I nod, but all I can feel is hardness circling my heart, encasing it, walling it in.

Clay drops his fork and excuses himself from the table. He heads our way.

"I'll be right back," I say, leaning to give my mother a kiss on the cheek. She frowns but says nothing. Great. She's finally back and I'm leaving. But, my anger won't let me drop this.

I angle past the tables and turn down the hallway to the bathrooms. I wait, my back pressed against the wall, running over everything I'm about to say in my head. I can't be too harsh, but Jesus, he told me he'd quit and there he is. If he didn't want to stop, why didn't he—

"Riley." He steps into the dark hallway with me. His voice is rabbit-pelt soft and apologetic.

I fold my arms over my chest and stand rigid like I'm made of stone. Maybe it'll harden my heart enough to stop him from breaking it.

He extends his hand to touch me, but sees my face and withdraws. A small red sore the size of a pencil eraser has formed at the corner of his mouth. I stare at it, my heart thumping. "They've already got you," I say, pointing.

He covers his mouth, embarrassment flooding his face. "They don't *got* me," he says, reaching for my hand. He pulls it to his chest. The strong, steady rhythm of his heart pounds into my palm. "*You* got me." His blue eyes peer into mine until they seem to be looking into my heart. I let him join. Encouraged him. How can I stay angry?

I fold into him as he wraps his arms around me. Still he feels miles away.

"We have to leave," I mumble into the folds of his shirt. He doesn't answer, just strokes my hair. I almost let it placate me. Almost. Finally, I pull away. "We *need* to leave," I say more forcefully.

His eyes flick down to my face and then upward at the cracked plaster for a long time as if divining the future in those lines like a palm reader. Finally he sighs. "'Member the story I tole you 'bout my baby brother?"

How can I forget? Clay's brother was murdered by marauders on the road while Clay watched. It's the burr in his saddle that he'll never be able to dig out.

"I keep havin' a dream," he says, his eyes still far away. "I dream that Cole and me is pullin' up to that sports car again. And deep inside, I know what's gonna happen, but I can't stop. I can't stop myself from puttin' my car in park and gettin' out. I can't stop us from slidin' up to that goddamned beautiful car." He swallows, his voice wavering. "And when Cole leans in, I can't look away when the motherless bastard grabs him and presses the knife to his throat. I can't—" He pulls back from me and presses the pads of his fingers to his eyes. "Riley, in the dream when I look up, it isn't Cole bein' cut." He turns wet eyes to mine. "It's Ethan."

I bite my lip, a chill sliding through me. "That *won't* happen."

Clay sniffs and turns away. When his hand reaches for mine, I lace my fingers through his strong calloused ones. If there's one thing his story reminds me, it's how very few moments like these we're allowed. The world doesn't announce its plans before it snatches your loved ones from you. It just takes them and leaves you behind, broken.

We make our way through the food court to the table. Mama smiles as Clay greets her with a gentle hug. Then she goes back to listening as Ethan drones on about the store he and Rayburn are staying in and how it must've been a game store because he found seven multicolored pieces in cracks along the floor and how he's creating his own game. And on and on.

I sit in a chair beside Mama, fatigue washing over me. I didn't sleep well the night before, or really the night before that. And for a moment, no one I love is in immediate danger. Mama's earthen aroma wafts by, reminding me of home. My heavy lids droop.

"Riley." I snap up. Mama peers at me from her chair. The boys have gone off and left us.

"Sorry. Fell asleep." I rub my eyes.

Mama nods, frowning slightly. "You look tired, baby."

I sit up. My neck feels like a kinked hose. "You're one to talk." I smile at her. "You look better, though."

She nods, her hands finding her swollen belly.

The belly hasn't grown any, thank God. "It'll be okay," I say, pointing to her stomach. "They said they slowed the growth."

"Slowed it, yes..." Her eyes find mine. "Not stopped it, sweetheart. I just want you to know. I want you to be...prepared." Her eyes are wet. She reaches out and grabs my arm. "I want you to be there to comfort your brother when...if I'm not—"

"Stop," I say, a chill running through me. "You're not dying. Clay joined their crew so they would save you." I grip her hand too hard and she winces. I let go. "You gotta be okay. They said you would be."

"I'm sure you're right." She won't meet my eyes.

I shake my head, a wave of nausea settling over me. "That goddamn baby."

She frowns. "Now, Riley—"

"No, really, it's killing you. If there was a way...a way to get it out without hurting you, I'd do it." I whip around and look at her. "Is there? Could Rayburn do it?"

She shakes her head.

"How do you know?" I lean forward, gripping the table. "There could be a chance. There has to be."

"Please," she says, tears welling in her eyes. "Seeing you upset just makes this worse for me." A tear traces down her burned cheek, trailing past the rippled skin like a river over rocks. "I hate that you're always the one to take on all our troubles. I'm your mama. I should be the one." She swipes her hand across her nose. "Why can't I be the one to save you?" She turns her face away, leaving me looking at her scar. The scar she carries because she once ran into a burning house to save me.

I touch her fire-ravaged cheek. She turns to me. "I love you," she whispers. "I know you'll watch out for your brother." Another tear. "He'll need you. Already he looks to you as his mother."

No. No, no, *no*. I'm shaking. The sounds of the cafeteria dims to a buzz. The heat in the room doubles and sweat trails down my back. The boys walk this way, laughing, but I can't take it. I stumble away. Where can I go? The bathroom. I nearly run. Once in a stall, I sit on the cool toilet seat and put my head in my hands. Mama cannot be dying. After all we did, after all we went through to get her out of the Breeders' hospital and she's going to die here with these freaks? I brush away tears with the back of my hand. No, I refuse to believe it. There has to be a way to save her. I'll talk to Rayburn. If he can't help, I'll go back to the Messiah. I'll offer myself up in exchange. I made a promise when I lost her the first time that if I ever found her, I'd never lose her again. I don't break promises.

I walk out into the food court, wiping my face on my sleeve. Mage and Ethan sit on the faded plastic fruit in the center. Mage hands him a folded paper flower in bright lemon yellow. He takes it, a smile breaking onto his face that I know all too well. A smile that says "here's my heart in my hands, take it and do with it what you will." Before I can stop myself I'm tromping over.

"Ethan, we gotta go," I say, my voice a razor's edge.

His eyes snap up. "Ri, Mage and I were just—"

"Mama needs to get back to her room." I reach for Ethan's hand. He leans away from me, anger seeping into his features.

"They already took her," Mage says, pointing. Our table's empty. I didn't even get to say goodbye.

"Well, then I need you for..." I grab his hand, "something else."

"Riley, stop." He eyes me angrily beneath his wave of dark hair. "What're you—"

"Come on." I tug him away. He tugs back, but not hard enough considering my brain's on fire. He protests as I drag him behind me. When we get to a quiet part of the hallway, I let him go. He pushes away from me.

"What the hell do you think you're doing?" he yells. He tosses his thin arms up in frustration, a spitting image of Arn.

"Saving you from heartache," I say, crossing my arms over my chest. I lean in and whisper angrily. "We're leaving here and that girl," I shoot a finger toward the food court, "is *not* coming with us."

He flashes his teeth. "Stop bullying me. Who says you can drag me outta there like that? You're not Mama."

His words are meant to cut me and they do, but not for the reasons he thinks. If Mama dies, he'll— I stare up at the ceiling, feeling gut-punched. "I'm not your mama, but you'll listen to me all the same." I lay a hand on his shoulder and take the steel out of my voice. "It's for your own good."

He shrugs my hand off. "You used to hate when Daddy said that to you."

His words feel like a slap. I rub my hands over my face and blow out a breath. "Ethan, getting close to someone who might not be on our side is only gonna get your heart kicked in." I peer into his brown eyes. "The only people we can trust is our own."

He studies me through the dark slash of hair, his mouth working. "So, what about Clay then?"

I pull back, feeling a prickle of pain around my heart. I force the words out, though they feel less true today than they did yesterday. "Clay's family now."

***

Garage duty is a welcome distraction and I fall into my work with the men and the cars. My second day I sort through rusting bins until my fingers ache. After an hour, I stand up, stretching my back. Crank looks over at me from where he lies on the ground, staring up into the underbelly of a car.

"Sore?" he asks, smiling. A splotch of oil darkens his cheek.

I nod, popping kinks from my shoulders. "You got something I can do to stretch my legs a bit?"

He rolls out on the little dolly and stands. He nods to Rayburn who's stacking old tires. "You two could hike out to the warehouse and pick up a couple more bins of scavenged parts we haven't sorted yet. Give you a chance to stretch. It'll be hotter than fried snot, though." He squints at me as he wipes his oily hands on a rag. He's cross-eyed, his left eye turning in toward his nose, giving his face an off-kilter appearance. I couldn't care less though. He treats me like a human being.

"I can deal with a little heat. You up for it, Ray?"

Rayburn gives a slow nod. "O-okay." He pushes the last knobby tire onto the lopsided stack and walks toward me. "It's the old toy establishment across the lot? The one with the giraffe out front?"

Crank laughs, nodding. "Yep, professor. That's the one." He points a finger out the garage door and across the sand-strewn parking lot. "Carry back as many bins of parts as you can lift. They'll be over to the left of the tech bins, I think." We head out and he hollers after us. "And snag me the best-looking battery in the stack."

110

"Will do." I say.

"And a nudie mag if they got any," he yells. Donut, behind him, gives a hoot of approval.

I give them a wink.

The sun hits us like a spotlight. It must be at least a hundred degrees, no wind. Rayburn shrinks in the heat like a turtle going into his shell. His sunburn has started to peel on his ears and cheeks. He crouches down and cups his hands over his face.

"Here, look," I say, digging back behind me to pull my T-shirt up and over my ears and neck. "It might look goddamn ridiculous and the shirt'll chafe under your arms something awful, but it'll keep your ears and neck from getting sizzled." I keep forgetting he was hospital grown and never learned to live out in the wild.

He pulls his undershirt up and over his head and neck and looks at me.

I laugh at the sight of him: his big round glasses on his big round face, poking through the hole of his t-shirt. He looks like a cartoon bookworm. I give him a playful shove. "Once you're outside enough, you'll brown up. Crisp like bacon, my Auntie used to say. Then you won't have to worry about it." I glance down at my arms as an example, but realize my tan, the one I've had since before I can remember, is starting to fade. I've been indoors too much. For some reason this really bothers me. Maybe it reminds me of being cooped up in the Breeders' hospital. Maybe I see it as weakness. Either way, this place is slowly eroding who I was. Who we all were.

"Those, uh, those men are awful trusting." Rayburn thumbs back to the garage. "Letting us come out here alone."

I squint behind me. Crank's shadow lies under the car and Donut is in the back working on something electrical, wires splayed out in a mess of colors. "Yeah. If the Brotherhood knew we were snooping around unsupervised, they'd pee in their giant panties." I waggle my eyebrows, realizing what I've just said. "Rayburn, we've got to make this trip count. How long d'you think we got 'til those guys expect us back?"

He shrugs, the shirt over his head making him look silly. "Twenty minutes. Thirty at most."

I pick up my step. "Hustle your bustle. We're gonna to search that warehouse for weapons, electronics, anything that could help us get the hell outta dodge."

He shoots me a worried look. "W-w-won't they n-n-notice?"

I grin at him. "Not if we're careful."

It takes a few minutes to jog across the boiling blacktop to the toy-store-turned-warehouse at the perimeter of the parking lot. The shop looks like it was once painted a rainbow of colors, but now the tile blocks are dulled and sand-blasted. The sign still reads TOYS, but the giant letters R, U, and S lie broken on the concrete, leaving behind faded outlines and twisted metal wiring. There's a large two-dimensional giraffe standing beside the door. The plastic figure has a goofy grin and round eyes, but time has warped its orange neck until the giraffe bows down in defeat. We step through empty, glassless doorframes and into the shaded stillness.

"Huh," Rayburn says, squinting into the dark. He pulls the t-shirt off his head and runs a hand over his shaggy curls.

"Huh is right," I say, walking slowly inside.

The warehouse looks like a roadside swap meet on steroids. Boxes, shelves, and bins run in rows as far as the eye can see. The far left wall is lined with blue plastic shopping carts filled to the brim. To my right, cracked monitor screens and keyboards with half the letters missing are stacked on top of each other. A bin at my feet is stuffed full of wires that twist and jut out like a basket of snakes. We walk through slowly, touching copper piping, old wrenches, screwdrivers, a rusted saw with missing teeth.

"Geez," I say, lifting a telephone with a cracked screen. I press dusty buttons. "What do they do with all this stuff?"

Rayburn sifts through a bin of medical equipment, his hand resting on one of those heart-listeners the doctors wore around their necks. He puts it on and then takes it off just as quickly. "They piece it out. Use, uh, use it for parts and the like. No wonder they, uh, have things running so smoothly. They have every spare part they could ever need."

I pass a bookshelf chock full of yellowed books and try to read their spines. "I've never seen so much stuff in one place. Most of the buildings we find have been gutted to the gills."

He nods, picking up a broken syringe. "Genius, really, to collect as much as p-p-possible. It's not like this stuff is, uh, is being produced anymore." He pushes up his glasses, hunches down, and peers deep into a suitcase on the floor.

I gaze around. The stacks and piles go on forever. How can we find anything useful in twenty minutes?

"We need to split up. No more window-shopping. You go left. I'll go right. We look for weapons, anything that could help us escape and get out of this place." Remembering Mama's situation, a tightness encircles my heart. "Look for medications, too. Anything that might help Mama survive on the road."

Rayburn offers me a sympathetic look. "I'll work on that. You look for the, uh, weapons."

I smirk, taking off into the dimly lit interior. Rayburn knows me too well.

I jog, scan, jog, scan. Bins of warped silverware. Cracked plastic tubs of clothes and shoes. Everything has a fine layer of dust. It's like searching through a museum. If I had the time, I'd rifle through each bin and touch each relic, turning it over with gentle fingers. A baby doll peeks at me from under a table, one eye gooed shut, the other staring at me behind her black lashes. So many treasures, yet I can't find what I'm looking for. I don't know if I expected a shelf full of guns and racks of bullets, but I find nothing. Not even a usable kitchen knife.

At the bottom of one bin, I find little brown cylinders the size of my finger tied in a line. At each end a little wick dangles. I lift them to my nose. They smell faintly of gunpowder. Mini explosives? I pocket them, along with two soggy packets of matches. They could come in handy if they still light.

"Rayburn!" I call from my end of the warehouse. He's hunched form the door, bent over a tub. "How much time?"

"Not much!" His voice echoes back to me.

Panicked, I run faster. When I get to the back wall, my heart sinks. This is our one chance.

To my right I spy a door. Gripping the worn handle, I tug it. Locked. Locked doors mean big prizes.

I run back, grab a couple small screwdrivers and some thin pieces of stiff copper wire. Then I set about picking the lock. It's the second time today that I'm glad I had Arn around growing up.

When the lock clicks, I'm sweating and my heart is pounding, but the door sliding open sends a shiver of joy through me. I'm greeted by darkness. Slowly, my eyes piece together a storage room. I feel around, hands extended until I bump into something at waist level. My hands fumble into a round drum big as a water barrel. It's heavy.

Gripping the sides I drag it through the doorway. Liquid sloshes inside. When I make it out of the storage room, I'm sweating.

Rayburn appears behind me. "What is it?" He leans over my shoulder.

"Don't know." The off-white opaque plastic holds liquid. Water, or something else? I twist off the round white plug. The chemical fumes that escape nearly knock me off my feet. I stagger back, coughing, my eyes burning.

"Cover it up!" Rayburn shouts, fumbling for the lid.

"What is it?" I ask.

"A caustic chemical. Some sort of hydrochloric acid maybe, or bleach." He looks up at me with worried eyes. "Whatever it is, we should l-l-leave it alone."

Symbols are scrawled across the sealed lid in a smudgy charcoal.

"What does it say?" I lean in.

Rayburn reads the dark, ominous letters. "'CAUTION: HF. DO NOT OPEN. FOR 14:13.'"

CHAPTER FIFTEEN

As the sun sinks low in the west, my mind whirs. I roll the black, slashed words around: CAUTION: HF. DO NOT OPEN. FOR 14:13. The CAUTION is simple enough. FOR 14:13 tightens my insides. Why would they keep a huge barrel of caustic chemicals locked in a room? What is 14:13? A time? A date? They've already been tampering with the water. Then I remember Mage telling me her father said it would be better to die than to go with the Breeders. Will they use this poison on us? How long do I have to figure it out until these lunatics dump it in our water and wipe us all out?

I point at the black scrawl, the smell of chemicals still hanging in the air. "What d'you think this is?"

He swallows hard and looks down at the barrel. "I...I don't know."

"You don't know? What do you think about the number 14:13? A certain time of day? Some sort of code?" I stare at his face in the dim light of the warehouse.

He blinks uncomfortably, pushing up his glasses. "Riley, I really, uh, don't know."

"Rayburn, seriously. This is important." I hit my hand against the barrel. The plastic vibrates and the liquid sloshes inside.

"Is it?" he says, dropping his eyes to the floor.

"Yeah," I say slowly. "I think it is."

He blows out a frustrated breath. "It could mean absolutely nothing, Riley. It could be someone's favorite number or their shoe size."

"Their shoe size?"

"You know what I mean." His eyebrows fold down and his stammer is nearly gone. His next words come out forcefully. "You are so busy looking for a way out maybe you haven't considered that we just stay."

I blink, taking in his words. This was the last thing I expected him to say. "Stay? Stay here? Rayburn, we can't—"

"Can't we?" he says, gripping the sides of the barrel. "We have food here. Shelter. I have meaningful employment. No one tries to shoot us. There are…" His eyes lock on a stack of hardcover books. "There are many benefits to becoming a member of this, uh, this well-formed society."

"Well-formed society?! I…I can't believe what I'm hearing." I nearly spit the words. "Why would you say this?"

"Why? Because I have so much to look forward to on the r-r-road?"

I stare at him, my mouth open. "What about Clay?"

Rayburn won't look at me. "Clay can take care of himself."

My anger flares hotter. "You've never liked him."

His head jerks up. "W-w-wait a minute. He never liked *me*. Not the other way around."

"That doesn't mean we let them take him." I shake my head, frustration building. We are running out of time. Crank and Donut will start missing us soon.

He turns and begins striding back to the warehouse front doors. "Good luck with your wild goose chase, Riley. Let me know when you g-g-get us excommunicated."

I grit my teeth and watch him leave. Then I shove the barrel back into the closet and lock the door. I don't care what he says; I have a bad feeling about that barrel. Above me, the giant metal beams, once shiny and new, have given over to rust and erosion. How long after I'm dead will those beams still be here, providing homes to birds? Generations? How can I keep fighting when the people I'm fighting for turn against me?

***

Our garage shift ends as the sun is trailing thick orange fingers over the parking lot. Rayburn and I walk together, our long shadows leading us in. We haven't spoken since our fight. Crank, Donut, and Lance crunch behind us too close for us to speak anyway. I look over at him and he drops his head. I kick at a rock in our path and watch it skitter into the weeds. Why does everything I do have to be so hard?

Inside, we split up and wash up in different bathrooms. Then we walk to the cafeteria, the throng joining us, making it impossible to talk. We stand in line, elbow to sweaty elbow, and receive our trays of stringy, boiled beans and a deflated wheat roll. Andrew wasn't kidding when he said they were rationing. My heart sinks at the small portion. After all that hard labor, I'm starving.

When I look up, I spot Ethan and Clay at a table not far from mine. The boys wave, but I don't move. Instead I look out across the bustling food court. It's easy to see why Rayburn wants to stay. He has a real chance at a life here and the road has been awful for him. He could work and make friends. For a moment I consider it, creating a life with these people. But then I think of Stephen, of Kemuel, of Andrew and his goggle-covered stare. I think of the sore already forming on Clay's lip. And the moaning in the hole. Rayburn might not believe me, but I know this place is poison.

My reason for moving on sits several tables down, waving for me. Them and Mama and Auntie. We can't stay here. No matter the cost, family is the foundation I've built my life on, and I'm not about to let them be killed by these monsters.

I slump down in a plastic chair beside Clay and Ethan. They're deep in some serious conversation and I lean in to hear it over the din.

"Just go up to her," Clay says, smirking, "and say, 'Hey pretty lady, wanna take a walk?'"

Ethan blushes. "I can't do that."

"Well then, I dunno. Figure out how to make one of them paper animals and give it to her. Or a flower or somethin'." Clay's eyes trail over to where Mage plays with the other children.

I clear my throat. "What're we talking about exactly?" I look at Ethan. "You ask him for girl advice?"

Ethan drops his head, letting his bangs hide his eyes. He shrugs his shoulders as his answer.

Clay throws an arm around me. "Old hoss has himself a crush. Perfectly natural. We was just having a man-to-man. I told him how I stole yer heart." He tries to plant a kiss, but I dodge it.

"I don't think it's good advice for him to get tangled up with Mage." I lean forward to get Ethan's attention. "Remember what I said? What good is it to get involved when we're just gonna leave?" I cross my arms over my chest. "Besides, you're only eight. Too young."

Clay barks a laugh. "Eight's a fine age for yer first crush. 'Sides, where else is he gonna see girls? Not on the road, that's for damn sure."

Ethan pushes back from the table. "I don't wanna talk about

this."

"Munchkin," I say, reaching for him, but he turns and runs off. I sigh in frustration.

"You baby him, you know." Clay's voice is matter-of-fact, and it bugs the hell out of me.

"You think he's just one of the boys, huh? Having a man-to-man. Well, he's not a man, Clay. He's eight." I gesture toward the kids on the play structure to make my point.

His eyes travel there. "I was riding on raids at 'bout that age," he says flatly.

"Well, I certainly don't want him raised like you were."

He shoots me a look. "Me neither." He frowns, leaning forward on his elbows. "I wasn't tellin' him to shoot up a road gang. I was tellin' him its okay to talk to a girl." Then he looks me over. "What's wrong with you today?"

Should I tell him about the barrel? What would I say? That I found some caustic fluid that I think might kill us, but I can't be sure? Clay won't believe me and I just don't have the strength left to try to convince someone else. Plus, if I'm honest, I'm starting to doubt myself. Maybe I always do jump to conclusions.

I look up at him and try a smile. "I've been fighting against the world for my whole life." I pause and take a breath. "Sometimes I forget I don't have to fight you too."

He caresses my cheek. "The fight in you is one of the things I love."

***

Before I go to bed, I walk down to the infirmary. The guard at his stool doesn't even stand up. He frowns at me, waving me on with his yellowing paperback. As I walk the infirmary hallway, the cots and mattresses are quiet. Patients lay still with their eyes closed. It's creepy here at night. I wish Mama was well enough to come back to our room and lay beside me.

An older man with yellow, cat-like eyes watches as I slip by. He sits up and continues to watch me.

"Revelations..." He trails off, his voice dying in his throat. "Revelations 14:13."

The black scrawled numbers on the barrel, 14:13! I turn toward him, senses alert. "What did you say?"

He reminds me of an old tortoise, his neck stretching like he could slip it back in his shell if he was spooked. I took him to be ancient, but as I get closer, I can see he isn't as old as I thought. It's just his puckered body, his yellow eyes, and thin hair that makes him look that way. Did the water do this to him? Fear scrambles up my spine as his eyes lock onto mine.

"What did you say?" I ask again, hardly breathing.

"The end... is nigh." His eyes pop open until they're nearly lidless. He leans forward, stretching his long neck. "Revelations 14:13. 'Blessed are the dead which die in the Lord from henceforth.'" He coughs and a glob of blood and saliva splatters his palm. He looks at it for a moment and then begins smearing it on his cheeks. "'Yea, saith the Spirit, that they may rest from their labors; and their works do follow them.'"

I pull back, horrified. And yet, what if he knows about the poison in the warehouse? "When is the end?" I kneel at the edge of his dirty mattress. He rolls toward me and I shrink back. I steel my will and look into his eyes. "What do you know about the end?"

He blinks at me. "The temple was filled with smoke from the glory of the Gods." He smacks his palm to his bloodied cheek with a sound like a snapping twig.

"Stop," I say, reaching for his hand as he pulls back to hit himself again. He smells like rot.

"And no man was able to enter into the temple." The volume of his voice rises as he slaps his cheek with his other hand. "Till the seven plagues of the seven angels were fulfilled!"

"What's going on?" A Middie jogs up, holding her billowing skirt. "You!" She points at me. "You let him go this instant."

I drop the man's arm and he slaps himself again. The crack is loud and it rocks his body back, almost off the mattress.

The Middie grabs me by the arm. "What have you done? Why did you make Brig so upset?"

I look down at Brig, who hauls back and slaps himself so hard the sound echoes through the store. "Maybe you should stop yelling at *me* and worry about Brig knocking himself unconscious." I point as he winds up again.

"Oh, Gods help me," she mutters, reaching down, trying to sooth him. She takes his hands and holds them to his chest. His head lurches back and forth in a tantrum. "Get out of here," she says to me over her shoulder.

I push up, my legs shaking. As I'm about to turn the corner, a slap echoes through the hallway. The Middie says, "Oh, Brig, Jesus."

Jesus is right. What was all that talk about the end and blessed are the dead? Was it a madman's ramble or was he really communicating something to me? And what's revelation? As I walk back toward my mama, I try to pin down everything he said to me. It might be nothing or it might be the key to our survival.

The fitting rooms are dim and silent. I slip down the dark hallway and push back her slatted door. It creaks on its hinges, and Mama stirs from her nest of blankets.

"Riley?" she says, rubbing her eye with her fist like a child.

I nod, squat down and fold myself into the corner beside her.

"What's wrong?" she asks, her hand already on my back, stroking.

I shake my head and lean into her. She smells like herself again, warm earth and clean linen.

"You can tell me, you know." She pets my hair in slow even stokes. "You're not too old to tell Mama what's wrong."

"You've got enough to worry about," I whisper, letting my cheek rest on her shoulder.

"What?" she asks, her voice rising. "I don't have anything to occupy my mind in here. A little worrying would do me good. Keep me from going batty."

When she says batty, the image of Auntie waving a butcher knife at a bat trapped in our cupboards floats to mind. Auntie. One more stake straight through my heart.

"Have you ever heard of revelation?" I ask. Outside someone moans. I wonder if Brig is back to slapping himself.

"Revelations?" she says, rolling the word over in her mouth. "You mean, like in the Bible?"

I sit up and look at her. "Revelations is in the Bible?"

She nods. "I think so. Bell would know. Your Auntie was quite religious when she was younger. Gave up reading the Bible when her eyes got bad." Mama smiles sadly and goes back to petting my head. "I hope she's okay."

"Me too," I say. "So, the Bible. Do you remember what it said about revelation?"

She shifts, a musty smell puffing from the old blankets. "I think it was predictions for when God came back to earth. For the end of the world."

Gooseflesh breaks out over my arms. I press my hands to the carpet, thinking. "So this part in the Bible tells about the end of the world." I pause, thinking. "Are all Bibles the same?"

"Pretty much, I think," she says, resting her head against the fitting room wall. "Why? Is this what's bothering you? Where did you hear about Revelations?"

"Just some crazy guy out there." I thumb toward the hallway. "Don't worry about it."

"Like I said," she sinks down, her eyelids drooping, "I like to worry about you."

Soon her eyes are closed. A few more minutes and her breathing evens. I slip from under her thin arm and ease myself out of the fitting room. As I slink out of the infirmary, the Middie who helped Brig glares at me from behind a checkout counter. At least Brig has stopped smacking himself. I slip by his mattress. Just as I think I'm clear, I see his yellow eyes on me. I nearly run to the exit.

The hallway back to my room is dim. Most have gone to bed. It seems ever since Stephen died and Clay joined the guard, no one is locking me in at night. No one seems to be paying attention to me. I might be able to get my hands on a Bible after all. Instead of heading to my room, I slip left down the hallway towards the Messiah's quarters. The question is, how do I get in?

***

I stand in shadow and peer out toward the Messiah's chamber. A burly guard sits outside the main door in a plastic chair. His wide hands cup his knees. I watch for long minutes, waiting for his eyes to sag, but they don't. I slink back into my pocket of shadow and press my hands to my head. Who am I kidding? Even if I slipped past the guard, Andrew, the Messiah, and any number of his Brotherhood are probably inside. What'll I do, just slip in and say, *Hey, can I borrow this?*

I hide and wait. The guard has a runny nose. He sniffles every ten seconds until the noise is so maddening I think about strangling him with my bare hands. I shift and something in my pocket digs against my hip. Reaching down, I draw out the mini-explosives I found in the warehouse today. I squint in the darkness and slowly read the word *Firecrackers* written along the side. Let's hope they do the trick.

Glancing down the hallway, I look for my target. These firecrackers might not blow anything up, but I just need noise, not destruction. A few feet down the darkened hallway a glass partition still stands. Glass exploding would draw attention, but could poke a couple holes in me too. At the end of the hallway, about twenty feet from my corner and another ten feet from the guard, sits a large ceramic flower pot with a fake plastic tree inside. I slink over and examine it. If the firecrackers really do their work, they could shatter the vase and set the plastic tree on fire. That would keep the guard busy. Meanwhile, I could hide in the dark alcove near the corner. With the guard tending to the flaming plant, I can slip right by him into the Messiah's room. It's not a great plan, but it's the only plan I got.

I walk to the flowerpot and dig out the firecrackers. With the two books of matches in my other hand, I dangle the red explosives into the ceramic pot and drape one end over the side. When I pull out a match from the booklet, my heart sinks. It's flimsy to the touch. Soggy. Holding my breath, I pinch the match tip between both sides of the matchbook and drag it across. Nothing. No sulfuric hiss. No bright pop of flame. I toss the spent match into the flowerpot and pull out another. Nothing. I run through the whole book with no success and my heart starts hammering. If this doesn't work, I have no plan B.

The second book seems more solid, but they're decades old and there's no guarantee they'll light. I pull out a match and examine the rounded red tip. *Please*, I think. I rip it and strike it against the matchbook.

A blue spark turns into a yellow tongue of fire. I'm so excited that I touch the flame to the firecracker without thinking. The wick catches with another hiss. I stare at it dumbly for a beat. Then I dive for cover.

Crouching in the dark alcove, I place my hands over my ears. How loud will it be?

A series of pops like gunshots explode through the hallway. Then they're done. That's it? No fire? No shattering pot? That's all I get? It won't take the guard long to—

"What the hell?" he shouts, from around the corner.

I fold up into a ball back as far into the dark corner as I can. Maybe he won't see me. Maybe my plan is half baked.

I hear the guard running toward me as the last of the firecrackers fizzle. His footsteps vibrate the floor until he's standing right next to me. I hold my breath. Any minute a big hand will reach down and drag me out of my hiding spot. Instead, he moves on.

"Paul!" I recognize the Messiah's voice, deep and commanding. "What's happening?" He heads this way just as the smoke from the firecrackers tickles my throat, making me want to cough. I squeeze my lips shut and fight the urge.

"Sir," calls the guard from down the hall. "Please stay in your room. I'll check out the wing and let you know when it's all clear."

Fingers trail along the wall as the Messiah passes my hiding spot and moves past me. "Paul, was that gun shots?" The Messiah keeps going toward the guard. Soon I can hear them talking down the hallway. Soon I can't hear them at all.

Now's my chance. I'm up and running before I can think. I sprint down the carpeted hallway and nearly slide into the outer doors. Palming the handle, the door opens with a smooth click. I slip inside.

Darkness. I fumble, hands outstretched through the antechamber, banging my shin on a plastic chair that scrapes across the floor. My hands find a smooth surface, another door. I take a deep breath and open it.

Candlelight flickers from the corners. The same thick scent of incense wafts in the air. I head straight for the Messiah's desk. It's a large table constructed out of two surfaces butted into an L. Parchments, books, scissors and pots of sticky glue cover the table. His latest creation of lines cut from many books is spread out in pieces on the right-hand side of the desk. The books he's cut from are stacked on either side. I walk over and examine them, sounding out the titles, cursing at myself the whole time for how long it takes me to read each one. *The Book of Mormon*, *The Qur'an*, *Torah*, *Dianetics*, and *Tao Te Ching*. Each yellowing text has been dissected here and there with little rectangular holes. He must have Andrew help him since a blind man couldn't do this alone. Tingles creep up my arms as I touch one of the pages. It's like looking at some gutted animal, though I don't know why. Maybe it's the incense swirling around my head. Maybe it's the fact that any minute the Messiah could burst back in and grab me. Forgetting his rambling cut-out text, I keep looking.

My hands fumble over a worn leather-backed tome. Flipping it over, I slow read "The Bible" etched in flaking gold letters. Bingo. I clutch it to my chest and whirl around.

"I thought I smelled you."

My blood freezes to ice. The Messiah stares at me with cold, milky eyes.

CHAPTER SIXTEEN

"Drop it," he says, pointing.

I can't move. The Bible is clutched to my chest and my heart thuds against it. "Drop what?" I say, slipping the book around to my back. If only I could tuck it in the waistband of my pants.

"Drop the book. The Bible, isn't it?" He sniffs, floating closer, bringing with him more incense. My head goes cloudy with it.

"You *can* see, can't you?" I say, still clutching the Bible. If I'm ever going to uncover what he has planned in that rotting brain of his, I need this book.

The Messiah's face hardens under his curly brown beard. "The cataracts make it nearly impossible to see anything but changes in light. But the Gods have given me sight in other ways." He dons a look of calm clarity. "Just like how I smelled you in the hallway. How I knew you'd come in here."

"What're you gonna do with me?" My eyes trace my path to the door. He's blocking it, but he's blind and frail, despite his girth. So what if he can smell me coming? He won't be able to stop me.

The Messiah slides over and sits on one of his plush couches. I take a step toward the door.

"Leave with that book and I'll have you all put out with nothing—no shoes, no water. Your mother, your brother, Clay." He draws the last word out, his voice cold and final. "That book is more precious to me than you know."

Slowly, sadly, I place the Bible back on the stack.

"Good," he says when my hand has left its leather binding. "Why do you want it?" He pats the couch as if he means for me to sit beside him.

"Just wanted some light reading." I stand rigidly and eye the door. "I hear the Jesus story is a humdinger."

"Hmm," he says, one corner of his mouth lifting. "Humor to lighten the mood. I find humor a waste of time." The Messiah folds slender hands over his knee.

"Yeah, well, we got nothing but time here, right?" I take a quiet step sideways.

He frowns. "Oh no. You are mistaken, child. Time is precious.

Time is not something we have in abundance."

I snort and take another tiny step sideways. "Seems like you got everything in abundance."

"You're in such a hurry to leave," he says sadly, shaking his head. He's noticed my movements. How does he do it?

I fake a yawn. "I'm pretty tuckered, working on your trucks and all."

"I've been meaning to talk to you alone, Riley," he says, rising. "I'm glad your thievery afforded us this time."

"Happy to pilfer any time," I say.

"Stealing is a sin," he says sharply. Beneath his flowing gown his veined biceps flex.

"Okay. But what do you want with me?" My eyes trek through his apartment. A carved wooden pole with strange animal faces leers at me from one dark corner. In another corner a metal cross angles up to the ceiling. Is that blood or rust on its crossbeams?

"Riley, it's not what I want. It's what the Gods want. What they want, we must provide. You know that, don't you?"

"Yeah, sure. Like how you butcher and burn those pigs. For the *Gods*." I can't keep the sarcasm out of my voice. "I hope they like pork."

"You don't believe in the Gods? That they can save us? That they need to be appeased?"

"No, I don't." I fold my arms across my chest, suddenly angry and unsure why.

"Why don't you believe?" He walks over and lifts one of the burning sticks, wafting more incense into the air. The smoke curls up in cloudy ribbons.

I take a deep breath and fix him with my eyes. "I don't believe because I see no reason to. The Gods have never blessed me one day of my life. This world is hell. I've seen people die. They're scared out of their minds. There's no glowing light. No joy." I stare at him, my heart pounding. I feel like crying, but won't give him the satisfaction. "We live, we sweat, we bleed. Then we go into the ground. That's it."

The Messiah stares at me for a moment. Then he pouts his lower lip. "How sad."

"Yeah, it's sad," I say, folding my arms over my chest like I need the barrier from him and his religion. "Life is a sad, sad thing."

"What of death?" He lifts one knee over the other, his robe rising with it. "Is there any joy in death for you, non-believer?"

"Who has joy in death?" I ask.

A wide smile breaks out on the Messiah's face. He leans forward with his elbows on his knees. "For the Believers there is much joy in death, for it is only through death that we fulfill our truest potential."

A chill breaks out over my arms even though it's nearly eighty degrees in the room. The Messiah's eyes are too wide, his smile too broad. I don't like how he's speaking about death. I think of the liquid in the barrel. "FOR 14:13" scrawled so violently on top.

"Do you want to die?" I ask slowly.

The Messiah turns on me. His face is stone serious. "Why do you ask?" He snuffs out a candle with the pads of two fingers. "Do you wish to kill me?"

I shake my head, forgetting he can't see me. "Nope."

"Many have, you know. Many have tried to kill me over the years." He shuffles back to the couch and sits. "They've all failed. Only the Gods can end me. And my days are marked." His gaze drifts off. "Just like Moses never seeing the glory that is the Promised Land, I will not see the deliverance of my people." He bows his head as if sorry for what's to come. Maybe the poison's only for him. Then again I note the wide, weeping sores on his neck, his hands. The red, hairless patch on the back of his scalp. Even with all the incense, he smells like something is dead inside him. He doesn't need poison.

When I say nothing, he turns in my direction. "Riley, your mother, you love her, yes?"

"Yes," I say without hesitation. "She thinks she's going to die." I clench my jaw. "That the baby'll kill her."

"Whatever the Gods will, that is what is to occur." He folds his hands on his lap again. One finger traces the skin around the open sore.

"Well, the Gods will have me to answer to if they kill her."

"Do you think," he says slowly, "that you'd be better equipped to save her if you were to leave here?"

"Yeah." I draw out the word slowly. Do I believe that? Could I save her on the road? "Are you giving us permission to leave?"

"I've never stopped you," he says, rising, the incense swirling up with him. He walks over and blows out a guttering candle. "You were always free to go."

I step back, taking in what he's saying. "But, the guards... They locked us in."

"For your own protection." He takes a step my way, enough that

I can see the flesh colored make-up on the sores around his face. So many sores. "Has anyone locked you in lately?"

Slowly, I shake my head. "No, but…"

"I cannot keep you prisoner. The Gods won't allow it." His voice is almost coy. "Did you know, Riley, I was not born in this mall?"

I shake my head.

"I was born in the back of a Volkswagen. At eight months old I was abducted, with my mother, by a road gang. I have no idea what happened to my mother. The road gang warrior who became my father of sorts never would tell me, so I can imagine it wasn't…pleasant." He pauses and looks up, his face tightening with the memory.

"The man who raised me was not a kind man. He wasn't raising me to be his son, you see. He was raising me to be a warrior." His hands fold together and squeeze. "I killed my first man at age eight."

Ethan's age. I swallow hard. The heat seems to intensify. Why's he telling me this?

"I grew up in the most vicious road gang in the area. We had everything: food, shelter, guns. But, even as a child, I knew this wasn't what the Gods wanted for my life. When I was fifteen, I was separated from my people on a raid. I wandered the desert until I knew I'd die. Half buried in sand, my hands clawing for life, the Gods gave me a vision of this mall. It was then I knew I was a prophet."

He looks at me, but I have no words.

"So, you see, I know the ways of the road. What I don't understand is why you'd prefer that to this." He spreads his hands wide, indicating his dominion.

I press my sweating palms together. "Can I be blunt?"

He nods, one strand of wavy brown hair cascading over his angular cheekbone. "Please."

"I think you're crazy." I take a deep breath. "I think you're gonna kill us all."

He pauses, and I wonder if I just spoke my death sentence.

He bobs his head slowly. "I see." When he rises, my body tightens, ready to fight or run, but instead he wanders to his desk, slides out a drawer, and lifts a book from it. He strides over and holds it out to me. It's a slimmer, more tattered version of the book I was attempting to steal. A Bible.

He holds the book out to me. "Consider it a gift from a

madman."

I slip my hand around the book and draw it slowly to my chest. "Thank you," I manage.

"You are free to leave any time." He swishes to another candle and blows it out. The room grows darker. I shift toward the door. I don't want to be in a dark room with the Messiah. "But, if you stay…" He smiles like a cat about to pounce.

"But, if I stay what?"

"Tomorrow night we have a communion ceremony. It is a very holy time for us. All I ask is that you participate. After that, I will give you a truck and some spare fuel." A dark smile finds his face. "We lunatics can be generous, too."

My jaw drops open. "Th-thanks," I stammer. None of this computes. Why's he being so kind?

He waves to the door. "You may go now. Just please try to keep out of trouble until communion." He smirks. "A large feat, I know."

"Yeah," I say, my tongue-tied. "Thanks."

Freedom. I can almost taste it, but then why is it so bittersweet?

***

The next morning I wake to the sound of gusting winds screaming, shaking the roof and rattling items outside. When I get to the dining hall, an effort to block the open roof is in full swing. Squinting through the dust, Andrew stands in the center of the food court, shouting above the wind. Men climb up ladders steadied by fellow Believers as they attempt to raise planks and nail them at mismatched angles over the opening. Dust whips their faces as they pound the boards in place. Already the air churns with fine particles of sand. One of the tarps that shaded the eating area rips from its ties and blows halfway across the food court. It wraps around a support beam and flutters.

I find Mage looking up with wide eyes, her hands stuffed in her jumper pockets, a strip of blue cloth tied over her mouth and nose.

"What's going on?" I shout over the racket. My lungs already laden, I pull my shirt over my mouth.

"Sand storm," she says, glancing at me. "Bad one. Papa says the Gods willed it."

I snort, but don't say anything. "It'll be over in a couple of hours." I pat her dusty curls.

She looks at me with solemn eyes. "No, Riley," she says without blinking. "I don't think so."

***

With breakfast suspended due to the storm, everyone is ushered back down the hall to the grow house. Farmers hand out plump round tomatoes and sugar snap peas for breakfast. I eat a hard, orange tomato, the juice spilling down my wrist, while I search for Ethan, Clay, and Rayburn. I find Ethan and Rayburn stepping out of line, handfuls of blueberries cupped in their palms.

"Did you get breakfast, Riley?" Rayburn says, as he lowers his head and awkwardly hunts for a few berries with his teeth. Blue juice dribbles on his lip.

I nod and put a hand on Ethan's shoulder. "Okay, my man?"

He nods, showing me teeth stained blueberry blue. Then he hacks until his lips turn a matching shade. This dust storm will be awful for his asthma. God, can it get any worse?

I gaze out over the dust-covered crowd. "We need a family meeting in ten minutes. Where's Clay?" Both boys stare at me, their faces twisted like they know a horrible secret they don't wanna tell.

"What?" I ask. They say nothing. "Where is he?"

My heart begins pounding and I don't know why. I swivel around and stare through the crowds of gritty people lined in rows. No Clay. I turn back and then I see him. Muscle-bound Brotherhood thugs are hauling bags of grain from the back of the grow house. Clay is one of them, though he seems to have dropped his grain bag off at the distribution table and struck up a conversation with the buxom brunette running it. He leans in, pressing his palms to the chipped tabletop. She smiles radiantly and tosses a long, chocolate-colored lock over her shoulder.

I want to kill her. I want to kill him.

"Riley." Rayburn's hand settles on my bicep.

I shrug him off. I'm stomping over to Clay, both fists clenched, before I know what I'm doing.

"Riley!" Rayburn calls again, though I can barely hear him over the wind and the pounding of my chest.

As I near, the girl notices me and her smile falls. Suddenly she's very interested in the lists she's made on a piece of an old bed sheet. Clay turns, his own smile fading.

"Hey," he says, his tone happy and false. "Mornin'," he reaches for me, but I stand stiffly to the side. "Did you get somethin' to eat?" he asks, nodding to the bag of grain at his feet. "I was asked to bring out some of the stored grain, so...I did."

"Yep." I stare. My arms do not leave my chest.

He swallows hard and runs a hand over the back of his neck. His injured hand unbandaged, something he never would've done on the road. "I'll be done in a little bit. We could..." he pauses, chewing his lip. "We could take a walk 'round the mall when I'm done."

"No thanks." I say flatly. "We're having a *family*," I flash the girl a look, "meeting in thirty minutes. Meet us at my mother's room."

He nods. "I'll probably be done by then."

As I walk away, I fight the urge to cry.

Rayburn, Ethan, and I walk through the hordes of wide-eyed people to the hospital wing. The guard at the entrance is gone, probably either nailing boards to the ceiling or slinging feedbags up from storage.

Rayburn eyes the empty stool, and his face tightens. "It's only a matter of time before I'm, uh, I'm called up to help with the s-s-storm." He pushes up his glasses. "We'd better make this fast."

"It's important," I say. The Bible rubs against my back where it's tucked in my waistband. Last night I skimmed through the ridiculously small print until my eyes crossed. I found Revelations 14:13. I tried to read the whole chapter, but it was dense and wordy. Today, with help, maybe we'll figure it out, but maybe we don't need to. Maybe we'll be out of here before he plans to use it anyway.

We find Mama sitting on one of the cots in the large open space that serves as the general hospital ward. Her cheeks are still sunken, her skin pale, but she looks a bit healthier. As we stride up, she hands a cup to an elderly woman in the cot across from her. The woman takes it and lifts it to her lips with trembling hands. That's my mama, nursing the sick even when she's hurting.

"Hi, my dears." She waves and then rises slowly. Her hand finds her rounding belly.

"Hi," I say, drawing up to her. Ethan wraps his arms around her waist. I lean in for a hug. The woman on the cot begins hacking.

My mother looks down in worry, but a Middie is walking toward the woman, ready to take Mama's place.

"We need a family meeting. Can we use the fitting room?"

"No one's been moved into it yet. I don't think they'll mind."

We follow her into the dark hallway and past the musty change rooms to the back. The fitting room is tight for four of us, but we all manage to squeeze inside, sitting Indian-style on the floor. Above, the howling wind sounds like it's tearing the roof off and the sand peppering the building is making me tense. I stare at the slatted door. Where is Clay? Should we just…start without him?

"What's going on?" Mama asks. She pulls Ethan into her, her arm around his shoulder. "Is it about the storm?"

I pause and look at Rayburn. "The Messiah's letting us go. Once their blasted communion ceremony is over tonight he'll give us a truck and gas." I look up at the three faces staring at me. A long pause. "We can get the hell out."

"He said this?" Mama asks, tightening her grip on Ethan. "He said he would let us go?"

I nod, folding my hands together, squeezing. "He said we weren't prisoners. We can get back on the road. Leave these lunatics behind."

Rayburn leans back, blowing out a breath. "I-I-I'm not going."

"What?" I dig my hands into the carpet. "You're really gonna stay?"

He nods, not looking at me.

"Rayburn," I say, pushing up onto my knees. "That's crazy. They'll make you join the Brotherhood. You'll get sick." I gesture out toward the mall.

His black curls jiggle as he shakes his head. "I can't go back on the road. I'll d-d-die out there. In here," he says, lifting his eyes, "Here I can live, work, even find a companion."

"But you'll end up like them. Believing every word that lunatic says." I run my hand through my hair. "I don't get it."

"I do," Mama says quietly.

I look over at her. "What?!"

"I understand why Ray would want to stay. We can't force him to go, nor should we. It's his decision." She runs her hand up and down Ethan's arm. "If we didn't have Auntie to go back for, I'd advise we all stay."

"I can't believe this," I say, slapping my hands onto my thighs. "These people are totally batty. The leader told me his days are numbered. We found a barrel with poison labeled for 14:13. I think he's gonna to kill everyone." I punch my fist into my thigh. "We can't stay."

Mama raises her eyebrows. "A barrel of poison?"

Rayburn shakes his head. "We have no proof it's for anything other than, uh, cleaning the f-f-floor."

I shoot Rayburn a pained look. "He told Mage that they'd be better off dead than with the Breeders."

Rayburn pushed up to his knees. "That has nothing to do with this."

"Enough fighting." Mama grabs Ethan's hand. "We aren't staying, poison or no poison. I'm just saying that the road is hard and dangerous. I hate to put you through that again."

Ethan curls into her arm. "I'm going where you and Riley are going."

"What about Janine?" Rayburn says, pointing to my mother. "They've slowed the fetus growth with the drugs they're giving her. On the road she'll have n-n-none of that."

"That's why we need you," I say, leaning across the dusty little changing room. "You *have* to come, Ray. You *have* to help her."

He shakes his head. "I can't help. It's beyond me."

"No!" I shout, clenching my fists. "I refuse to believe that."

"What's going on?"

We swivel. Clay stands in the doorway, hands on his hips, looking down at us. The concern on his face is real. So is the red, nickel-sized sore at the corner of his mouth.

"Clay!" Ethan says, brightening. Then his brow furrows. "Riley says we're leaving."

"We are?" he asks, turning to me.

I nod, flicking my eyes to a spider-webbed corner. "After the ceremony."

His frowns and pushes up the hair on his crown, his unconscious gesture of thumbing back his hat still clinging to him even when the hat is gone. "Can we just hold our horses for a minute?"

"We gotta go," I say, standing. "I think the Messiah's planning on killing everybody. Rayburn and I found a barrel of something I think is poison, big enough to wipe out New Mexico. We think he's gonna use it soon. Don't know when, but I got this." I pull the slender Bible from under my shirt and hold it up to him.

He stares at it, confusion flooding his face. "A book?"

"The Bible. There's gotta be something in here about when he plans to wipe out everyone, but I can't find it. Maybe if you'd help..."

Suddenly heat's burning up my cheeks. Why does it embarrass me to ask my boyfriend for help? Maybe it's because our relationship is as thin as my threadbare shirt.

"Do ya know how plum crazy you sound? The Messiah's not gonna kill his people," Clay says, shaking his head. "I talked to him this mornin'. He was busy organizin' the workload to batten down for the storm. Why would he care if he was gonna end 'em all?"

I open my mouth, but no response comes out.

"Maybe he just wants to kill the bad guys?" Ethan offers.

"Maybe, little man." Clay crouches down and smiles at Ethan. "We don't got to worry none. I got us covered."

I scoff. Clay flashes me a look. "You got something to say?" he asks, anger finally creeping into his voice.

Is that what I wanted all along? To stir him up just to prove I still could? I shrug, looking over at Mama. Now it's her turn to stare at the carpet.

"Say it." He steps forward until his chest is a foot from mine. "Go on. Say it."

I grit my teeth. "Just because you party with them doesn't mean that they won't smoke you the *first time* you fall outta line." I meet his eyes and, for once, am not melted by them. "They're *bad* people, Clay. They only care about themselves."

"Bad people who saved yer ma?" He shoots a finger at her.

"For a pric—"

"Bad people who fed you, clothed you, kept you safe." He hits his palm with his fist with each item on the list. "Who let you do whatever the hell you please." His tone slings more venom than I've heard in a while. This isn't what I wanted.

"They locked us up like *animals*." My own hands curl into fists.

"That was for their safety and ours. But you ain't locked up now, are ya?" His blue eyes have lost their fire. Now they're cold, a temperature much more terrifying. Is that disgust on his face? Does he hate me now? My anger folds like a chair, leaving me teetering on the edge of tears. This isn't supposed to be happening. My gaze falls on the sore at his lip. I drop my head. How can I blame him for seeing their side when I'm the one who let them open his eyes?

"I gotta go," he says, turning.

Ethan pulls out of Mama's arms. "Wait, Clay!" He throws himself onto Clay, skinny arms cinching around Clay's waist. For a moment Clay's stiff, but then his hands fall on Ethan's head.

"It's okay, little man," he says, his eyes turning to me. "This isn't the end."

CHAPTER SEVENTEEN

Sand. Sand covers everything: coating the floor, the tables, thickening the air that we suck into our lungs. We tie scraps of cloth over our mouths and noses. Still, we nearly drown in sand. People disappear into their rooms. Dunes have begun to pile up near the doors and all over the food court, drifting against tables and up around the restaurant kiosks until the whole place looks like a ghost town swallowed by the Mohave. Even though it's only noon, darkness has descended throughout the mall, plunging us all into a murky twilight. The power keeps flickering off and on, everything choked by sand.

After the meeting we all agreed to leave the morning after communion. We won't be able to leave tonight with the sandstorm raging outside anyway. We'll have to wait until it dies down.

With no one around to make a fuss, I bring Ethan and Rayburn into my room. We sit on the stained mattress and eat rough grain cakes that stick between our teeth. Between the gritty air and the dry cakes, my mouth feels like an old boot buried in the desert. I chew the last of my cake, swallow, and cough.

"God, those things could be used as artillery. If we run out of bullets, we'll just chuck these," I say, cleaning my teeth with my tongue.

Ethan doesn't laugh at my weak joke. A dusting of sand covers his skin and hair making him look like a kid made out of mud. He's been hacking more than I'd like. This dust storm has to die down or he'll hack up his lungs.

Rayburn swallows a lump of grain cake and makes a face. "At least we aren't, uh, out in the, uh, storm."

"Knock it off," I say, the anger from our meeting rising up in me. "I don't want to fight about this right now."

"Riley, you have to see reason," he says, pressing both palms into the mattress.

I fold my arms over my stiff, dirt-caked t-shirt. "Haven't heard anything reasonable this whole damn time."

Rayburn opens his mouth to sass back, but a figure appears in the doorway. Mage's curly head dips below the partially lowered grate and comes into the room. The sand's gotten to her too, reddening her normally sparkling eyes and dusting her golden curls into a dirty blond. She comes over and sits on the mattress, facing us. Beside me, Ethan sits up straighter.

"I wanna come with you," she says, looking each of us in the face.

A long pause. I know what she's asking, but I want to hear her say it. "To where?" I ask slowly.

She cocks her head sideways like I'm an idiot. "Out there." She points wildly behind her. "You know," she leans in and drops her voice to a whisper. "On the *road*."

I furrow my brow. "How do you know we're planning to leave?"

She shrugs, her jumper slipping down her shoulder. "I overhead my papa talking to Andrew about you wanting to go after the communion ceremony." She leans forward, her eyes wide. "I want to come too."

Beside me, Ethan nods.

Rayburn shakes his head, dust trickling from his hair. "You can't mean that. The road is awful. You have a great, uh, great life here." He spreads his hands to indicate the mall. "Why would you ever leave?"

"Because," she says, with wide, serious eyes, "my papa's been crying in this room. I hid and overhead him praying. He says the plagues are here, the Gods are going to kill everybody and there's nothing he can do to stop it." She looks up at me, her eyes bloodshot and wet. "I don't want to die."

"When, Mage?" I grab her arm. "When does he think the plagues are coming?"

She turns her tear-filled eyes to mine. "They're already here."

***

I run through the abandoned hallways, my boots spraying sand in front of me. I have to find Clay. The dust-filled air burns my lungs. I hack a couple times and keep going. I know I can make Clay see reason. Then we can get away from these lunatics and I can get Clay back. My Clay. The Clay who wouldn't hurt me.

I skid around a corner and peer down the sand-clogged hallway. The shops are deathly quiet; many are covered with cloth or tarps that hang heavily over the openings. People huddle together in the near-darkness. In a former clothing store, two women sit on a pile of rags, moaning. The elder—a woman I've seen before in the food line—lifts red eyes to me, silent tears streaming down her dust-caked cheeks. Do they think the plagues have arrived?

We gotta get out of here.

I run down the men's wing and it's just as eerie and quiet. As I walk down the hallway, a dark shadow steps in front of me. Andrew.

His goggled eyes are dust caked and there's finger marks on the lenses from where he's swiped them clean a couple of times. His rainbow clothes and gold jewelry are muted by sand. He grins, flashing me his rotten teeth like pebbles in his gums. I turn to run away, but two more of the Messiah's Brotherhood step out from the shadows. I'm surrounded.

"What's this?" I ask, wheeling around. The men fence me in, arms extended.

Andrew smirks behind his patchy beard, making the scar that cuts through it look like a second smile. "The Messiah wants you put up until communion."

"Put up?" I take a step back, my eyes searching for an exit. The men close in on me. My heart begins to thud.

He nods, coming toward me. His giant eyes crinkle up as he steps closer. "He wants you locked away for a few hours where you can't get into trouble."

"Did he say that? That's so thoughtful, but I'm fine. Now if you boys will just leave me be..." I smile. Then I rush at him, screaming.

He reaches out with giant arms, but he's slow. I duck under and scramble on my hands and knees on the worn carpet. Behind me, Andrew swears. The other two men clomp forward.

"Move!" he yells at them.

They pound toward me. I'm up and on my feet in an instant, bolting for the common area. If I can get to the food court, maybe I can hide.

A hand grabs for my shirt, but I duck sideways and pull free. I can smell them, hear their thunderous footfalls on the carpet. Down the hall a kid about twelve turns the corner and his eyes go wide. He slips into an open storefront as I tear past him.

Soon I can't hear them. I chance a look over my shoulder.

Andrew holds a pistol in his hand and is aiming it at me. My insides twist. A gun? I thought they didn't carry guns.

"Stop or I'll shoot you!" He locks his elbows and closes one giant goggled eye.

Does he have bullets? I skid to a stop and turn. Slowly I raise my hands in surrender. When he walks over and puts his meaty mitt on my wrist, I wish I'd just kept running.

"So," I ask as nonchalantly as I can, "Where you gonna put me up? Not many hotels round these parts."

"Shut up." He shoves the gun between my shoulder blades roughly.

I turn and head where he pushes me. Hating Andrew won't change how this goes down, but I do it anyway.

He walks me through the sand-choked food court. I pull my T-shirt over my mouth as the dunes drift across the floor. In the darkness, it's like being inside one of those snow globes. Someone's shaken us and we're swirling about, disoriented. And the sand's still lashing against the planks they've fixed to the ceiling. Suddenly the idea of being stuck here forever weighs heavy on me. What if the winds never stop? All the sand storms I've ever experienced only lasted a few hours, but that doesn't mean this one will. I squint through the gritty air and suddenly feel like I'm suffocating.

"Move." Andrew shoves me again. The other two guards have peeled off, no longer in sight. I wonder if he'll do something to me once we're alone. My heart thumping, I steel myself for a fight.

He shoves me past the food court and into the dark recesses of the mall where I know the hole to be. My heart pounds faster.

"Look," I say, swiveling. "Whatever it is you think you're doing, you can forget it. Clay's in tight with the Messiah and so's Mage. You can't do anything to me without getting in serious trouble." I plant my hands on my hips and try to look fierce.

Andrew barks a cold laugh. "I don't want to *do* anything to you." He shoves me into the dark and clicks on a small electric lantern. The beam does little to break up the deep, thick shadow.

He points to the hole. "Down the steps."

I shake my head. "No."

He cocks the gun, a smile on his face. "I was hoping you'd resist. Which foot's your favorite?" He aims down.

"Don't!" I say, shuffling back and heading toward the hole. My heart is banging into my breastplate and I'm sucking lungfuls of dust-clogged air. Coughing, I descend into darkness as thick and terrifying as a grave.

We wind down the rocky decline, into the heart of the crevasse. It's cooler and less sandy here, but it doesn't soothe my panic. Why is he taking me into the hole?

We stop at the base and I turn to him. "You've scared me, okay? Now take me up and lock me in wherever the Messiah told you to."

Andrew sniffs, shining the lantern around the cavern. "He just said to lock you up." He pulls the lantern close to his face so I can see his awful sneer. "Never said where."

I stare into the penetrating darkness around me and feel light-headed. Andrew reaches around the wall until he finds what he is looking for: wrist manacles attached to a chain that's anchored to the concrete. He jingles them, smiling.

"You can't be serious." I back up until I hit the far wall. He grabs my wrist and drags me forward. I fight him, but it's no good. He's stronger. He wrestles one wrist into the metal manacles and clicks the padlock shut. I hit him with my free hand, but he laughs and wrenches the other wrist into the manacle. The second padlock closes with a sickening click.

My wrists strain against the cold metal, my panic swirling like the dust outside. I'm going to suffocate. I'm going to die.

"Please." I'm begging, silent tears streaming down my cheeks. A terror I can't even name is choking me, tightening my throat. "Don't leave me down here."

He laughs like a rabid hyena. "Hope the creatures that live down here already had their supper." He holds the lantern up to his face. The red sore on his mouth seems to pulse like a sick, bloody heart. "For your sake."

Then he turns, still laughing and takes the light up the incline with him.

My chest is heaving. *Stay calm, stay calm,* I think over and over. *It's only the dark. There's nothing down here. He's just trying to scare me.* I stare into the wall of darkness, willing my eyes to see. The crevasse smells like mildew and old bleach. Above, the howling wind sounds a thousand miles away. If I focus I can hear the drip, drip, drip of water.

I shuffle back and lean against the wall, letting the broken concrete cool my flushed skin. The manacles on my wrists cut into my flesh, but it'll only be a few hours. He'll have to come get me before the ceremony, right? Someone would miss me. But then, they'd never look down here. Not in a million years. I settle in to wait, trying not to see the awful images in my head. Instead I think about Auntie and her famous bread.

A low, agonizing moan rolls out of the dark recesses of the cave.

I snap my head toward the sound. The pitch blackness is terrifying.

For a moment everything is quiet. Maybe I imagined it all.

Footsteps sound down the tunnel—heavy and dragging on the floor like whoever is coming has a broken leg. Whatever it is, it's lurching toward me fast.

This can't be happening.

I tug at my chains, yank my arms back and forth until the pain radiates up my shoulders. Footsteps drag closer. Oh God, it's coming. It's coming for me!

Don't move! Don't move! I think. *Pleases don't let it find me. Don't let it know I'm here!*

Hot and rancid breath hits my face and a hand cinches on my arm. I scream.

CHAPTER EIGHTEEN

I tug away from whatever has me, but with the chains, it does no good.

"Help!" I lurch and scream. Still it stands there, waiting, my heart pounding. The smell rolling off this thing is awful: rotten meat or rancid garbage. I pull away.

Still it holds me, saying nothing.

"What are you?!" I scream at it. "Say something!" Nothing. Just darkness and panting. Terror courses through me, weakening my legs. How could someone live in this ungodly dark? Is it some sort of...beast?

"Clay! Rayburn!" I scream upwards, hoping someone, anyone will hear me. I can't think. Can't breathe.

Something wispy like hair brushes my cheek. My skull scrapes on the concrete as I pull away. Nowhere to go. I start to pray.

Raspy breath pushes against my ear. "Tell *themmm*." The voice is human, but garbled as if whatever is speaking has lost the ability to work its jaw. "Tell *themmm*."

I stare into the pitch blackness at the voice, trembling. "Tell who? Tell them what?"

"Tell *themmm*...we're *ssssstill* here." His voice rattles like his lungs are filled with fluid.

"I...will. I'll tell them."

"Tell *themmm*," the voice says. It moves beside me now. Something brushes my arm and I yelp. There's a jangling of something metal and then my wrist is tugged sideways. I pull away and my hand is...free?

"Who are you?" I ask.

The thing, the person, moves beside me and yanks on my other cuff. My hand falls free and the chains clank against the concrete. I can't believe it. It freed me. I shuffle sideways, wanting to run, but not wanting to bump into the thing again. "Who are you? Why are you down here?" I ask again.

"Tell *themmm*," he says one more time. "We're *ssssstill* here."

"Who should I tell? The Messiah?" I slide along the concrete wall, my palms gliding over the rock. It doesn't answer or follow me.

When my feet find the slope, I run up the incline as fast as I dare in the dark.

When I reach the top, I crumple into a ball and tremble. Breathe, breathe, *breathe*. The voice scrapes around my head. Does he live down there? Are there more living in darkness?

I pull myself up and glance toward the hole. Why doesn't he just walk up here himself? Maybe he's a deformed monster they've banished into the darkness. I pull my groaning body up. I need answers and I know where I'll find them.

***

I stand outside the Messiah's chamber, the solid doors all that separate me from the madman that runs this asylum. I want to hear what's going on right from the horse's mouth. No more lies. It's time to peel back the mask.

I push through, into the antechamber. The candles flicker on wall ledges, casting wavering shadows. A guard, sitting in one of the hard plastic chairs, pops up when I enter.

"Stop!" His hand goes for his knife and he draws it out of his belt. "You can't go in there!"

"I need to see him." The Brotherhood guard, Lavan I think his name is, was one of our attackers that morning at the diner. His clouded left eye and missing front teeth remind me that I once hated him. I glare as voices, laughter, and even music spill through the crack behind us. I take another step. "I'm going in. It's urgent."

Lavan raises the knife.

"Stop!" I yell.

On the other side of the door, the laughter stops. The interior door cracks open, leaking the smell of incense, and the Messiah's face appears. "Lavan, what seems to be the trouble?" His cloudy eyes search the room as if he could spot me.

Lavan shakes his head. "It's the dust. She wants an audience. I was about to escort her bac–"

"Let her in," the Messiah says, sliding back into his chamber.

Lavan glowers at me, but steps aside.

The Messiah's men lounge on the couch and chairs, drinking, laughing. A few of the prettier women hang off them, tossing their long hair off their delicate, pale shoulders. Drinks and food are stacked on end tables. There's even a spread of fruit on the floor. All

144

this abundance when we're rationing food for everyone else? The Messiah heads toward the back and the mess of papers spread across the table. And Clay's standing by the desk as if guarding it. Clay's face floods with concern when he spots me.

"I need to speak with the Messiah," I blurt into the stillness.

When he spots me, Andrew stands and the girl on his lap falls to the floor. He eyes me like a ghost.

"What're you doing out..." His eyes slip over to Clay. "This is a private party. I'll take you back." As he strides at me, the gun in his belt winks in the candlelight.

"Don't touch her!" Clay says, coming after Andrew.

Laying a firm hand on Clay's shoulder, the Messiah draws him back. "I would like to hear what Riley has come to tell me." As he's pointing to the door, his face tightens as if in pain. His hand presses to his abdomen, but he draws it back quickly. He smoothes the look of pain away and turns to me. "Riley, I'll speak to you in the hall."

I ignore Clay's concerned looks, swivel on my heel, and push through the doors into the hallway. Outside the chamber, the air feels heavy, like the sand storm is burying us.

The doors swing closed behind the Messiah. As he turns to face me, I take in his sallow complexion and the dark bags circling his eyes. His normally shining hair looks lank and unwashed. He looks terrible.

"What's down in the hole?" I ask when the weight of the silence threatens to choke me.

The Messiah cocks his head, a strand of long hair slipping over his robed shoulder. "The lake. Our source of holy water. Why?"

"*Why?* Because Andrew locked me down there, that's why." I shoot an accusatory finger toward the doors. The anger I tried to bury breaks the surface.

The Messiah folds his sore-pocked hands into the sleeves of his robe and shakes his head. "I thought he might do something like that."

"You did? Well, next time when you get an inkling, maybe send someone else to put me up!" I'm nearly shouting, but I know there are ears on the other side of that door. I drop my voice to a dangerous whisper. "He chained me in complete blackness like an animal."

The Messiah nods sadly. "I apologize for his behavior. He won't hold his position long."

"Who lives in the hole?" I ask, remembering. His breath on my neck was like cold, unwelcome caress from a corpse.

The Messiah furrows his brow. "No one."

"You don't need to lie."

"I do not lie! The leader of the free people and the prophet of the Gods does not lie!" His voice is booming, his face fierce. Either he's a great liar or telling the truth. He doesn't know about whoever's down there?

"Someone in the hole told me to tell you that they're still here." I watch his face carefully. The look of confusion is still rooted in his features.

"No one lives in the hole." He runs a hand through his beard, once trim, now scraggly. Then he turns his eyes skyward. "It won't matter soon anyway," he mumbles.

I lean in close enough to smell the death on him. "Why d'you keep on saying stuff like that? You're gonna kill everyone, aren't you?"

His face betrays nothing, not a twitch, not a flicker. "I'm not planning on killing anyone." He unfolds his arms and his gown flutters. "The Gods, well…" he raises milky eyes to mine. Gooseflesh gathers on my arms. "That's a different story."

I shake my head. "You're not going to pin this on the Gods. Anything you do, *you* are responsible. These people depend on *you*. They want *you* to protect them." Frustration throbs through the veins on my forehead. I want to hit something.

Despair darkens the features of his face. He grabs both of my arms. "Don't you think I've tried? Don't you think I've asked them *over and over* to spare us?" He shakes me with his words. "Listen to it outside. They've spoken." He holds a hand up to where the wind howls like a cyclone. His sleeve falls back, revealing small scars running down his bicep. Has he been cutting himself?

"You have a choice," I say, pulling my arm from his grasp. "We all have choices."

The Messiah falls to his knees. "Oh Gods," he folds his hands beneath his chin and shakes them, "take this cup from me!"

The shouting sends his guard barreling out. Andrew draws his gun. The Messiah grips Andrew's arm and uses it to pull himself up.

"It is time," he says, straightening his white gown, brushing back his hair. All traces of his despair are gone.

Oh, masked man, I think, *what game are you playing now?*

The Brotherhood peels out in different directions. Clay wraps his arm around me. "I should take her to her room to rest," he says.

I let myself fold into his warmth.

"No," the Messiah says. "Bring her. Bring everyone. The time of communion has arrived."

CHAPTER NINETEEN

Drum beats echo down the hallways, a syncopated *boom, boom, boom* copying the beat of our frightened hearts. People shuffle out of their rooms and down the hallways behind us. I walk with Clay's arm around me. Right now being next to him seems like the best idea in the world. With the drums and the sand and the sad-eyed people, I feel it in my bones—we're being marched to our deaths.

We walk through drifts into the food court. The wind above has died down and with it the swirling sand. Above us, the hazy sunset slices through the wood panels. Soon it will be dark.

We should run, but the guards walk behind us like dogs herding sheep. Where's the rest of my family? How can I get them out of here?

The Messiah steps up onto the carousel. Clay and I settle near the front of the crowd. The rest of the men arrive, still banging the drums with a *boom, boom, boom* that cuts through my chest like a blunt chisel. My cheek brushes against Clay's shirt collar and the smell of him fills me with comfort. God, please don't let them kill us. All I want is the open road with Clay and my family. We could mend the brokenness between us.

Andrew joins the Messiah on the carousel steps. He's wearing a white gown similar to the Messiah's although more tattered at the seams. He holds the bronze wine bowl in his palms. Beside him sits a barrel of water.

My heart pounds as my eyes catch the dancing reflection in that bowl. The poison we saw in the warehouse. Is it in that barrel? Is this the end?

I pull away from Clay and shoot him a desperate look. "Clay, it's the poison!" I whisper through my teeth. "We gotta get out of here!"

He frowns and brings his lips to my ear. "What're you talking 'bout? That's the same water we been drinkin'."

I stare at the barrel. It looks the same as the one I saw in the warehouse and yet this one bears no scrawled warning on top. But then they wouldn't label their poison here for everyone to see, not if they were going to secretly kill us with it.

"It's *not* the same water," I say, snapping my head back and forth. "He's going to kill us all!"

Clay rolls his eyes. "Don't start that again. He wouldn't do somethin—"

I grip his forearm. "Mage heard him say it. She confirmed it for me." I step away and whirl around, panicked. Where's Ethan and Ray? We gotta run.

"Mage confirmed what?" Clay asks, but the rest of his words are drowned by the frenzied beat of the drums. The crowd chants. A woman behind us wails like a wounded coyote in a language I don't understand.

I tug Clay with me toward the back, but I'm stopped by a wall of muscle. Several Brotherhood guards stand around the crowd, shoulder to shoulder.

"Let us by." I try to shove past and a hand cinches around my bicep.

"Hey!" Clay yells, but they grab him. Andrew steps up, his hand on the butt of his gun. Clay's eyes drop to the revolver and his face tightens. "What d'you want?"

Andrew points toward the carousel. "You're being inducted. Time to drink."

No. No, no, no. I look at the barrel of shimmering liquid. When I swore to participate in his communion ceremony, I didn't think I'd pay with my life.

"I changed my mind." I shove forward, but one of them grips my shoulders and spins me around. Rayburn, Mama and Ethan are being shoved up onto the carousel, too. Terror blares through my brain. The giant jug of poisoned water jiggles as I step onto the platform.

My heart thumps wildly as I search for a way out. The Brotherhood circles us. The people keep chanting. I can't think. I look into the faces of my loved ones. I won't let them die. I don't care what I have to do. The *boom, boom* cuts through me until I'm sure I'll scream. I scan the crowd looking for Mage. Looking for any help, anything. The crowd is frenzied. One old woman drags fingernails down her face, leaving red welts. One man tears at his shirt. And oh God, the *chanting*. "Sight, sight, sight," echoes through the space and fills my brain like sludge until my thoughts are mired. Do they know what's coming? I look at women clutching their children on their hips. They can't know. Otherwise they'd all be running for the door. All these innocent faces. He can't be planning to kill them, right?

Then I remember the terror on his face when he cried, "Dear Gods, take this cup from me." He thinks it isn't up to him. It's up to the Gods. And these Gods are vengeful.

The Messiah holds his hands up and the drumming stops. A silence snaps through the crowd, leaving the air empty and vibrating with tension. Beside me, the Messiah has broken out into a sweat. His gown clings to him like wet paper. His golden necklace with its many religious symbols rests on his sharp collarbones. He lowers his trembling hands and clasps them at his waist.

"Children, the time has come to induct these outsiders," he waves his hand at us, "into the fold. Though they will be leaving us tomorrow, tonight they will perform the rite of passage into our brethren and become one with us. Then we will drink the communion water and pray for another year of the Gods' grace. They will pray for the Sight as will we all. Sight to deliver us from this plague. Tonight, everyone will drink, women, children, babies. All." He surveys his people, nodding. They nod back, their eyes obedient like cattle.

No. This can't be happening.

He turns to Andrew. "The bowl, please." Andrew dips it in the barrel of water. I watch in horror as the water fills the silver drinking bowl. The bowl meant for me. I look at Ethan, my mama, and her swollen belly. How can I stop this?

He turns milky eyes toward me, his mouth moving in silent prayer. I stare at the rippling water. What would it feel like to die slowly from the inside out?

He lifts the bowl. "Drink."

I shake my head. "No."

The crowd murmurs. Andrew takes a step forward, his palm on the gun.

The Messiah offers the bowl again. "Drink."

I reach up for the bowl, my hands trembling. I look over at my mama, my baby brother. If I drink, will they let them go? Could they leave even if I died?

I slam my hands into the bowl and splash the water onto the Messiah. He stumbles back and bangs into a carousel horse.

Andrew grabs my arm. He yanks the gun from his hip, points it at my head, and begins to thumb down the trigger.

Clay shoves between us. His chest is inches away from Andrew's gun barrel. The awful black eye of the pistol hovers near Clay's heart.

He keeps his eyes on Andrew. "Put the gun down and no one has to get hurt."

They stare each other down. My heart's pounding into my ears. Please don't let him shoot Clay. Please.

Andrew swivels and aims at Mama on the other side of the platform. "Riley drinks," he says, "or her mom takes the bullet." He walks over and presses the muzzle of the gun into my mother's temple. My blood sizzles like fire.

"Don't touch her!" I yell, stepping around Clay. His hand slips over my wrist, but I shake it off.

"I'll drink!" I shout, my chest heaving. "I'll drink your poison, if they don't have to." I point to my family. I drop my heavy arm as the weight of my words sink over me. "I'll drink if you'll let them go."

Brushing wet hair off his forehead, the Messiah steps up. His white gown clings to his chest, revealing dozens of sores underneath. "The water isn't poisoned," he says, folding his hands.

"Ha!" I turn to the crowd. "I know you plan on killing everyone."

Someone in the crowd gasps. A little child begins to sniffle.

The Messiah looks shocked as if he has no idea what I'm talking about. "Why would I kill my people?"

"Because the Gods told you to. You believe time is up. But what kind of Gods would want that kind of sacrifice?"

A tiny smile reaches the corners of his lips before he can pull it down. Apparently *his* Gods want that kind of sacrifice. "I'll prove it." He turns to the crowd, arms wide. "I'll prove the water isn't poisoned." He takes the silver bowl from the carousel floor, dips it in the barrel, and raises the rippling liquid to his lips.

No one breathes. We watch, stunned, as he slowly, slowly he drains the whole bowl.

Someone shouts, "See?" Another shouts, "Make her drink."

Was I wrong? Or is he willing to be the first to die to carry out his insane plan?

He fills the bowl and turns toward me.

Heart pounding, I take it in my hands. The clear liquid looks so much like water, but yet, there's a smell I don't like. Chemical, like the water in the underground lake. I look over at my poor mother, the gun at her temple reddening the skin. She stares at me, silent tears streaming down her cheeks. I feel the weight of a hundred pairs of eyes on me as I lift the bowl to my mouth.

There's movement behind me. Clay dives for Andrew. Andrew turns, but it's too late. Clay's body rams into Andrew's, sending them both flying into the horses. They rock the platform and the bowl falls from my hand and crashes to the floor. There's a scramble of arms and legs. Clay slams his elbow into the side of Andrew's head with a sickening crack. Andrew's fingers claw for Clay's eyes sockets.

Where is the gun? I search the floor. If only I could grab it.

Clay jumps up, the gun in his hands. He presses the black revolver to Andrew's skull.

"I should pull the goddamn trigger now," he says through gritted teeth, pressing the barrel harder into Andrew's temple. "After what you done to my girl, I should paint this stage with yer brains." He digs the barrel into Andrew's head until the bastard cries out.

"Stop!" the Messiah yells, striding up. "Any violence against my men and you will never be allowed to leave."

Clay pushes up, leaving Andrew cowering on the floor. He turns and aims the gun at the Messiah. The crowd gasps.

"Step back or I'll shoot!" Clay yells. The Brotherhood obey, but their eyes could kill.

Hands raised in surrender, the Messiah shakes his head. "I thought you were one of us, Clay."

Clay shakes his head. "My allegiance is to her," he nods my way. "Always to her."

The Messiah lifts a sad smile. "I understand. Now, put down the gun, and we'll let you walk out of here."

Clay shakes his head, flashing his teeth. "Not so easy. You'll come with for insurance. Then, when we're a mile or two down the trail, we'll drop you off and yer boys can come pick you up."

The Messiah shakes his head. He takes another step forward, until there's only a foot between him and the gun barrel. My breath comes in shallow, strangling grasps. I flick my eyes between Clay and the Messiah. Does Clay really think we can take the Messiah hostage?

"Back up or I'll shoot." Clay's eyes are cold steel. He means every word.

The Messiah's face remains unchanged, though he's a foot away from a lead death. He takes a deep breath. "It's time to go," he murmurs, more to himself than to Clay. He raises his eyes to the ceiling. "Not my will, but Yours."

"Hell yeah, my will." Clay wiggles the gun to the left. "Let's go, magic man. We need a truck," Clay looks at Andrew. "Best get that ready."

The Messiah drags his eyes from the ceiling and centers them on Clay. His sore-pocked face has taken on a sadness I don't understand. Everyone member of his Brotherhood looks like he wants to rip Clay's head off, yet the Messiah looks like he's just…disappointed. The Messiah takes a step forward, his gown swishing around his ankles. "If the Gods have willed it, so it shall be."

Clay nods, but a raw feeling of dread has been spreading in my heart. Something's wrong. I place my hand on Clay's arm. "Let's just go."

"Yes," the Messiah says, his voice faraway and robotic. "Time to go home."

With one step, he closes the gap between himself and the gun. His hand shoots out, wrapping around Clay's hand. Clay's mouth drops open in surprise. What is he—

His finger curls over Clay's on the trigger. Before Clay can pull away, the gun fires, a flash of light and a puff of smoke. The bang rings in my ears. Blood sprays from the right half of the Messiah's head, so red in the setting sunlight streaming between the boards above. Hot liquid dots my face. The Messiah falls like a stone onto the carousel platform. It rocks beneath me and the floorboards vibrate. My eyes lock on his body: the white gown growing red, the bloody scalp, his brown hair clumping in red tangles. And the blood. Oh the blood, it gushes like a hose all over the wooden boards. It spills through the cracks and patters on the floor beneath the carousel.

The Messiah is dead.

CHAPTER TWENTY

Clay's face is white, his hand slack. His eyes are glued to the body. The gun sags to his side and droops as if it weighs a hundred pounds.

The crowd stirs. "He killed the Messiah!" a voice yells. "Papa!" calls another. It must be Mage, though I can't see her.

Clay's eyes flash toward the voices. It doesn't matter that the lunatic killed himself. Some of the crowd didn't see clearly and the rest will be easily swayed. Only those of us close enough to see know the truth. It'll be the perfect way to get rid of us, a mob frenzy fueled by hatred. They'll draw and quarter Clay. They'll let the buzzards peck at his bowels while he watches.

I grab his arm and yank. "Run!" I shout. "Run!"

His eyes find mine, fear replacing shock.

Andrew falls out of his trance. "Get them!"

The men come out of their stupor and charge up the steps. I grab Mama's arm, pulling her along with me. Clay scoops up Ethan and limp-runs beside me. Rayburn skitters up behind. The platform jiggles as we jump off. The Brotherhood is steps behind.

Clay reaches back and shoots. The gun cracks and sends a bullet slicing through the crowd. I look over my shoulder, expecting blood, but Clay shot to scare, not to wound.

"Then next bullet won't be a warning!" he shouts as he runs beside me. Already his breath comes in raged gasps. His leg. How will we make it out? It doesn't matter. We must. To stay is death.

When I don't hear stomping footsteps behind us, I turn. Half of the men are heading off down another hallway while a group keeps a boiling crowd at bay. I look into Clay's face, hopeful. He shakes his head.

"They're gonna get the guns. The Messiah didn't allow 'em, but now that he's dead it'll be open season. Soon's they return, they'll mow us down like a combine through a field. We gotta get somewhere safe and pronto." He wrinkles his brow, flicks the revolver's chamber out, and does a quick-count on bullets. Four bullets. He frowns and shakes his head at our meager firepower. My

155

heart sinks like a boulder into my stomach. Beside me, Mama labors just to keep jogging. We won't get far. We'll be gunned down in the hallway.

I shake my head. We don't give up. Not ever.

We stumble into the unlit hallway leading to the hole. No exits. The only thing here is the deep dark crevasse.

"We have to go down," I sputter, wishing I could think of anything else.

"Go down?" Ethan slips out of Clay's arms and drops to the ground. He points to the dark, yawning hole. "Go down *there*?"

"Riley, no." Clay shakes his head. He opens up the revolver and examines his bullets like if he looked harder there'd be more than four.

Footsteps pound behind us. They're coming. This time they have guns.

"Go," I say, shoving them forward. "Go!"

They stumble to the incline. I take the lead and slip down the dark spiral, one hand on the wall to keep me from falling. Behind me, their shuffling steps let me know they've followed.

"This way," I say over my shoulder, trying to keep the terror out of my voice. The truth is my heart's doing jumping jacks in my chest. I hate this hole. Sensations from the last time trail over my skin: rancid breath on my face, wispy hair on my shoulder. Whatever lived down here saved me, but the fear still clings to my skin. I fight my panic and keep my feet moving forward. One hand on the rough stone, I walk down the circular incline for what feels like forever. Each step is terrifying in the dark. I keep picturing myself falling off the incline and dropping to my death.

My foot strikes something and I stumble, my hands skidding over the concrete. When I sit up, there's an ache in my shoulder, but I think I've reach the bottom. I stand, hold my hand out and call to them. "This way." A hand fumbles into mine and a yelp escapes whoever just bumped into me.

"It's me," I whisper. "Rayburn?"

"Yeah," he says, his body pressing close in the dark. Then he rocks forward and there's an *umph* behind him. "We're stopping," he says to those behind him.

"Riley?" It's Mama. She sounds scared.

"Yeah. I'm here. Is everyone okay?"

Four yeses echo in the dark.

"So, what's the plan?" It's Clay's voice. His hand fumbles for me and then slips around my arm.

"I don't know." I try to pick out any shape in the blackness and come up empty.

"You down there!" a voice calls from above.

I jump. Clay's hand twitches on my arm.

The voice above echoes down. "We're posting guards! If you come up, we'll shoot. If you know what's good for you, you'll stay down there and starve to death."

I squeeze Clay's hand to tell him not to bother to answer. Nothing we say will make a difference. They're not coming after us. It's great news and yet, somehow I don't get it.

"Why wouldn't they just run down and kill us?" I whisper.

"Maybe they don't have guns after all," Clay muses.

"Or m-m-maybe there's monsters in here that will, uh, eat us and save them the t-t-trouble." Rayburn's voice shakes.

"That's enough of that." It's Mama's voice. "There's no such thing as monsters."

I think of whatever freed me and say nothing. Better not to scare them yet. First, we need light. "Anyone hiding a flashlight in their pocket?" I ask.

"Anyone have m-m-matches? A lighter?" Rayburn asks.

Matches! I dig out the matchbook and find the little green Bible in my pocket beside them. I pull the book and the matches out. "Hold this," I say to Clay, pressing the book into his palms. "Open it to the middle and hold it out for me." He does as I ask. Then I pull a match out and strike it, holding my breath.

There's a hiss. A little orange flame dances on the end of my match, barely lighting the thick darkness. It's enough to see Clay and the Bible cupped in his palm. I set the little match tenderly on the pages.

"I'm sorry," I whisper. Who am I apologizing to? The book? The gods that supposedly inhabit it? The Messiah whose blood has dried on my face?

The little book catches flame, the first pages coiling and crinkling. Clay looks at me with wide eyes.

"Set the book on the ground," I say. "We need to look around before the flame goes out. Anything else to burn?"

Rayburn offers his T-shirt and it gives us a little more time. We shuffle outward, circling the walls of the crevasse. The stone is rough and useless. I find the spot where I was chained and skirt around it, the fear creeping up my neck. A child's shoe is overturned in one corner and it reminds me of Mage. How is she doing with her dad's death? Will I see her again? I drop the shoe into the flame. Clay produces a very old newspaper, which burns up, smelling foul. Ethan runs up triumphantly, a huge smile on his face. In his hands he holds a lantern.

I reach for him. "Where did you find this?"

"Hanging on the wall over there." He points.

"Just hanging there?" It's a little electric lantern like the one I used when I came down after Clay. I look down at the black toggle switch on the front. "They must store one down here for emergencies."

Ethan nods, his face beaming.

"Don't get too excited. It might not have batteries," I say. When I flick the switch from off to on, a beam of yellow light joins the orange of the sputtering fire. I kiss Ethan on his head and swing the light around the cave.

The walls are mostly gray rock. There are large cracks that zigzag up to the surface. Boulders lie in the corners as if this hole was forged by an earthquake or a sinkhole. As I aim my little light forward, a dark tunnel leads out toward the lake where the men took Clay. Even though that water is likely poisoned and will make us crazy, it is our best bet for finding whoever is down here. Whoever lives down here will know if there's another way out. And if not, they might be willing to help us fight against our common enemy.

"So, we go on then," Clay says, half statement, half question. He sidles up to me, close enough to feel the heat of his body. I put my hand on his arm.

"We go on," I say, sounding less sure than I'd like. My brother takes my hand. Rayburn and Mama slide up beside us and stare at the pitch-black tunnel. "I'm looking for someone who lives down here. He might be able to help us find a way out."

They stare at me. "Someone *lives* down here?" Rayburn and Clay ask at the same time. Clay's hand floats down to the revolver tucked in the top of his pants.

I shrug. "Think so. When that bastard Andrew locked me down

here, someone came and freed me. He was a little…crazy, but maybe he can help."

"These caverns could go on forever," Mama says, tightening her grip on Ethan. "How do you know we'll be able to find him?"

I shrug. "He needs water, right?"

Rayburn's brow furrows. "If there were other, uh, other exits, wouldn't he have used them?"

"Maybe," I say. "But, it's worth a shot. We don't got a lot of options."

Clay nods, pulling out the revolver. "Doubt he got any firepower." With his revolver in his hand, Clay's face settles into his battle-hardened stare. It's amazing how much that comforts me.

"What's down there?" Ethan whispers, pointing into the blackness.

"A lake." Clay flashes me a look, but doesn't say how the water turns you into a drugged lunatic or that it slowly kills you from the inside out. What'll we do if we can't find clean water? We'll have to drink eventually.

"How far is it?" Mama asks. Her face looks sunken and pale.

"Not far." I reach up to pat her arm. Voices sound from above. I can't tell if they're coming closer. "Let's go before they decide to finish us."

We shuffle slowly ahead, bodies touching. None of us wants to be the one who slips off into the darkness alone. The little light illuminates the path a few feet ahead. Darkness, thick and heavy as cowhide, lurks beyond the reach of my lantern, making my insides turn loops. Maybe there are other creatures trapped down here that aren't as friendly as the one who freed me. Maybe they're all mad. I picture arms reaching out of the darkness.

"You okay?" Clay whispers in my ear. His hand presses on the small of my back.

"Stay close." I pull even tighter to my family.

"I don't get it," Clay says, his voice echoing slightly in the cave.

"Get what?" I ask.

"The Messiah pulled that trigger. Not me. His finger jammed mine down. I felt it." He turns confused eyes to mine. "Why'd he kill himself?"

"Maybe he knew he was gonna die. You saw the sores all over his body. Flesh peeling off." I think of the Messiah's sore-covered

159

skin showing through his wet robe.

Clay shakes his head. "With what they did for yer ma," he nods back to Mama, "you'd think they could do something for their beloved prophet."

"Maybe he was sacrificing himself t-t-to the Gods." Rayburn's voice travels up to us.

I look over my shoulder at him. "He put a bullet in his brain-pan to appease his Gods? I thought he was going to kill everyone else to do that."

Rayburn shrugs his hunched shoulders. "The most important story in Christianity t-t-tells of Jesus sacrificing himself on the cross for the sins of, uh, mankind. The Messiah dressed like Jesus. He clearly read his book." I think of the little green Bible we burned. Rayburn continues. "Maybe he thought if he k-k-killed himself, the Gods would spare everyone else."

Clay snorts. "Or maybe he was baked in the brain from one too many cups of crazy juice."

I mull this over, remembering the look of sadness on the Messiah's face when he gripped my arm in the hallway and asked the Gods to take this cup from him. Was he acting out Jesus's last days? It makes his death much more heroic.

I turn to Rayburn. The lamplight shines off his glasses as he trudges behind me. "Never knew you were religious, Rayburn."

His mouth quirks up. "We covered religions in school." He shrugs. "Among other things."

"Huh," I ask, stepping over a large rock.

"I grew up in the hospital. I was born there. A dud, actually. I was supposed to be a girl." He blushes. "All I ever wanted was to be a doctor. Prove I could be useful. When I f-f-finally finished school and learned what they were really doing... I guess being a doctor wasn't, uh, wasn't exactly what I thought it would be."

I picture a little Rayburn running around the hospital, the nannies chasing him for a bath.

"We learn something new about you every day," Mama says to him, smiling.

He grins, the first in a long time.

Up ahead I hear the trickle of water.

"Lake's this way," Clay says, taking the lantern from me and striding a bit faster.

Clay, Ethan, and Rayburn walk ahead a little, but I hang back with Mama. I offer her my arm and she takes it.

"You doing okay?" I ask, trying to keep inside the Clay's lantern light. I can barely see Mama's face in the dark.

She leans hard on my arm. "I'm...fine."

I shake my head, my heart calcifying. "You never tell me the truth, do you?"

A sad smile touches her lips as she looks at me and presses her palm to my cheek. "When you have children, you'll understand. You'll do anything for them. Give your life if need be."

"Don't talk like that." Thinking about what may be happening inside her makes my own insides twist. I can't stand to see her pain.

We walk in silence. The sound of trickling water grows louder as many little streams flow toward the underground lake. Ahead, Ethan hoots at the sight of it, his voice echoing around the cavern. Clay shushes him.

We catch up and stand next to the boys, the lake at our feet. I had forgotten how the cave opens up here, a three-story ceiling dripping with cones of rock that dangle above like fangs. The lantern light dances on the surface of the water. Ethan steps toward the lake and leans down to touch it.

"No!" I say, grabbing him.

He shoots me a confused look as I drag him away. "What? I'm thirsty."

"This water isn't..." I look at Clay. He frowns. "This water might not be clean."

"Not clean?" Ethan says, stepping carefully toward the shore. "What's wrong with it?"

Clay clears his throat. "The Messiah's men brung me down here during their little induction ceremony. We drank this water." He nods toward the lake, his eyes growing hard. "After a while, I felt real strange: dizzy and not...right in the head. It made me feel like I could do anything. Then I..." He looks at me. "I don't remember what happened that night."

I nod, not wanting to remember his rough hands on me, dragging off my clothes.

Rayburn peers around. "We'll need water soon. If there's not another source, we'll be forced to go back up the way we came down."

161

Everyone frowns. I shake my head. "Let's find the guy who helped me and make a plan from there." I survey the water, thinking. There's so many caverns. So many dark passageways. Well, the only way to begin is by beginning, as Auntie would say. "Okay, so we'll walk around the lake in two groups."

Clay swings the lantern, making the light waver. "We only got one light."

I point to the torches on the walls. "We can light those." I hand him what's left of the matches.

"So, me, Mama, and Ethan will go this way," I point to the left, "and Rayburn and Clay will go right."

Clay frowns. "Don't like it. Rayburn should go with you. Me and little man can stick together." He smiles at Ethan. "Right, little man?"

"Yeah!" Ethan says, jumping out of Mama's arms. He latches onto Clay's intact hand. "Let's go."

I purse my lips, but say nothing. Too late to ruin their fun. I turn to Mama. "You ready?" She nods reluctantly, her eyes searching the dark corners.

Clay and Ethan march off, the torch painting their path with its dancing orange flame. Rayburn, Mama and I head the other way, our lantern throwing steady yellow beams onto the rock walls. Even though I've put on a good front for my family, my heart patters. The rancid creature's breath still seems to cling to me, although it was hours ago. What'll he look like? I picture dripping skin, pocked flesh, rotting eyes. *Stop*, I tell myself. Imagination has to be worse than reality.

We reach the halfway point around the lake and I shoot a look back at the boys. The torchlight disappears around a corner. They must've found another cavern. I hope they don't go too fa—

A scream tears across the lake. Mama, Rayburn, and I exchange terrified looks and turn toward the sound.

Two gunshots crack through the cave. Clay's gun. My boys are in trouble.

CHAPTER TWENTY-ONE

Why would he fire? Clay knows how precious bullets are. He would only shoot if they were in danger. Danger. The word sparks in my head like a match. I sprint over the rocks, my lungs burning.

I tear around the lake toward the boys. Rayburn straggles at my heels. Mama is somewhere behind.

Another scream. It's Ethan's. Then a moan. I hurdle a small rock, a prayer on my lips. *Please, God. Please.*

Two forms explode out into the main cave. Clay with Ethan on his hip. Clay runs with his loping stride, Ethan clinging to his neck. Terror is plastered on their faces. Clay waves me back, the revolver still clutched in his hand.

"Run!" he yells. "They're coming!"

"Who's coming?" I shout, skidding to a stop, rocks flying.

He doesn't have to answer. Grotesque, mangled creatures lurch out of the darkness. Their skin is pocked with weeping red sores. Their hairless heads and wide, sightless eyes make them look like…like walking dead. The one in front has a raw stub where her hand should be. Another behind her is naked, her sagging breasts, pale and puckered in the torchlight, the only indication of her gender. Two, three, four of these monsters straggle out, hands reaching, slack mouths moaning awful. More appear behind, just as grotesque, just as angry. How many are there?

"Holy shit!" Rayburn yells behind me. He turns to run.

Terror bursts through my body. I turn and run. How can we get away? Where will we go?

Rayburn and I sprint around the lake, Clay trailing behind with Ethan still in his arms. The moaning echoes through the cavern until it sounds like they're everywhere.

"Are they…z-zombies?" I yell through panted breaths.

Beside me in the dark, Rayburn shakes head. "No such thing. The water…"

I shoot a glance over my shoulder as we run along the lake shore. They're slower than us, held back by their deteriorating limbs, but they're determined. One growls at me when its eyes lock with mine. Its teeth look like fangs. There's at least a dozen of them. They must've been hiding when we came in, hoping we'd go away. They aren't hoping for that any more. Now they want to kill us. On my count Clay has three bullets. And these monsters have nothing to lose.

"Why're they so angry?" I ask through ragged breath.

"Killed one." Clay looks back, shudders and keeps running. "Pissed 'em off."

"You shot one?" My boot splashes into a wet puddle, spraying water up my leg.

Clay nods. "They came right at us. What was I supposed to do?"

We reach Mama, who's standing at the lake's edge, terrified. "What are they?!" she asks, grabbing my arm.

I look at the mob. They sneer at us from across the lake and keep coming. One decrepit woman splashes through the water, cloudy eyes wide with anger. She gnashes her remaining teeth.

Clay raises his revolver, aims, and squeezes the trigger. I cup my ears. Across the lake, the first creature falls. The others pause for a moment and stare at the downed body. Then they turn and lurch at us again, mouths curled in awful sneers. Clay raises his gun.

"Don't!" I say, tugging down his arm. "You only have two bullets and all you're doing is pissing 'em off!"

He whirls on me, his eyes wide. "What d'you suggest? Stand here and die?!"

I shake my head, looking around. These monsters can't be very bright. In front of us, a tunnel winds away from the lake. "Come on," I say, grabbing Mama's hand.

My little lantern swings wildly as we tear into the dark. The path forks right and I take it. A few feet up, the path splits in two. "Right," I whisper. The moans are farther away. If we can just find a quiet spot to lay low…

A few more minutes of terrified running and I spot a rock ledge about three feet from the floor. It's big enough for the five of us to squeeze into and off the beaten path so that those monsters can shuffle by.

"Up here!" I whisper, gesturing them forward. Rayburn clambers up the rock wall, pebbles trickling down as he scoots onto the shelf and tucks himself into the back. Clay lifts Ethan into Rayburn's awaiting arms. I whirl around for Mama.

She's crouched low, her arms around her pregnant stomach. Perspiration dots her forehead and slides down her neck. She lifts her face to mine and the expression of pain is unmistakable.

"What is it?" I say.

She looks up at me, her eyes afraid. "Whatever they did to slow the baby down… stopped working. It's awake and…" She looks down at her stomach. It gives a violent jerk. "It's moving."

"Oh God." I reach for her. Moaning echoes down the hallway. They're coming.

My heart is going to explode. I look up at Clay.

"I'll get you up," he says, taking Mama's arm, drawing her to him.

She winces, but nods. Her belly jerks again, the baby rolling inside her.

The moaning draws closer.

Clay lifts Mama while Rayburn pulls her up. I run over and bounce on the balls of my feet, anxious to get up there.

"Douse the light," Clay whispers.

My fingers stray to the switch, but I don't want to turn it. Pitch darkness with those monsters coming toward us? Oh God.

I flick the switch and darkness falls. My hands find the ridge and I pull myself up, banging my knee on what must be a rock, scraping my palm. I reach down for Clay. My hand swings through empty air a few times and then it connects with his. He pulls himself up.

Five of us crouch on the rocky shelf about the size of a walk-in pantry. The ceiling brushes my skull as I shift. Clay's body settles next to mine. A hand, Mama's I think, snakes around my arm. The darkness is total. And they're coming.

In the dark, the moans are terrifying. A mob of great wails, inhuman and angry, echoes down the cavern toward us. How many were there? Twelve? Twenty? My brain supplies fifty, all missing skin, eyes, and fingers. Their fanged teeth snap up and down.

They're closer now. Almost to us. My heart pounds so hard my chest hurts. Mama's hand tightens around my arm. She needs help and I can't do anything about it.

They arrive in a wall of sound and smell, decaying flesh and toxic chemicals. Their loping shuffles echo through the cavern. As they begin moving past our ledge, I don't breathe. One passes by so close I can smell his breath as he exhales. I squeeze my eyes shut. Beside me, Clay is a stone. Mama squeezes my arm until it's numb.

They are passing. Their awful noises recede down the tunnel like a gaggle of tortured animals. Why can't I think of them as people? They were once, weren't they? People like Kemuel who were cast out, dropped down here to die, yet somehow hung on to live like the walking dead. Why else would they be down here?

We wait for what seems like hours, until we can no longer hear them, until we are sure they are long gone. Clay turns to me.

"What now?" he whispers.

I shrug, forgetting he can't hear me. "I don't know. My plan is ruined. Maybe we—"

A hand reaches out of the darkness and drags me off the ledge. I fall, smashing into the ground. My wind gone, I suck air. Hands grip my arms and yank me up. A body, smelling like death, holds me tight.

"Did you tell *themmm*?" the garbled voice breathes into my neck. "We're *ssstill* here."

CHAPTER TWENTY-TWO

I fight against my attacker, but his arms are steel. The smell of his rotting skin makes me gag. His breath on my neck makes my knees weak.

The lantern flicks on and I slam my eyes shut against the assault of light. When I can open my eyes, Clay stands before me, his revolver aimed above my head.

"Let her go!" The gunslinger look is back, the determination flashing in his eyes. I lash back and forth against my attacker, but he holds me tight. He fits his body behind me, giving Clay nothing to aim at.

"We are here," the creature behind me breathes. Hearing his voice, the monsters rush back down the cave. They look just about as awful as I remember: lesion-covered skulls shining, open sores dripping. A dozen of them lurch toward us. And they look pissed.

Clay flashes the lantern at them and they shrink back, covering their eyes. They advance with their eyes closed, hands reaching. Fear floods Clay's face. On the ledge, Mama cradles Ethan in her arms.

"What d'you want?" Clay yells at the one holding me.

The thing behind me draws a wet, rattling breath. "We want *vengenccce*," he says slowly, drawing out the word like it's holy.

"I'm sorry. I shouldn't've shot ya. You came at us like...like animals."

"We are not *animalsss*," he hisses. His hands flex around my biceps.

"Okay, okay," Clay says, lowering the gun. "You're not. Sorry."

"*Sssorry* will not *raissse* the dead," the thing behind me says. I don't like his tone. It sounds like he's smiling.

The monsters fall on Clay, a tangle of ruined arms and legs. Clay cries out. The lantern drops, throwing crazy shadows everywhere. My attacker's hands loosen as he watches his people struggle with Clay. This is my chance. I yank away and his hands slip off. He howls. I duck to the right as he claws at my shirt. Then I dive into a pile of rancid bodies and reach for Clay.

I punch. I kick. The smell of rot is awful. I try not to breathe.

The lantern rolls, throwing light around so I can't tell who I'm fighting. A beam lands on the shelf where my family sat. Only now the creatures are dragging them off. Mama screams as they pull Ethan from her arms. Then the lantern rolls away. In the darkness, Ethan cries out.

"Ethan!" I yell, abandoning this scrum of bodies. I grope in the dark for my brother. My hand reaches the rock wall. Ethan, he must be somewh—

Something huge and hard smashes into my skull. Stars explode in my brain. My legs unlock and the ground slides up to meet me. I lie there, fading out as heat sears my skull. Then a faraway pain. Then Ethan crying. Then nothing.

***

I wake to darkness. Pain radiates from the top of my skull down into my spine. It throbs with the slow, steady beat of my heart. My arms are bound behind my back by what feels like rough twine, pinching and twisting the skin. With my eyes closed, the smells and sounds wake me to the horror. We've been captured by these monsters. Their rancidness clings to every inch of this space.

I open my eyes and the pain in my head flares like a rocket. I am lying on my side. The ground is rough beneath me. We're still in the caves, though God knows where. Ten feet away a fire sputters, lighting the cave in orange and black. Whatever they're burning smells like hot feces as it crackles over the fire. As I lift my head, Clay turns toward me, relief flooding his face. I open my mouth to speak, but he shakes his head, a quick snap to tell me to keep quiet. His eyes flick sideways and mine follow.

The monsters move around on the other side of the fire. One skins a small black bat and its fuzzy skin peels off like a sock. Another slump-shouldered woman with one stumped arm uses a flat rock to drop more of whatever they're burning onto the fire. The stink of hot waste makes me gag. They're definitely burning feces. How can they stand it? I tuck my mouth into the collar of my shirt.

My eyes rove the clearing for the rest of my family. Rayburn and Mama sit a few feet to the left, their wrists also bound. I search for Ethan, but he's nowhere. What have these monsters done with my brother?

One of the creatures lurches into the light. I recognize my attacker from the cave fight. He's also the one who untied me when Andrew left me chained. Where has his kindness fled to?

Now that I look him over, I realize it's not a he, it's a *she*. Her voice was so garbled I couldn't tell, but now in the light, her female form shows through her ragged clothing. Her body shows less decay than the others. There are a few patches of white-blond hair on her skull, long and stringy like corn silk. She has working use of all her limbs, a fairly amazing feat down here. When she opens her mouth to breathe, she reveals empty gums with four remaining teeth that hang crooked and yellow. Her clothes are strips of fraying material that only cover her most private parts.

When she whirls toward me, my insides go cold. Too late to feign sleep. She narrows her eyes and lurches over.

"Awake," she rasps, leaning down to look at me. One puffy lid droops over her left eye. I pull back as her breath hits me.

"Yes," I finally manage. I force myself to look her in the eyes. "Where's my brother?"

She glances over her shoulder at the group behind her. Most have stopped working and are focused on us. My insides curl like orange rinds. Then I notice something else. Most of the creatures are female. No, not most, *all*. I shoot Clay a look to see if he's noticed, but the speaker leans into my line of vision.

"Your *brother'sss* being kept. For *insssurancccce*." She lisps the words like her tongue is a dead thing.

"I want him back," I snap.

She shakes her head. "Not yet."

I frown. "Why are we tied up?"

"You attacked *ussss*," she rasps. "You killed two." She holds up two dirty fingers.

Behind her, the group mumbles angrily. One mutant, with a few strands of hair clinging desperately to her head, lurches forward and shakes a fist. Her one working eye rolls angrily. "Kill, kill!" she shrieks. The others howl in agreement.

Clay snaps up, heat flaring into his cheeks. "I tole you. You came at me like rabid dogs. What you 'spect me to do?" He shoots me a pained look. "If anyone's to blame, let it be me. Let the rest go. I'll pay for my crimes."

"Clay, no." I haul myself to a sitting position. Pain knifes

169

through my skull, but I manage to ignore it. "It's not his fault." I turn to the speaker. "What's your name?"

The woman hovering over me looks surprised. "Name?" She grinds her four teeth together. "We are...the Forgotten."

Behind her, the rest of the women nod their ruined heads.

I try another strategy. "I remember you," I say quietly. "You helped me. I told the Messiah you were still here."

At the mention of the Messiah, a shriek echoes from the group. I cringe as the awful moans reverberate around the cavern. The speaker hunches down, covering her head with her hands.

"We do not *ssspeak* that name. He *isss* the one who decreed we be put out."

When I heard they "put people out" I assumed it meant the road and the blazing heat of the desert. Somehow this fate seems worse: trapped underground, your only water source the poison that'll eat at your guts. But, why are they all women? I look around the crowd. They're listening to me. Maybe if I can talk them into seeing things our way, they'll forget that Clay killed two of their own. If only I can figure out what they want. "The Mes... I mean, the leader put you down here?" I ask.

The speaker shrugs her skeletal shoulders. "*Hisss* men did. An...drew," she says, slowly as if uncovering the buried memory from under yards of dirt. "He *usssed* to bring *usss* food. Now he left *usss* to die."

I mull this over. "The leader might not've known what Andrew was doing." There's an angry mumble from the crowd. One woman with an empty eye socket shakes a fist at me.

The speaker nods slowly. Her few hairs waft up and down. "Andrew will be *punissshed*."

"Good." I nod with her. So, we have one thing in common. If I keep her talking, maybe we'll find more equal footing. "How d'you, er, ladies survive down here?"

The speaker points to the lake and then to the woman skinning the bat. She's slicing open the bat's bloody body and removing small, squishy innards. My gorge rises, but I swallow hard and continue. "Bats?" I ask.

She nods, her moldy-fruit tongue roving around her remaining teeth. She points to a mound in the corner that I'd mistaken as a mound of dirt. As I look closer the mound reveals itself to be dozens of fuzzy, winged bodies. Dead bats. This time I visibly shudder. Clay clears his throat beside me, clearly trying not to gag.

"That's awful," I say. The speaker narrows her eyes. "I mean," I say, "it's awful they made you live this way."

Behind the speaker, a few of the mutants nod.

"Is there any other way out of the tunnels other than up into the mall?" It's my most important question, the one I've been dying to ask. Hope rises in my throat.

"No," she says, dropping her head. The firelight gleams of the hairless patches. "*Sssome* have tried to find the *sssun*." She takes a deep, ragged breath. "They've not returned."

My hope sinks. I drop my eyes. What do we do now? A tunnel out was my only plan. To know that there's no way out… The cave walls seem to close in until I'm having trouble breathing.

"You ever tried to fight yer way out?" Clay juts his chin at some of the rock tools stacked beside the fire. "You could do some damage with those."

The speaker glares at Clay. When she's angry, all of the humanity washes out of her face and once again she's the monster, lurching after us. "We are weakened." Her ruined voice warbles. "If we fight, we die."

"If you stay, you die," Clay snaps.

A few of the mutants shoot Clay sharp glances and bare their teeth.

"He's trying to help," I say, scrambling to think. I'm losing my footing with them. I need to get it back. A thought flits in my mind. Should I tell them? As I'm mulling it over, the snarling woman picks up a sharp rock, the size and shape of a dagger. She lurches toward Clay with it.

"The Messiah is dead." The words jump out of my mouth, before I've realized what I'm doing.

A gasp from the crowd. A few push in to peer into my face, as if mulling over my words. The woman with the rock dagger stops in mid-stride.

"It's true," I say to everyone. "Clay killed him."

Clay stiffens and shoots me a look. I nod slightly and turn back to the group, holding my breath. The enemy of my enemy is my friend.

The speaker studies my face. "The *Messssiah isss* dead?"

I nod. "Just now."

"Why are you here?" she asks. "To tell *usss thisss*?" Her cloudy eyes follow my every movement.

"They want to kill us." I look at Clay unsure of my next words. "For killing their leader."

The speaker looks at me and then lopes over to the group. The dozen mutants fold into a huddle. Their ruined voices struggle to form sentences, but can't make out what they are saying.

Finally, the speaker lumbers over, but I don't like the look on her face.

"What?" I ask, leaning forward. "What did they say?"

"We *sssay*," she says slowly, "the time for remembering *isss* here. We go up and reclaim our place. While they are *weakessst*."

I nod. "Okay. Let's go."

She shakes her head. "You'll go. We trade you for our freedom."

CHAPTER TWENTY-THREE

We walk between burning torches with mutants on either side. They shove us forward, back to the very people who swore to kill us.

The group was ready to leave in ten minutes, fastening torches, smearing guano on the torch tops so now we trail the rancid burning stench with us. They have pulled out sharpened rocks, as pointy and dangerous as daggers, likely honed in the dark with vengeance in mind. They peppered us with questions: Who's left in charge? What weapons do they have?

I hang my head in shame as my feet navigate over the rocky terrain. My gambit failed and now the mutants think we are worth something to the people upstairs. I tried to tell them Andrew wants us dead and doesn't care how. He'd be happy if we languished like them, eating bats and stinking of guano until we go crazy from contaminated water. But the group is not exactly logical. If their skin and hair has decayed this much, I can only imagine what their brains look like. Still, if I hadn't told them about Clay killing the Messiah, we might not be in this predicament. I kick a stone, feeling like dirt.

Mama lumbers in front of me, her steps slow and painful. Even from behind I can tell the baby is moving, invading her body. My chest constricts with the weight of our situation. How can I save Mama? How can I save anyone?

Ethan is walking somewhere behind us. I caught a glimpse of him before we headed out. Some wizened old hag with most of her nose missing dragged him out of a cave, a leather thong around his neck like a dog. These people may have been compassionate once, but all humanity has been leeched into the darkness.

We reach the base of the incline that winds its way up. A shove from behind sends me skidding into the rock wall.

The speaker inches along the incline and leans into my ear. "You go *firssst*," she whispers, her dead breath pulsing on my neck. "Tell them the Forgotten are here...to make a deal."

"What if they shoot me?" I whisper, looking into her eyes for some compassion.

The whites of her eyes are yellow like custard. "That *isss* none of our *concccern*."

"Great," I say, frowning. "And what if they don't give two rips that the Forgotten are here?"

She ponders this for a moment as if the thought never crossed her mind. She scratches a nail-less finger through her remaining strands of hair. "Tell them we have the one who killed the *Messssiah*."

I stare up at the dim light filtering from the mall. "Yeah, well, they might not care about that either."

She prods my back. I shuffle up the incline and cringe when my eyes crest over the tunnel's top. I stop and survey the mall floor. No one around. No sign of the guards who were supposed to be posted here. Son of a... We could've just climbed back up and walked out?!

I stride up the rest of the incline, listening, looking. The mall is quiet as death. I thought the people would still be wailing about the death of their Messiah. I'd pictured an all-night candlelight vigil. But nothing? The skin on my arms crawls. It doesn't feel right.

"Back I see."

"Who's there?" I whirl around, my bound hands held out in front of me. They're weaponless, useless and all I have. "Who are you?" The voice sounds like—

"Lavan," the voice says. One of Andrew's Brotherhood guard. He hiccups. Is he...drunk?

"Where are you?" I step toward the voice. In the entryway of an empty storefront, Lavan lies slumped over, his head lolling against the cracked concrete wall. In one hand is an empty drinking bowl. A liquor smell wafts from him. As I step closer I see a rifle gripped in his other hand.

"Whoa!" I say, shuffling back.

"Can't run," he slurs. He makes no move to lift the rifle. Instead, he laughs darkly. "None of us can."

That something-isn't-right-feeling steals over me again. "What d'you mean?"

He hiccups and chuckles. "Might as well go out with liquor in my belly." He pats his stomach and a dull, sloshy sound echoes from inside. "Might as well go out feelin' good."

I step closer. "What do you mean 'go out'? Where are you going?"

He draws his bloodshot eyes up to my face with some effort. "Home."

"Home?" I ask, my heart pounding harder.

"Yeah," he says, smacking his hand on the concrete floor. He points toward the heavens. "Tonight we're all going home."

I back away, my hands shaking. It's the end. With the death of the Messiah, they must've decided it was time to… I don't want to think about the end to that sentence.

I run back to the hole, my heart tearing around my chest. I skid down the decline and almost bump into the speaker. "They don't want to barter," I pant. "The end is here. They're going to kill everyone." The words spill out of my mouth in one long, unpunctuated strand. Everyone stares at me. I bang my hands against my knee. "We have to get outta here!"

Slowly, the mutants come unstuck and start murmuring. The speaker skirts past me, hugging the wall as she slips back to discuss this with her people. Clay, Mama, and Rayburn scuttle up to me. I can't see Ethan.

"W-w-what's going on up there?" Rayburn nods up toward the mall. "Th-they dead?"

I shake my head. "Only one guard is up there, but he's a mess. Drunk. He told me all the Believers are going *home*. Rayburn, the barrel of poison we saw. They must be planning on using it tonight. We have to warn the people and get the hell out."

In the dark, Clay's face wrinkles with concern. "We're still tied up and they got Ethan. We need to talk these freaks into freein' us."

I nod. "The speaker's the one. She has more heart than any of the others."

Clay nods. "I'll talk to her."

I frown. "Maybe I should."

Clay glowers. "You *always* think you should be the one. You never trust me. The only thing I ever did right was shoot and now I can't even do that." Even in the dark, his blue eyes flash like jagged pieces of glass.

I drop my chin. "You help a lot."

"Not one damn thing I done so far has helped!" He leans in, wrapping one of his bound hands around my wrist. "Let me do this. You gotta try trustin' me at least once to know it ain't a good idea."

I shut my mouth. Nod once. He stands a little taller as he faces the speaker who's pushing through the mutants toward us. She does not look happy.

"We don't believe you," the speaker says, forming her ruined hands into fists. "You're lying. If you lie again, one of you *goesss* over the *ssside*." She points at the dark drop below.

"No," I say, but Clay's hand on my arm silences me.

"She's not lyin'." He stares hard at the speaker. "And you know it."

"We do not kno—"

"No, not *we*," Clay points at the speaker's chest. "*You*. You know this ain't right." He holds up his bound hands. "We ain't cattle and y'all are not like these monsters up here." Clay nods up toward the mall and where the Believers live. "If you was, you'd still be up there."

The speaker pauses, mouth open, her swollen tongue showing. Some of the mutants grasp at her sack clothing, but she waves them away.

Clay continues. "You know you should let us go. That together, *we*," he circles his bound arms around to indicate us and the mutants, "should take these bastards down."

For once the crowd is silent. The speaker stares at Clay as if she's just seeing him for the first time. She rubs her hand through her remaining hair. "I..." she says the word slowly, testing it out. "*I* hear you. I agree," she says more boldly. She faces the mob of questioning faces on the incline below.

"We will *ssset thessse* people free," she says, arms wide. There are murmurs of dissent, but some heads nod. "We will follow them up." More murmurs. Many of the mutant's faces looked scared, but others look enraged. One woman with warts on her cheeks shakes her fist in the air.

The speaker licks her cracked lips. "We will go up and reclaim our *placce*." Now they are nodding, smiling. The speaker nods with them. "We will do it when they are *weakessst*. We will take over and we will kill those that have *sssentencced usss* to death."

"Wait, only the Brotherhood, right?" I ask her. When I get no response, I turn to Clay.

Clay calls after the mutants. "You don't want to hurt everyone."

But it is too late. The throng of mutants surges forward, a wave of stinking flesh. They brush past us and I cringe as their bodies touch mine. *Zombies*, my brain thinks. They look undead.

The speaker slips out a rock dagger, grabs my wrists, and yanks them up. I pull back, but she's sawing at my bonds. When the rope splinters and my hands fall free, she thrusts the rock-knife and Clay's gun in my hands. I hold them delicately, my jaw slack.

"Free the *othersss*," she pants, her yellow eyes following her people. "Then join *usss*. We will avenge all who've fallen."

"Wait," I say, thinking of Mage. "You don't have to kill all of them. They aren't all guilty!"

But she's gone, lurching up the steps with a vigor that sends shivers over me. Ethan, free of his leather leash, runs up and wraps his arms around my waist. I hug him. For a moment, the five of us stare at each other.

"What did we do?" I whisper to Clay. He doesn't answer, just looks up at the trickle of light.

Then the screaming begins.

My hands tighten around Ethan as cries of terror cascades down the hole. Who's screaming? Clay tugs on my arm. "Go," he says, his eyes wide. "Run to the closest exit." He looks at Rayburn. "We need a truck."

"The garage," I say, remembering. "They got trucks."

Rayburn nods vigorously.

"What about Mage?" Ethan asks, pulling away from me. "We just can't leave her."

I stare up at Clay, searching his face for answers. He nods slowly. "We'll look," he says. His tone of voice says we'll look for a minute and then we're outta here.

As we crest the floor surface, I see who's screaming. A few of the mob have fallen on Lavan. One of the mutants bites his arm. Another beats on him with a small hunk of concrete. She rears back and smashes the concrete into Lavan's knee. He screams.

"They'll kill him," I whisper under my breath. Do I care? The Brotherhood have been awful to us, but he's drunk and the fight is totally unfair.

"Riley, we can't," Clay's eyes are sad. "We gotta go."

But if Lavan dies it'll be our fault. I can't take his screams. I run at the mutant who's about to smash the concrete into Lavan's head. "Get off him!"

Clay grabs the mutant's hand and stops the blow in mid-air. "Go find Andrew," Clay shouts. "He's the one who put you out." The mutants snarl, but back away, rotten teeth flashing.

We stare down at Lavan, moaning in a bloody mess on the floor. None of the cuts look life threatening. What's more life threatening is whatever the Believers have planned.

"We, uh, we should question him," Rayburn says, pointing a shaking finger at Lavan.

Clay kneels down, grabs Lavan's shirt collar, and draws him into a sitting position. His head lolls back, a trickle of blood dribbling into his dark hair. "I know yer busted to hell," Clay says, "but we need to know what you meant by it being the end? Is there poison? Are you gonna force people to drink it?"

Lavan's eyes roll back in his head and he murmurs something.

"Speak up!" Clay says, shaking him a little.

Lavan opens his mouth and vomits down his shirt. It falls with a wet splat onto the floor.

Clay let's go of Lavan and wipes his hand on the guard's soiled shirt. "Well, he ain't gonna be much help."

"You're right," I say. "We gotta find Mage."

"Where do we look?" Mama asks. Her mouth tightens, a sure sign of the pain she's trying to hide.

"We start with the girl's hallway," Clay says, heading that way with Ethan in tow. "At least some of the mutants went the other way."

He's right. Shouts and smashing sounds come from the men's hallway. There's the pop of a single gunshot. We all jump. Clay waves us in the opposite direction.

We peel out into twilight streaming down from the food court ceiling. Some of the boards and canvas sheets they nailed up have fallen down. Sand still lurks in the corners and collects on the foam play fruit. My eyes trail over the giant oranges and apples and sadness sinks my heart. Will they try to kill everyone? The carousel is empty. The Messiah's body is gone, but his blood remains in dark puddles. I've watched him die at least a dozen times in my mind and seeing the blood brings those images flooding back. I focus on running through the food court without drawing attention. Everyone in this mall is our enemy now.

Running down the women's corridor, I see clumps of Believers huddled together. One woman sits alone in the middle of an empty shoe store staring out at us. Her clothes are torn and something black, ash maybe, covers her face. Her hollow eyes follow us as silent tears plow through the dark smudges.

They don't need to be warned the end is coming. They already know.

We slip silently past several more empty stores until we come across the Willow Room. Inside Prema, my cranky boss from my days as washerwoman, and Yusuf, the middle-aged Willow Room teacher, hover around half a dozen frightened children. A crown of golden hair appears behind the crowd.

"Mage!" I yell. A few of the children duck behind the adults as I barrel into the room. I hold my hands up apologetically. "We're here to help."

Mage's eyes fall on us. "Help?" she says slowly.

"Lavan said…" I look down and see two pairs of little eyes staring at me from behind Yusuf's pant leg. I lean in close and whisper to Mage. "He said it was *the end*."

There's a flicker on her face, almost imperceptible, then it's gone. "Lavan's drunk. He took my papa's death real hard."

Didn't she take her dad's death real hard? I stare into her face, but it's stone. I put my hand on her arm. "The Forgotten are here. The people Andrew put out." How long until they descend on this room? Would there be enough human being left inside them to keep them from harming these children? I think of Ethan wearing a dog leash around his neck. "We gotta get you out of here."

Mage's face tightens and a frown creases the corners of her mouth. "That's gonna be a problem."

She walks us out of the Willow Room and down the hall to the exit. It's the door leading out to the garage. There are two giant, armed Brotherhood guards at the door. They point the rifle barrels at us as we approach.

"Turn around!" The guard waves his rifle toward where we came from. "Go back to your rooms and stay there like you were instructed. Our new leader will tell you when it is safe to come out."

Somewhere down the hallway there is a crash. A scream. The mutants are tearing the place to pieces and these men do nothing to stop it.

I step forward and one of them points his rifle at me.

"Step back!" he shouts. They're dressed plainly with thick boots and tough denim pants. Like they're ready for battle. Who are they going to battle with? "Go back to your rooms," he says again.

I spread my hands out in a show of surrender. "Why are you doing this? You have to let us out."

"By order of the Messiah and our new sovereign leader, Andrew, no one is to leave this building until instructed. It's been foreseen."

Mage is as stiff as a statue beside me. "The Messiah is dead."

"His spirit lives on," says the one to the right. His voice is robotic. "We must follow him home."

"What about the children?" I ask, unable to keep the disgust out of my voice. "Are they to follow him home, too?" How can these men sentence their own children to death? I swallow hard and lock eyes with one of them. He won't look at me, but there's worry in his face. The other sets his rifle into his shoulder socket and raises it at me.

"I'm gonna count to ten," he growls. "Ten. Nine." His finger curls around the trigger. "Eight."

"Fine!" I yell. "Let's go."

"Seven. Six."

We run back to the Willow Room. When we get there, all eyes turn on us. My gaze falls on the children, their round cheeks and giant pleading eyes. Mama holds a little boy in her lap and gently strokes his straight brown hair. All the children are boys, now that I think about it. A three-year-old boy with golden hair like Mage clings to Prema's knee. Two preteen boys sit with their backs to the wall, their eyes downcast. It's odd that they're all boys. And the Forgotten are all women. It feels like I'm missing something. Something important.

Prema waddles over to us, her brown face puckered like a raisin. "What did those cowards say?" Her frown is the same, etched into her skin, but her eyes look different somehow. Like she really sees me this time. The last time we spoke she was scolding me about my plunge and scrub technique. Now she peers at me like she really wants to know what I have to say.

Mage shakes her head, her shoulders slumping.

"Why are they doing this?" I ask no one and everyone.

Mage's gaze drifts off in the distance. "It's what we've always feared. The evil ones are coming."

Her words strike my chest like a hammer. "The evil ones?"

"Yes," Mage says, large eyes meeting mine. "The people from the hospital. The Breeders."

I gasp. Beside me, Clay whirls at her words. "The Breeders? They're coming here?"

So many thoughts whirl through my head: poison, suicides, the Breeders. I can't catch my breath. My hand circles the ankh brand on my wrist over and over. What will they do to us if they catch us? I can't begin to imagine.

"We have to run." The desperation in Clay's voice is immediate and frightening. He leans down and levels Mage with a serious look.

"How long 'til they're here?"

Mage nods. "Tomorrow. That's all I know."

I think about Dr. Nessa Vandewater's cruel blue eyes and awful images flash through my mind. We can't be here when they arrive. None of them should be either.

"We need a way out and fast." I start to pace back and forth across the room. We could go for weapons, but they're all in the hands of the Brotherhood. We could try to break out of the mall, but that would take more time than we got. No one knows when the Brotherhood plans to poison us. And the Forgotten are on a rampage.

Clay steps in front of me, breaking my thoughts. "We fight," he says, punching a fist into his palm. "We don't roll over and die."

I place my hand on his. "We got one gun."

He frowns. "Then we find a way to bust out."

I look from him to Mage. She's standing with her back to the wall, furiously folding a paper animal, though it's a sloppy mess. I walk to her. "Mage," I say quietly, touching her frantic hands, "We need you. You're the one who knows your dad's mind."

She crumples the paper animal in her fist.

"You might not want to think about him, but it's the only way we can save the children." I point to the wide-eyed kids in the back. One is sobbing into Prema's large chest.

Mage looks up at me, her eyes growing round. Is she thinking of her dad? How he looked as he pulled the trigger on Clay's gun? I want to spare her this, but I can't.

"What does your dad have planned? How would he have them take out the whole Citadel in one swoop?"

She shakes her head and points to the corner. "Ask Lavan."

Lavan? The last we saw him he was being attacked by the Forgotten. A body lies slumped in a heap, facing the wall.

I walk over. "How did he get here?"

Yusuf rubs a hand over his wrinkled forehead. "He limped in here while you were out negotiating with the guards." Yusuf scrunches up his piggy nose. "He's a bloody mess and smells terrible. We put him in the corner."

I walk over, Clay at my back. Lavan lies curled in a fetal position, knees to his chest, arms wrapped around his legs. There's dried blood on a gash in his hair and vomit on his shirt. We tried questioning him before and got nothing. I look up at Clay. "How did he get here?"

Yusuf rubs a hand over his wrinkled forehead. "He limped in here while you were out negotiating with the guards." Yusuf scrunches up his piggy nose. "He's a bloody mess and smells terrible. We put him in the corner."

I look at Clay. "You think it's worth trying again?"

Clay screws his mouth down and sighs big. "What choice we got?"

I kneel beside Lavan. Yusuf is right, he smells awful. I breathe through my mouth and try not to look at the vomit on his shirt. "Lavan." I shake his shoulder. "Lavan!"

He moans and his dark eyelashes flutter. I shake him again. This time when the lashes flutter they slowly reveal bloodshot eyes.

"Hi there," I say as kindly as I can. "It's me, Riley. Remember?"

Confusion fills his face. His swollen lips work over some word that never makes it out of his throat. Instead, an awful-smelling burp escapes.

"Wish you hadn't drank all that wine," I mumble as I bat the smell away. I shake his shoulder again. "We need you to sit up, okay?"

He frowns, but I give him no time to protest. I pull him up by his soiled shirt collar and get him into a sitting position against the wall. His eyes roll back in his head.

"Lavan, we need to know about the Messiah's plan." I lean closer, my tone not so nice anymore. "Look at me!"

His eyes flutter open and his pupils dilate. "Dust girl." The corner of his mouth twitches. "Andrew hates you."

I frown. "I'm sure he does." I lean back from his breath. "Lavan, what's the Messiah planning? We need to know. Now."

Sadness fills Lavan's face. He shakes his shaggy head and grits what's left of his teeth. "Andrew wouldn't even give me a mask. Or a gun. Gave me hole duty without a gun." His lead slips down to his chest. When he starts to sniffle, I shake his shoulders again.

"What do you mean give you a mask? What kind of mask?"

"Gas mask," he says, sniffling. He runs a hand sloppily under his running nose, smearing a streak of snot on his cheek.

I grip his shoulder until he snaps his head up. Then I stare into his eyes. One is cloudy like the Messiah's; the other is a surprising green. "Lavan," I say slowly, "why would you need a gas mask?"

He looks up at me, his chin quivering. "It's the plan for the end. The Messiah's emergency plan for if the Breeders ever came." Lavan hiccups, burps, and continues. "We all go home." He drops his head. "It's better than becoming an abomination." His eyes flick to my mother.

I lean back, my head buzzing. Then it's confirmed. They do plan on poisoning everyone. The group has gathered behind me. They all look down with scared faces.

Mage nods. "Papa said if the bad people ever came, he'd never let them get me."

Clay puts a hand on my shoulder. "So he'd kill them all to keep them from the Breeders? Mage said they're coming tomorrow. Is that true?" Clay asks Lavan, his hand squeezing the life out of my shoulder.

Lavan shakes his head. "Dunno. After the Messiah died, Andrew said the Messiah killed himself to show us all it would be okay. That we should follow."

"How does he plan to do it?" I ask Lavan, my heart slamming into my chest. "How could he kill everyone in the mall at once?"

Lavan doesn't lift his head, so his next words are hard to hear. "Sprinkler system."

"The what?" Clay asks.

Mage points to the ceiling. A rusty silver arm protrudes from a pipe there. I've seen the pipes in other parts of the mall too.

"What is that?" Ethan asks, coming over and peering up at the circular metal wheel on the rusty pipe arm.

Rayburn jumps up. "The sprinkler system. Oh, Jesus." He grips his curls in his hands. "The Messiah would've, uh, would've had to find the main water line and hook up his drum of corrosive liquid. Acid maybe if he found the right type." Realization dawns on his face. "HF. Hydrofluoric acid." He slaps a hand to his cheek. "That's why it would be stored in a p-p-plastic container. He could, uh, could deliver it through the sprinklers. It would eventually eat through the metal, but not before killing everyone in the m-m-mall." He squeezes his fists together. "We'd be d-d-dead in minutes."

Mage nods. "My papa was working on the sprinkler system a lot last year. He wanted Andrew to test it and fix the lines that were clogged." Mage slumps down the wall, her knees tenting her jumper. "Why would he do this?"

I follow the sprinkler pipe with my eyes until it disappears beyond the wall. "Where's the main water system?"

Mage lifts her head, sniffing. "Don't know. In the back, maybe."

"Lavan?" But his eyes are closed again and no amount of shaking rouses him this time.

"It's in the basement." Prema pushes up and points a brown arthritic finger at the sprinkler. "I've seen it. We had trouble with the wash water last season. I walked down to the filtration system to speak to the engineer."

"So, we go to the basement." I stand. "Clay, Mage, Rayburn, and I'll go down and disconnect the acid. Then we find a way out."

Mage looks up with wet eyes. "If the acid is down there, it's gonna be guarded. If I know my papa, he would've planned for someone to try to disconnect it." She stares up at me, her eyes round gray orbs. "Riley, he really believed he was helping us by sending us home. He won't care who's killed. Walking in there'll be a death mission."

I look at Clay, a sick unease settling in my stomach. "It won't be our first."

CHAPTER TWENTY-FOUR

Gunshots and screams echo down dark hallways. We sneak through the passages, barely breathing. We pass a storefront splashed with blood. The smell of smoke spikes the air as we slip by a large department store. This whole place is a ticking time bomb.

Clay limps silently beside me, his face locked tight, jaw rigid, eyes flitting back and forth as he scans for enemies. He glances at me, nods and then points at a scuffle going on twenty yards from us. Two mutants attack a male Believer in one of the storefronts. The crazed mutants claw and bite. The Believer fights back with what looks like a chair leg, clubbing mercilessly. The mutants take the blows like they can't even feel them. They throw themselves on the man like a pair of rabid dogs, with flashing teeth and sprays of blood. I clutch Mage's arm and pull her away.

Mage leads us to the back of the mall, an area so poorly lit we nearly collide into one another when one of us stops. The walls are empty of the faded posters and flashy signs that decorate what's left of the stores. Here it's bare walls and hard tile. Small black doors line the hallway with plastic signs that read, "EMPLOYEES ONLY," and "SECURITY AND SURVEILLANCE: AUTHORIZED PERSONNEL ONLY." It's quieter here, nothing but an electric hum that buzzes my teeth. I'll take buzzing over screams any day.

We follow her to a door that reveals an even darker staircase. We step into darkness, palms running along the cool metal railing. The four of us bump to a stop at the bottom, squinting into the dark. Down the long hallway, the hum is louder and there's another noise too, a mechanical whir like a fan. A hand touches my arm and I flinch. Mage wraps cold fingers around my wrists. I reach for Clay. Rayburn scoots up behind us and his hand touches the small of my back. Then, linked together, we shuffle down the hallway toward the sound.

Ahead, a triangle of light cuts into the hall from an open door. We creep up to it, press our backs to the wall and listen. No sound, no voices, but that tells us nothing. From what Mage says there should be guards. What if they're heavily armed? We got one gun and two bullets.

Clay leans over and whispers in my ear. "I'm going in."

"Don't!" I whisper.

He pulls away from my grasp.

"No, Clay!"

He leans his head into the light.

I squeeze my eyes shut, my heart pounding.

Silence. Clay takes a step forward, peering into the room, gun aimed. Illuminated like this, he looks stunning. I stare at his handsome face and love slams into my heart. My life would shatter if I lost him and I'd have little reason to pick up the shards. How did I let us grow so far apart? How was I so stupid?

He turns and smiles at me. "No guards," he says. "Come on."

Rayburn slides into the light next to Clay. There's a noise from inside the room. They turn and their faces contort into an expression of ... fear? I step forward as if in slow motion, my hand reaching. "Clay!"

A gun explodes.

I watch in horror as both the men fall, a spray of blood arching into the light.

I stare, unable to process. Clay said it was fine. There were no guards.

I fall to my knees and grab for Clay. My hand reaches for his bunched shirt. The click of a trigger sounds from the open door. Another gunshot cracks through the air. I duck. The wall behind me explodes, peppering my neck and back with debris. I dive to the floor and curl into a ball. My ears ring. My heart pounds. I need to get away. I need to get everyone away.

Someone screams. Mage. She's screaming in the hallway. I uncurl and flick a glance at the shooter. He's a Brotherhood member in plain denim and heavy boots. His hair is thick and messy like a beaver pelt. His shaggy beard curls wildly from his chin and cheeks. He's fumbling with the pistol, trying to reload with slow fingers. He looks like he's never loaded a gun before. He shakes a lock of damp hair out of his eyes as he fumbles a bullet into the open chamber.

Movement beside me. Clay jumps to his feet. In two strides he's on the gunman, snatching the gun with his good hand and punching him in the jaw with his wounded one. The gunman's head snaps back, coarse curls flying. His legs unlock and he tumbles onto the concrete floor. Clay takes the gun, flips it around, and smashes the pistol's handle into the man's head with a horrible crack. The skin on his forehead opens up like an overripe peach.

The gunman is still.

I push up, standing on shaky legs. Clay breathes a heavy sigh of relief, his chest heaving through his sweat-soaked shirt. But, he smiles. Thank God he's okay. I run a hand over my body. I'm okay. Mage steps into the light. I expect relief on her face, but there's something else. I follow her eyes to the floor and my heart reboots in my chest.

Rayburn lies in a pool of thick red blood. His face is ashen. His glasses are broken, split in two halves that dangle off the left side of his face. His mouth lies open like he's screaming. But there's no sound. No movement.

I drop to the ground. "No! Rayburn!"

His shirt is already soaked in blood. The fabric peels back to reveal a jagged red hole in the center of his chest. The flesh is flayed open like a punctured can. Inside is a bloody mess. My hands flutter over the wound, unable to help, unable to repair the destruction one cylinder of lead did to his heart.

"Rayburn." I lean over him. His eyes are open, irises staring up. The trickle of blood at the corner of his mouth slips down his neck. "Rayburn!" I press my hands to his chest to stop the flow of blood. My hands are instantly slick. I have to make it stop or he'll die. "Rayburn!"

I look into his eyes, a deep chocolate brown. They're beautiful, actually, though I've never really looked at them. Never really looked at him until now.

Clay's hand is on my arm, pulling me up, but I can't go. I keep pressing on Rayburn's wound. Maybe if I hold him like this he'll…wake up. Maybe if I just stay here in this moment none of this will be real.

"Riley," Clay's shaking me. "Riley!" A yank on my arm draws me out of my trance. "There's nothin' we can do."

I stare at Clay. Mage steps behind him, her eyes thick with tears. Why is she crying? Rayburn never saved her life. He never took care of her when she was ankle-deep in hell. I turn back to Rayburn. My friend. My family.

"Riley!" Clay yanks my arm again.

I throw him a tortured look. "We can't just…leave him," I manage to choke out. My head is buzzing. I can't think. I lift my hands. So much blood.

Clay takes my arms and draws me to him. He folds me into an embrace and gently whispers in my ear. "We gotta save yer ma. We gotta save Ethan."

An image of them floats into my mind, pushing out some of the fog. "What do we...do with him?" I ask. "We can't just leave him," I repeat.

Clay looks at Rayburn's body, his face lined with sorrow. "We'll tuck him in safe here and then come back later. 'Kay?"

I feel myself nodding, though I'm anything but okay.

We carry Rayburn into the room. Lifting his feet, a wave of nausea hits me. More blood dribbles from his shirt onto the floor. His hand flops down. The hand he used to help me pull Clay into the van when we were fleeing the Breeders. The hand that stitched up my gunshot wound and Clay's. That helped my mama come back from death's door. The sadness crests, ready to drown me, but Clay locks me with a solid glance and I manage to get Rayburn's body into the room. We lay him out, his arms folded on his chest, his eyes closed.

I pinch the bridge of my nose and try to focus as tears slip down my face. I think of Mama. Ethan. Rayburn wouldn't want them to die.

Clay shuts the door with a quiet click. The water room is the size of a master bedroom and houses pipes of all sizes, angling from several metal machines. The pipes are painted blood red, but have a thick layer of dust coating them. I stare at all the valve wheels and yards and yards of pipe. The far wall holds a huge metal box, its open door revealing rusting wires threaded through like tangled yarn. On the top there's dozens of red and black switches, none of them labeled. I shove my hands into my hair and pull. There's no way we'll be able to figure out which one shuts off the sprinkler.

"Shut-off valves," Mage says, pointing, bouncing on her toes.

Pipes the size of three trunks run up from the floor. Giant orange wheels are attached at waist level. We walk over and stare at the six-spoked metal wheels, their paint worn around the edges where countless hands have gripped them.

"Do we just...turn one?" Clay rests his hand on the wheel. Some blood from his palm streaks the grip. Rayburn's blood. I will myself not to turn and look at my dead friend.

Mage shakes her head. "This doesn't seem right." Her eyes follow the pipes upward, one finger tapping on her chin. "There would have to be a tube or something spliced into the system. I don't see anything like that." She turns to me. "Riley, didn't you say there was a drum of poison? It would have to be down here, hooked up."

I press my palm to the cool pipe, trying to think. If the poison isn't here, where would it be?

Suddenly an alarm shrieks down the hall. We run to the door and pull it open. The loud, incessant beeping drills into my ears. Did we trip an alarm? Is there a fire?

Down the hall a watery hiss begins. A sprinkler turns on above the entrance to the stairwell.

We're too late.

CHAPTER TWENTY-FIVE

"The sprinklers," Clay says, staring. It's the one enemy he can't fight with bullets.

Mage pulls up behind us, her body trembling against the fabric of my shirt. "Maybe it's just water."

I look up, hopeful. Yet, the mist floating from the sprinklers is starting to make my eyes water. A deep burn begins in my nose. I pull my shirt up over my face.

"It's not water!" I yell into the fabric. "We have to get out!"

Mage looks at me, frantic. "How?! Our exit is being blasted!"

She's right. The spray from the one working sprinkler at the end of the hall is saturating the stairwell with caustic water. The walls sizzle with acrid steam. If we run through, we'll get doused. It'll burn through our clothes and skin. But we can't just sit here and hope they run out of acid. Mama and Ethan are upstairs and God knows what's happening to them.

My eyes do a quick scan of the room. It's bare except for poor Rayburn and the guard that Clay knocked out. He wears thin clothes, threadbare shoes. Nothing to cover us.

Clay pulls out the gun he took from the guard and aims at the sprinkler.

"No!" I say, putting my hand on his arm. "Save your bullets. You'll only bust it and make the acid spray faster."

My eyes skip past the box of switches, but then I see the door on the electrical box. It's at least three square feet of solid metal, wide enough for all of us. I run over and examine it. The door is screwed into the electrical box with huge screws. The hinges are solid metal too, but they're covered in a heavy coat of rust. I grip the metal lip and yank the door up. The hinges groan.

Clay's face slides into my line of vision. His damp hair clings to his forehead as he frowns at me. "What're you doing?"

"Help me!" I yank up on the door. It squeaks like hundred-year-old car brakes. The metal lip digs into my palm, but I pull with every ounce of my strength. When I stop, Clay takes over, heaving up with a grunt. One hinge lets go. He yanks down, his jaw locked. There's a metal *twang* and it pops off, clattering to the ground. We run over and pick up the bowed door.

Clay looks at it, shaking his head. "It won't be enough. Hold on." He runs over to the unconscious guard and begins stripping him.

"How's that gonna help?" I ask, striding over. I look away as Clay tugs off the hairy man's jeans.

Clay tosses me a stiff shirt. "Find a faucet that works. Make sure it's clean water." He throws Mage the guard's jeans. "We soak these and wrap 'em 'round any exposed skin. Our faces. Hands." He holds up two socks, nodding. "It might not stop a direct hit of the stuff, but'll protect us from the mist."

With Mage's help, we find a little wash sink in the back. The water seems to run clean, so we soak all the extra clothes and begin mummifying ourselves. With the wet material over our faces, it's hard to breathe, hard to hear. And the small slit for our eyes makes it nearly impossible to see. I hope to God we don't run into any more guards. We'd be sitting ducks.

Mummified, the three of us huddle under the metal door and lift it over our heads. It seems much smaller once it's hoisted. Shoulders and arms could easily be exposed if we aren't careful. Clay looks at us through his shirt turban. "We move as a team. Always together. No one leaves cover," he nods to the door over our heads, "got that?"

I nod. Mage's small round head wrapped wet denim nods. She looks up at me for reassurance. How can I be the one to reassure her? I can barely keep breathing through the fear tightening around my throat.

"Ready?" Clay asks.

My whole body screams no, I'm not ready to walk into a cloud of acid. Yet, I find myself walking alongside Clay with Mage in the middle. Clay and I lift the door, keeping our palms up inside the metal sheet. Then we step into the hall.

The hallway air burns my eyes like fire. My nose and lungs seem okay for now thanks to my T-shirt mask. Will our eyes burn out before we can escape? A horrible image of us stumbling through the mall with empty eye sockets flits into my brain before I can stop it. But all thoughts die away as we get to the hissing sprinkler. I huddle closer to Mage and Clay as the first drops ping against our makeshift umbrella. Will it eat right through?

The drops ping loudly on our heads and then cascade over the sides in a poison rain. The sizzling on our roof worries me, but for now the sheet of steel holds. The outside arm of Clay's shirt starts to smoke. We've only taken six or seven steps and we have to get all the way up the stairs. I blink tears out of my burning eyes and will myself into the man-eating cloud.

My toes bump the staircase. At least we've made it this far. Moving together, we manage the first step. The second. The third step is puddled with liquid. Mage slips, her shin banging into the stair. Water flies up, pelting us, but surprisingly the water doesn't burn. If only Rayburn were here to explain why. What will this air do to Rayburn's body? Then I realize Mage isn't moving. I look down. Crumpled on the steps, her hand rests in an inch of water. She starts wailing.

With one hand, I draw her to me, holding the door up with the other. Huddled together, the water pinging off our metal cover, her little body shakes as she cries. She holds her hand like an injured animal. Clay's blue eyes meet mine. We have ten more steps to go and then the rest of the mall to run through. "We don't stop." He looks at me pointedly. "We *don't* give up."

I nod. "Mage," I say, "we're going on. Your hand'll be okay."

Sniffling, her damp curls poking through her turban, she presses her face to my shoulder and nods once. Onward.

We move in sync, a being with six legs and three thumping hearts, up the stairs. My eyes tear up until the landscape is a blur, but we move mostly by instinct. Finally, through the tears, I see the open doorway. And the pinging on our metal roof is subsiding.

We crest the stairs and enter the ground floor. I look up, expecting a horrible acid rain, but some of the sprinklers are broken or haven't turned on. A few spray here and there and the air still burns my eyes, but it's better than I expected. The hallways are silent as a grave. I see no one. Well, no one alive. Fifteen feet down, a body lies under one of the working sprinklers. The smoke curling off his red, blistering limbs makes my heart lurch up into my throat.

"We left Rayburn," I whisper, not sure who I am speaking to.

Clay's jaw tightens. "We'll come back for him."

But one look into his face tells me it's a lie. The living doesn't go back for the dead when doing so might mean handing over their lives. Rayburn would've understood. Still, a sob stutters in my chest. I bite my lip. "Let's get the others and get the hell out."

We let the metal door drop. The top is corroded, but luckily no holes show through yet. I hoist it in front of me like a shield. My muscles ache, but we might need it again. Clay carries the guard's pistol with six bullets inside. His revolver, tucked in the waistband of his pants, holds one bullet. Better odds than we had before.

He lifts the gun and nods to the right. "We go light and fast. Any working sprinklers, we get under the lid. Keep yer eyes open for believers or mutants. We grab the rest and then we get the hell out."

"What about the other kids?" Mage asks, her voice muffled by her denim head wrap. She holds her blistering hand against her chest.

I look at Clay. "We get the kids out. Prema and Yusuf too. And anyone who isn't trying to shoot us." I look at the body slowly sizzling away under the sprinkler. "No one deserves to die like this."

Mage says nothing, but her face says it all. How could her father be so cruel?

We run. My irritated lungs struggle with the contaminated air and my eyes feel like someone has set them on fire, but we run. A few times we have to duck under our metal lid to slip under the sprinklers, but then there are large stretches where the sprinklers aren't on. I only hope Mama and Ethan were so lucky.

We pass another body, this one lying in a pool of blood. Mage shifts closer to me, but we don't stop. We don't give up.

It's takes much longer going than coming, but we make it to the Willow Room. In the dimness, the colorful children's drawings and murals look sad now. Thankfully, there are no sprinklers here, but the air is plenty toxic. The room seems empty and panic blooms in my chest.

"Mama!" I choke out. "Ethan!"

Movement in the back. Yusuf pushes up out of a mound of sheets. Chairs and a piece of plywood are leaning against the back wall, forming a tent. A few more heads peek out. Mama heaves herself up, her shirt pulled over her face.

"Couldn't shut it off?" she asks through her shirt. Her eyes are bloodshot and watering.

I shake my head. "We gotta go."

"Rayburn?"

I look away, feeling a stab of pain. I left him. I left his body to rot in the basement.

"Oh no!" Her hand flutters to her mouth.

We say no more, and follow her back to their tent. Inside, there are eight children, Yusuf, Prema, Lavan, and Ethan. Add in me, Clay, Mage, and Mama. We have sixteen people. Three of us are able-bodied enough to fight if it comes down to it. I stare into the dark mall. If any guards are roaming, they'll pick us off like baby rabbits.

Yusuf grabs the sheet of plywood and lifts it like our metal door. The acid will probably eat through that much faster, but we have no choice. Ethan coughs over and over as he slips out of the tent. His body curls with the effort of trying to expel this awful air out of his lungs.

"Come on," I say, waving them all out. "We run for it."

Clay hands me the sheet of metal and draws his gun. "Head for the doors. I got seven bullets." His eyes behind his head wrap are deadly calm. "I'll make 'em count."

We move: Clay in front, me, Ethan and Mama and Mage. The children run behind her, their eyes so wide and fearful it skewers my insides. Prema follows, pulling Lavan along, and Yusuf brings up the rear. The hallways are silent. Many of the sprinklers have stopped spraying, so the air is our biggest problem. Breathing is painful, like sucking lungfuls of acid even through the cloth on our faces. Beside me, Ethan draws in a straggling breath through the fabric over his face. Dear God, let him keep breathing. Help us get out of here in one piece.

In a few minutes we're at the same entrance we stood at less than an hour ago. Now only one guard stands at the door wearing a gas mask. His mask makes him look like a monster with bug eyes and an elongated nose. He raises his gun as we come into sight.

"Go back." His voice is muffled by the mask. He points back toward the mall with his rifle. We curl behind the wall and pull into a huddle.

Clay looks at me. "Keep 'em back," he says, nodding to the children. "Let me handle this."

I shake my head, worry strangling my heart. "Clay, he's got a rifle and a gas mask. You can barely see."

He tears the cloth head wrap off and shakes out his hair. His bloodshot eyes find mine. "I got this." In his left hand he holds the guard's gun, an ugly black pistol. His right hand flutters toward the revolver in his pants, the beautiful wood-gripped revolver of his father. But he can't draw both. Not anymore. His injured hand reaches out, slips down my head wrap and strokes my cheek.

"Clay, give me the other gun." I pull my head wrap off and hold my hand out.

"Riley," he says, his lips parted, his blue eyes staring deeply into mine until my chest starts to buzz. "I can still take care of you."

He kisses me hard on the mouth, his lips locking on mine. I wrap my arms around him, my fingers weaving into his hair, my body digging into his. When he pulls away, I cry out.

He thumbs down the safety and charges around the corner.

CHAPTER TWENTY-SIX

Clay runs around the corner, raises the pistol and fires in one smooth motion. The gunshot explodes through the quiet hallway. Behind me a child screams. My eyes are on Clay, stock still, the gun an extension of his body. His eyes are the blue steel of reckoning.

The stunned guard's shirt blows open and a spray of blood jets out. The guard drops to one knee, his gun sagging, his gas-mask-covered head drooping like a stomped-on insect. Clay waits, his pistol still aimed, watching his opponent like he's got all the time in the world. The wounded guard struggles to set his rifle into his shoulder socket. Clay aims the gun and fires at the same time as the guard. Twin shots crack through the hallway.

Clay crumples. The guard goes down too, the rifle clattering and then his skull smacking on the concrete floor.

I slap my hand over my mouth, my breath stuttering in ragged gasps. I run to Clay, skid to a stop beside his body. On my knees, my hands probe his chest, feeling for injury, blood. I can't find any. Slowly he blinks up at me. Then a smile.

"Oh, thank God," I whisper, relief surging through my veins. Then I slug him on the arm. "How many times are you gonna scare me like that?"

He smiles. "That idiot couldn't hit the broad side of a barn." His hand reaches to my face, but before he can draw me in, his eye widen at something over my shoulder. He drags me roughly to the floor as a gun explodes.

Something zips over my shoulder in a hot rush of air and then the far wall puffs up in a spray of plaster. The guard sits, blood running from two holes in his chest, the rifle in his lap. With the gas mask torn away, his hair stands up like a handful of straw. A trickle of blood runs from the corner of his mouth and seeps into his shirt collar. His chest is heaving wildly as he tries to steady his rifle enough to fire on us again.

Clay rolls over and snaps up to his knees. His left hand is a blur. The crack is loud. I wince. The guard's chest tears open. He falls, the rifle spilling once again to the floor. Clay strides over and fires a final time. The body jumps and then is still. I stare at the dead guard. At

197

Clay standing over him, the gun in his hand still curling smoke, at the hard set of his jaw, the flint in his eyes. He saved my life. Again.

Yusuf pokes his head around the corner. "Is he...?"

"All clear," Clay says. "Let's get these doors open."

The doors to the outside are chained and padlocked. Clay takes the guard's rifle and starts hammering at the padlock with the butt. My eyes follow the tiny beams of light trickling in through the boarded windows.

"Here," I say, digging my fingernails under the wood and tugging back.

We pull. Slowly, the thick wood creaks backward, more light spilling into the dark hallway. The nails groan as they slowly tear out of the plaster. I'm pulling, my arms aching, my eyes watering, when I hear a cry. Mama falls to the ground.

I drop the board and go to her. She's on her hands and knees, her head bowed. I put my arm on her shoulder. "What is it?"

When she looks up at me, I pull back. Dark blue veins stand out on her forehead like a road map of pain. She looks like a withered fruit someone has sucked dry. "I can't..." she whispers.

I can barely hear her. I lean in. "We'll get you help," I whisper, not knowing what to say. My relief at beating the guard is replaced by sheer terror. I stroke her cheek. Behind me the boards peel back, letting in more light. A child shouts for joy, but inside my heart is crumbling. Rayburn is dead. Almost everyone in the mall is dead. Who's left to save her?

She moans, rocking forward. Ethan appears at my side. His pale face and bloodshot eyes make him look sickly. "What's happening?" he asks, choking on tears.

She shakes her head, tucking into a ball. Her spine curves through her thin shirt.

"What's going on?" I ask.

She rocks back and forth as if she could lull the creature inside her back to sleep. "It's wrong."

"What is?" I lean into her, pressing my shoulder into her. I peer down until I can see her eyes. The vein on her head pulses as she looks up at me.

"Whatever's inside me." She blows out a hot breath. "It shouldn't be born."

I place my hand on her head. "You're exhausted. We'll get you outside, and—"

"*Nooo*," she moans. "We have to get it out. Where's Rayburn?"

I drop my eyes, staring at the pitted cement floor. She's forgotten what happened to him. "We'll ... we'll get you outside."

I can't breathe. I can't even look at her. I stare helplessly at her face and watch as she begins rocking again.

Light spills into the entrance way as a giant piece of plywood clatters to the floor. Dusty air spills into our chemical-clogged space. I squint into the light. Even though the air is hot and dusty, it's clean. Freedom. I slip my hand under Mama's bicep.

"Come on." I tug. "We *don't* give up."

She lifts her head, giving me a look that says I have no idea who I am talking to, but finally she pushes up.

Slowly the sixteen of us slip out of our poison prison.

Standing on the sand-caked sidewalk, everyone takes a deep breath. Night has fallen. The navy sky sprinkled with stars is so beautiful that tears spring to my eyes. So many stars. The air is thick with sand and grit, but that stinging burn in my nose is gone. Fresh air. Beside me, Clay takes Ethan's hand with a look of relief on his face. Ethan tosses a lock of black hair out of his eyes. "The moon," he says quietly. "I forgot what it looked like."

I nod, hugging him. "We all did."

"What now?" Clay tucks the pistol beside his revolver in the front of his pants. His eyes track the sand-covered parking lot.

I point toward the dim building in the distance. "The garage," I say. "The trucks are there. Fuel too. We can get somewhere safe. Who knows if anyone is still alive?" I nod back towards the mall. What has happened to the Forgotten? I gotta believe they're all dead too.

I support Mama's hunched form as we walk. In the fresh air, her breathing is less ragged, but she doesn't look up at the moon, doesn't smile. Her hands circle her stomach, which seems to be pulsing. What if she's right? What if whatever's inside her is evil? But I was a Breeders' baby. That baby in there didn't ask to be what it is any more than I did.

The garage looms in the distance, the dark doors shut to keep out the sand. Hopefully the trucks we tinkered on are still here. There were four, enough to get my family away from here and give Yusuf and Prema something to take the children away in. I wonder where they'll go. Nowhere will be as safe as the Citadel was before the Messiah went completely insane

When we make it to the garage, I leave Mama in Clay's arms and walk to the side door. Ethan and I scoop away the sand clogging the entrance with cupped hands and then I yank on the door until it twangs open.

"Once we get the trucks, we can grab whatever supplies we need from the warehouse across the lot and then be on our way." I peer into the dark interior. "After you," I say to Prema.

She steps into the dark. Her scream cuts through me like a blade.

Before I can process Prema's scream, a hand reaches out of the dark and yanks me into the garage. Panic blares through my head like a fire alarm. An arm circles around my neck, gagging me. I claw, kick, bite my assailant. My elbow lands somewhere soft, but the arm chokes, chokes, until stars dance in my vision. I gasp for air. My heart beats out of control. Is this how I die? Vaguely, I'm aware of Clay shouting. Blinding lights snap on.

Two dozen men aim guns at our group. In the center, staring at me, is Andrew.

"Let her breathe," he says reluctantly. He smiles, his goggles flashing reflected light into my face. The arm at my neck loosens. I suck in a straggling gasp.

Most of the Brotherhood are here, armed to the teeth and dressed for battle. Across the garage sit twenty to thirty women and small girls. Some are bound with rope. Others stare at us with wide eyes and clutch their daughters to them. A few of the boys we rescued run to their mothers and fall into their laps. There's a lot of sobbing. The scene is emotional, touching, but I'm not moved. All I can think about is the fact that every fertile woman from the Citadel is sitting in that corner.

They never intended to "go home" with the poor souls inside. They let everyone die while they saved themselves and their families. Those bastards.

"How could you!" I say, whipping toward Andrew. I glare at him, but my barbed looks do nothing. He instructs his men to push my crew into the garage and shuts the door behind them. Some of the children cry. I don't want to cry. I want to shoot Andrew in the face.

Prema steps forward, waving an angry finger at Andrew. "It was your job to protect us and you all ran? Cowards!" She makes some sort of sign on her forehead and then spits on the ground. Several men drop their eyes. One shrugs bashfully. Andrew glares back at

Prema through his goggles.

"Watch your words, old woman. Every breath you take depends on me not killing you." He flashes teeth like dirty pebbles. "So, be nice."

Prema pulls herself up to her five-foot height and puffs out her chest. "I stopped being nice years ago and I won't take orders from you!"

Andrew smiles as he digs his hand under his tunic and pulls out a large gold necklace decorated with charms. The Messiah's necklace.

Prema gasps. Her arthritic finger points at the necklace resting on Andrew's collar bones. "You...you have no right."

Mage stamps her foot. "Take off my papa's necklace!"

His fingers trace the gold charms, as if soaking in the feel of them. Of the power they bring. "As second in command, I have the right to wear this necklace, as well govern the people of the Citadel."

"The people of the Citadel were supposed to follow our Messiah home," Yusuf's voice warbles as if he might cry. "You told us so yourself. Now we find this?" He swings his hand out toward the guards and their wives. "I don't understand."

I grit my teeth and fight against the arms that hold me. "Were the Breeders even coming?"

Andrew's face becomes falsely solemn. "It was the will of the Gods." He spreads his hands, palms up, a great impersonation of the Messiah. "I am but a humble servant to their whims. I foresaw that the Brotherhood should not go home, but stay and fight the Breeders' attack."

"Bullshit!" I yell, struggling against the guard who holds me. "Then why would you save them?!" I toss my head at the women and girls. "My friend is dead because of you, you motherless bastard!"

"A lot of people are dead because of you," Clay snaps, his jaw tight. He struggles against the man that holds him. "You didn't even have the balls to kill 'em yerself!"

Andrew steps over to Clay, peering up at him with his over-large eyes. "You killed the Messiah. Men, you know what we need to do with these outsiders."

"He didn't." Mage pushes through the crowd. "I saw it. My papa pulled the trigger, not Clay."

A woman in the back nods. "I saw it, too. He did it himself."

Andrew puffs out his cheeks in a frustrated breath. "It doesn't matter what happened. This traitor was one of us," he points an accusatory finger at Clay, "and now he's inciting a riot against Gods' people! We should execute them all."

Clay narrows his eyes, staring at Andrew. "I never been one of you." In a lightning-quick movement Clay's arm slips out of his captor's grip and grabs for the gun in Andrew's hand. The two men fumble for the black steel, hands scrambling, teeth gritted, until the guard yanks Clay's arm back. Andrew holds up his gun triumphantly, smiling giddily like a child winning a toy. Then he pulls the pistol back and smashes it into Clay's face.

"No!" I yell.

Clay staggers, a bright line of blood spreading across his cheek.

"Stop!" Mage says, stepping up to Andrew, glaring at him with her hands on her hips.

Andrew leans down until his goggles are only inches from her delicate face. "Your daddy isn't here to step in on your behalf, you meddling little magpie." He places a hand on her shoulder and begins squeezing.

"Leave her alone." It's a gravely voice from the back. Lavan limps into the light.

His eyes look a little clearer, but his hair is a disheveled mess and the rancid crust of vomit on his shirt doesn't help his appearance.

Andrew places both hands on his hips and looks Lavan up and down. "Thought you were dead."

"You tried to kill me." He lifts bloodshot eyes. "Wanted to make sure I didn't tell."

A flicker of emotion crosses Andrew's face. Is it fear? Surprise? Then his awful sneer returns. "You're drunk out of your head. You have nothing to tell them."

Lavan runs a hand through his messy hair in a vain attempt to straighten it. He burps once and then straightens his face again. "Don't need to tell 'em nothing. I can show 'em."

"Show us what?" One of the Brotherhood guards steps forward, the pistol clutched tightly in his fist. He's tall, with hairy arms and a broad chest. He flicks a confused glance at Andrew and then turns back to Lavan. "Show us what, Lavan?"

Lavan's bruised face tightens. "I can show you the women Andrew was keeping for the Breeders."

"The women?" Another guard steps out of the crowd. He has a cut on his cheek and red creases where his gas mask would've sat. He points a finger at Lavan. "What are women gonna prove? We have our women here."

Andrew throws his hands in the air. "He's crazy."

Lavan flicks some dried vomit off his shirt and clears his throat. "I can prove Andrew made a deal to sell all the women to the Breeders. That he planned all this long before today."

There's a gasp from the crowd. The women in the back shoot worried glances at their men. An older girl curls into her mother's arms.

Yusuf steps forward, his chubby face trembling with rage. "Is it true, Andrew?" He wipes tears away with a thick finger. "I want answers." He looks around the room at the Brotherhood. "Don't you?"

The men behind Andrew shift uncomfortably. A few let their guns sag.

Andrew shakes his head, a look of panic creeping into his features. "It was the Messiah's plan." He speaks rapidly, waving his arms. "You heard him. He wanted to go home."

"If the Breeders were coming, why wouldn't he have told us before he died?" I say, thinking about him reaching for Clay's gun, the explosion of blood. "Unless he never knew they were coming." I look over at Mage who's nodding slowly. I turn back to the crowd. "The Messiah was afraid of the plagues. He saw the sandstorm of a sign that end times were coming. I think he gave himself to appease the Gods. He knew something bad was going to happen. He just didn't know it would come from his own people."

All eyes turn to Andrew. He seems to shrink beneath our stares. "That's not true!"

Lavan clears his throat, his eyes on the concrete. "Most of the Brotherhood made a deal. Their families would be spared if they kept everyone in."

"It was that or death!" a man in the back with a long black ponytail and sideburns blurts. When we turn to look at him, he drops his head in shame. "Couldn't let my children die."

Prema grits her teeth. "So, you'd kill the rest of us?"

"You were willing," the man with the cut on his cheek says to Prema.

Yusuf puffs out his chest in rage. "Not if I knew it was all a lie!"

"What about your sons?" I ask, looking around.

A few of the men shake their heads. One man steps up, sorrow lining his pale, beardless face. "I was told he ran when the sprinklers came on."

Another steps up, veins pulsing in his thick arms. "Andrew said no one could find him." He whirls on Andrew, anger flaring in his eyes. "Where's my boy?"

The men look at each other, anger building in their faces. Voices rise until I'm sure they'll all turn on him.

Andrew holds a gun into the air and fires. A woman screams. The people's new leader lowers the smoking gun, smiling like a snake. "Brothers, we don't have time to entertain lies from dusts and drunkards. Lock them up." He nods his men forward.

The Brotherhood shuffles uncomfortably, glancing from face to face. A man holding a cloth to his bloody head steps forward. "I want to see Lavan's proof."

A few others nod.

Andrew points wildly at the Messiah's necklace. "You don't need proof! I'm the word of the Gods. You do what I say."

The men of Brotherhood shake their heads. "You aren't the Messiah," one says. "I want proof," says another. Others nod in agreement.

Andrew clenches his fists, his face contorting. "He has no proof!" His voice is high-pitched, childish like a toddler in a tantrum.

Lavan straightens his posture. "I do."

"Where?" Andrew asks, whirling on him. His fists are clenched, the gun trembling in one hand. Will he shoot Lavan right here? What will the men do if he does?

"Inside," Lavan says, nodding back toward where we came. "We have to go back in the Citadel. We have to find the Forgotten."

CHAPTER TWENTY-SEVEN

We walk back in the twilight, all eyes alert. Andrew, Lavan, and six other guards with guns circle Clay, Mama, Ethan, and I. Much of me wonders why Andrew insisted in bringing my whole family into this. The only reason that makes sense is that he'll take us back inside and kill us all. And the Brotherhood is still mostly following Andrew's orders because they don't know who to trust. I look over at Lavan's face as he shuffles a little drunkenly beside me. How sure is he about this evidence? Won't the Forgotten all be dead? And, in the end, will it matter?

Beside me, Mama staggers to one knee in the sand, her hands circling her belly. I drop down beside her.

"You have to let her rest," I say, looking up at Andrew. "Her pregnancy is making her weak."

"Get her up," he says, annoyance in his voice. The Brotherhood hasn't stripped him of his pistol, which bothers me. I look at the gun at his hip and his eyes follow mine there. He shoves me forward.

"Mama," I wrap my arms around her, "you can do this. Just a little longer."

Sweat trails down her forehead. "Take care of them," she whispers. "Take care of your brother."

My heartbeat stutters at her words. "You'll take care of him." Tears well in my eyes. I slip my arm around her back and let her lean on me. "We stay together," I whisper. She says nothing.

The mall doors we pried open are still gaping wide. The dark hallway looks like an endless black tunnel and still smells like acid. Every atom in my body fights going back in there.

"This is ridiculous," Andrew says, coming to a stop just before the entrance. "We don't need to listen to this drunkard. Why go back into this death trap for no reason?"

Lavan straightens his shirt. "They want proof. The proof is inside."

Andrew's small mouth tightens in a look of disgust. "It was foreseen. Don't you believe anymore?"

Lavan's hand strays to the gun one of the Brothers gave him. "We go forward or the Brotherhood strips you of your title." His eyes land on the Messiah's necklace resting on Andrew's collarbone.

"Then wait a goddamned minute." He reaches inside his pants' pocket. Lavan raises his pistol, but Andrew pulls out a long, slender device with a large antenna and shows it to him.

"What's that?" the guard with the cut on his head asks. He snatches the thing from Andrew. "How do we know it's not a bomb?"

Andrew rolls his eyes. "Why would I go to all this trouble just to blow us up? We can't go in there with acid in the air. This turns on the ventilation system remotely."

The guards exchange glances. Finally, the one holding it presses the button. We all cringe.

Deep inside the mall, motors whir on and fans begin chugging. Air breezes out of the open doorway, carrying with it the smell of acid. When the smell hits my nose, my body recoils. I don't want to go back in there. The group steps away and waits while the system cleans the air.

When the air smells clear, Lavan disappears through the open door and into darkness. Lavan leads with a certainty that makes me believe he knows where he's going. Part of me wonders if he's bluffing, but then why would he risk the Brotherhood turning on him if he didn't have proof? Still, what will the Forgotten tell us that would implicate Andrew?

We're shoved in after him, then Ethan and Clay. As the Brotherhood fills in behind us, my eyes adjust to the dark. The sprinklers are off and so is most of the power. The air is pretty foul, but doesn't feel as corrosive. We draw our shirts up over our faces just the same. With the smell of chemical fading, the rancid stink of death begins to eek out of the corners. Corners where friends and family lie dead. If Lavan can prove that Andrew is responsible and did it for his own selfish reason, they'll turn on him faster than a scorpion on its prey.

We see no survivors in the desiccated hallways. A few bodies fester in acid puddles, red sores and flayed skin marking their deaths. The guards' drop their eyes as shame floods their faces. Some look shocked at the horror. Good. They should be.

Lavan leads us back toward the hole and the mood in the group shifts. Guards' hands itch toward their guns. Will any mutants be alive?

"This is far enough!" Andrew says, skidding to a stop a few feet from the hole. "Whatever you're playing at, Lavan, I suggest we get on with it." He adjusts his goggles and puts on a bored expression. "Get to some real business."

"This is real business," Lavan says through swollen lips. He points at the dark crack in the earth. "The evidence is down there."

Andrew peers into the dark. "What're you talking about? There's nothing down there but muties and bats."

"Muties!" Lavan shouts. "The fact that they exist proves you disobeyed the Messiah. He told you to put those women out and instead you stuck 'em in a hole underground to live a horrible life. You kept the women because you were planning a deal with The Breeders all along. Except they got sick from the water and weren't fertile anymore. So you needed more women." He turns to the Brotherhood. "Our women. That's why he saved them and no one else. He's going to hand them over to The Breeders."

Andrew crosses his arms over his chest, making the Messiah's pendant jitter. "That's not hard facts and you know it. He knows it," he says, turning to his men.

The Brotherhood look between Lavan and Andrew. "You're gonna have to do better than that," the guard with the cut on his head says, hefting the rifle onto his shoulder. "Is that all you have?"

"No. The Forgotten can tell you themselves. Once I convinced them to stop attacking me, one told me of Andrew's plan. How he tricked them into taking sanctuary in the hole and staying quiet instead of being put out. He took them food, promised them safety, but when he found out the water poisoned their insides, he abandoned them. They were no good to the Docs in Albuquerque, so why care? By then they were too weak to fight back". He looks around the dark area. "We just have to find the one I talked to. She'll tell you."

He's so convincing it has to be true. I look around at the men, hoping. But then, the Forgotten are likely all dead. What if we can't find one? And even if we do, will it be enough to convince the Brotherhood Lavan is telling the truth? Will they even care?

The guard with the big hairy arms turns to Andrew. "Is it true?"

Andrew's face is pale. He shakes his head. "Course not. All this was the Messiah's plan. He told me so himself." Andrew gives a weak smile. Suddenly he aims his pistol wildly, somehow centering on Ethan's head. All the men draw guns, but Andrew's already pulling my brother roughly into a bear hug. Ethan claws at Andrew's arms, his dark hair flying. But Andrew's grip is fierce. He drags Ethan with him toward the hole and uses him as a human body shield.

My vision narrows to a pinhole as I struggle forward, panic lighting up my body. "Stop!" I scream. "Let him go!"

"Ethan!" Mama cries.

I lurch forward, but Clay grabs my arm. "Don't," he snaps. "He'll throw him over."

The guards raise their guns, unsure of where to aim.

"Let him go," Lavan says. "We can work this out."

Andrew shakes his head, his goggles making his eyes bug crazily out of his head. He tugs Ethan back another step. My vision strays to the deep, dark drop and my heart somersaults. No one would survive that fall.

Andrew throws crazy looks around the crowd, spittle forming at the corners of his mouth. "It was for our own good." His voice is uneven, frantic. He searches his guards' faces for sympathy. "We were being poisoned. We didn't have enough food to last the rest of the year, but did *he* care? No!" He gnashes his rotten teeth together angrily. "The Messiah never listened to me! No one would listen to me. We were all going to die!" His voice reverberates around the concrete.

I take a step forward. "We understand." Ethan's eyes meet mine. Afraid.

"Shut up, dust!" Andrew says, his forearm tightening around my brother's neck. "It's your fault we're in this situation. Your fault the Breeders started paying attention to us. They told the Messiah to pick you up. That you had the Sight. And he believed them! He always believed his Gods would save him, that fool. I took one look at you and knew you were nothing special."

Clay inhales sharply. Cold prickles crawl up my arms. "The Breeders told him to pick us up? Why?"

Andrew grits his teeth. "You think I care? All I know is you were five extra mouths to feed. I knew the hospital freaks were using us. The Messiah's been benefiting from their technology and their insights for years. They taught him how to hook up the power. They gave him his precious prophecies that made him seem connected to the Gods. He's been communicating with them through a radio for years. Taking with no intention of paying back. But they were coming. He wanted mass suicide. I struck a deal to save some of us."

He looks at his men, a sadness settling on his face. The wildness drops out of his voice until he's pleading with his men. "I did it for you. So we could have a chance. So some of the women and children could have a chance. They'll take us in as guards. Otherwise, when they come here, they'll slaughter us all."

I shake my head. "What they'll do in that hospital is not a chance you should take."

Lavan's swollen face tightens. "You didn't do this for us." He shakes his head sadly. "You hated the Messiah. You thought he was an ignorant fool. You were giddy when he died." He drops his head. "The Gods will surely punish us now…"

Andrew blinks, crocodile tears welling in his eyes. "It was the only way. Otherwise everyone would die like the muties."

"Like *usss?*" A garbled voice rolls out of the dark. Slowly a figure lurches into view. The acid has eaten away her face, exposing raw muscle and sinew. Her lips are peeled back over what's left of her teeth and her nose and ears have shriveled to blistered nubs. She looks like a walking corpse. How's she's still standing I don't know. Maybe all those months of living underground. Maybe the contaminated water makes her stronger just like it does the Brotherhood.

The speaker, set to kill, draws a ragged, wet breath and zeroes in on Andrew.

"Shoot her!" Andrew squeals, ducking down behind Ethan. His feet shuffle within inches of the cliff's edge. Ethan's eyes go wide. He begins clawing at Andrew's arm at his neck.

"Let him go!" I shout, stepping as close as I dare. Mama grips my arm. I can hear her panicked gasps.

Beside me, Clay's eyes are blazing. "Don't be a coward, Andrew. Let Ethan go."

Andrew's arm is like a steel bar on Ethan's neck. He backs another step toward the cliff's edge. Gravel skids down the side and cascades to the bottom with a sickening ping. "I'll toss him in! I'll do it!"

Ethan's mouth drops open in terror. I reach out, my heart slamming in my chest. Ethan's only a few feet away and yet the distance seems like miles. "Please! He's just a kid!"

The speaker shuffles forward, lurching and gasping. She seems not to hear anything but the rage in her heart. She stumbles on, hell-bent on the destruction of the man who ruined her.

"Shoot her!" Andrew screams, pulling back from the speaker.

He takes another step back. More stones tumble down the crevasse. "Shoot her now or the boy goes over!"

The speaker grabs for Andrew. Lavan raises his rifle. I focus on Ethan, his face searching mine for help, a rescue. I grip my face, unable to move. I have to save him. How?

Movement catches my attention out of the corner of my eye. Another mutie? A guard? Mama tears past me, running at a speed I wouldn't have thought possible.

It becomes suddenly clear what she's going to do. "Mama, no!" I reach out to stop her.

All those times she wished she could be the one saving us instead of us saving her.

She slips past my outstretched hand, running, her clothes fluttering, her black hair streaming like a glossy ribbon.

She can't. She can't.

I take a step after her.

It all happens in slow motion. Mama hits Andrew from the side, jarring him. Surprised, Andrew stumbles and his grip on Ethan loosens. Ethan topples forward, his dark hair falling into his face. Mama reaches for him. For a moment I think she'll embrace him, but instead she shoves him back toward us, away from Andrew, away from the hole. He stumbles and skids onto the concrete. She smiles.

Then Andrew grabs her.

A tangle of arms and legs, Andrew and Mama tilt out over the dark abyss. Andrew's hand grips her shirt, his other arm slicing through open air as if he could fly. Mama's hands pry at his fingers, but she's teetering. She's going over with him.

Dear God, no!

Andrew falls, disappearing. I jump, stretching my body the last few feet to the lip of the hole. I reach for her leg as she begins to plummet. My fingers brush skin and my heart surges. I have her. Then my fingers slip off and my hand slices through open space.

"Mama!" I scream.

This can't be happening.

I hit the ground hard, my lower legs and torso on the concrete's edge, my chest and arms tilting into empty space. As I fall, my eyes lock on Mama below me. Her hair flutters against her cheeks. Her eyes, which I expect to find terrified, have lost their fear. She smiles at me, her mouth open. I'll fall with her and she'll tell me the last thing we'll ever know and I'll be with her in the dark vastness and whatever waits beyond. I reach for her.

A hand slams on my ankle. My elbow smacks into the crevasse's side. Mama is still falling, down, down. I'm losing her to shadow. My fingers drag against the rock wall. "Mama!"

For a moment that is both forever and a single second, her beautiful face is illuminated by light. She offers me one more smile, her dark eyes shining with tears. Then the darkness swallows her.

I squeeze my eyes shut and try not to hear. Yet the thud, when it comes, is so loud it shakes every inch of me.

I roll into myself. My body feels gone. My brain too. Maybe I've died. Maybe I'm floating forever through black space. Yet there's pain. Pain pressing at my heart. Hands draw me up and pull me in. Arms surround me, but I can't open my eyes. I can't live in the world where that just happened. It didn't happen.

Clay holds me. Holds me, holds me, holds me. Murmurs things into my ear.

I push away, detaching from his arms, and open my eyes. He stares at me, fear in his. "Riley, are you—"

I turn and run from him, down the incline, down into darkness. "Stop!" he calls, but I don't. I run. Run into the dark. I run until my foot strikes something hard and I skid into the wall. When my feet hit the bottom, I stand in the blackness, panting, not knowing what to do.

Clay thuds down the incline, a lantern bobbing from his hand. "I'm coming," he says, his tone firm. "Yer not doin' this on yer own."

My heart hammers so hard in my chest pain radiates up my breast bone, but I take the lantern from him. I both need and fear its light. But I have to see my Mama. See if she's...alive somehow.

Slowly, I scan the light over the dark hole. The beam falls on a pair of black lace-up boots. Andrew's. My gorge rises. Slowly, my hand trembling, I move the beam up, up his broken body.

His eyes are open and staring through goggles that have splintered into spider webs. His mouth is slack, as if surprised. A trickle of blood meanders from his nose. His thin blond hair is pink in the back where his head has cracked like a bird's egg. I turn the beam away from the mess of red behind him.

Clay walks up and pulls something off Andrew's neck. The Messiah's necklace. "For Mage." He tucks it in his pocket and turns to me. "Let's find yer ma."

My head swims. I'll faint. I'll die. I have to do this.

I flick the lantern left and the beam trails over a pale, slender hand. My own hands shake so badly the beam dances, yet I draw closer. I know those fingers. How many times have they stroked my hair or rubbed away the sting of some reckless wound? How many times have I held that han— I choke on a sob hitching up in my throat. Clay puts a hand on my shoulder. Then, slowly, he lifts the beam to her face.

Her eyes are closed. Her face looks…peaceful. Her raven hair fans out behind her head in a black halo. Trembling, I kneel down and touch my palm to her cheek.

"Mama?"

Nothing.

"Mama?" I lean down, placing both hands on her face.

Beside me, Clay kneels and presses two fingers to a vein in her neck. I don't want him doing that. I shake her a little. "Mama?"

His face morphs from serious to somber to total, awful sadness. He shakes his head. I push him out of the way. "Let me," I say. My fingers ply the tender skin on her neck and hope for the quick pulse beneath the pads of my fingers. Nothing. I shift my fingers.

"Riley," Clay whispers. Then firmer. "Riley."

I shake my head, still searching for a pulse. "No," I whisper. "No."

"She's gone." He places a hand on my shoulder.

"No." I stand, wringing my hands. Clay bends down to lift her and her arms fall lifeless to her sides. On the ground, a stain of blood has spread.

I turn and vomit. Lurching spasms rock my whole body. For several moments I can do nothing but convulse, gripping the wall. When it's over, I open my eyes. Clay slowly carries Mama's body up the incline.

I scuttle up to the surface behind him, a thrumming in my head that makes every movement, every breath feel like they belong to someone else. Somehow I reach the top. Lavan, the guards, and Ethan stare. They look at me. I don't like the looks on their faces. I want out of here.

"Riley," a small voice. Ethan. I feel his hand on mine. "Riley, is she…" He doesn't finish. I hear the tears in his voice.

I fall to my knees, drawing him in. I hug him and shake uncontrollably. I bury my face into my brother's chest. He holds me and cries, his body shaking, his tears falling into my hair, hot and wet. I don't know how long we stay like that. I don't know what else is happening around us.

When I finally look up, they're all waiting. Even the speaker, who looks more human now, less monster. Even her ruined face offers me a sympathetic look. Clay stands behind me. On the ground is a body covered in a jacket. Mama was alive a moment ago. She gave herself up to save Ethan. To save us all. I should've been the one. I should've have gotten to her in time. She can't be gone. She can't.

"We...we have to bury her," is all I can manage. My voice sounds like broken concrete.

Clay nods, his hand stroking my arm over and over. The only comfort he can offer. "This morning we'll honor her sacrifice."

CHAPTER TWENTY-EIGHT

Dawn in the desert brings no comfort. Today I bury my mama.

I stand, barely on my feet, as the Brotherhood gathers stones to entomb the woman who birthed me. Ethan is clutched under my arm, staring into the bright burst of pink light in the East. He hasn't talked since he asked me if she was dead. I don't blame him. I don't want to talk. I want to crawl into a hole and die. Over and over I feel her ankle brush against the pads of my fingers. Over and over I picture myself one second faster, my hand cinching around her leg, holding fast, drawing her up into my arms.

I could've saved her. Somehow I should be able to go back. I just need one more second.

They gather stones, large sand-colored boulders and, beside them, smaller gray ovals. The stack grows before my feet and yet it feels like they're piling them on top of my chest. I'll be buried here beneath the rocks and stones, entombed in this desert, and it'll be okay.

If I'd been one second faster...

We place her body on a sandy hill a quarter mile from the mall. Rayburn will lie beside her. I stare out at the foreign landscape. This isn't right. We can't leave her here. But Clay keeps insisting this is what we have to do. He comes over to me now, his eyes wary like a dog that's displeased his master. He places a hand on my cheek, but I can't be touched. Not with my mama's body growing cold beneath a tarp at my feet. I pull away.

He says nothing, just looks at me morosely and then goes back to hauling stones. Sweating and toiling for me. For my mama.

Her ankle brushing against my fingers. Then empty space.

When the rock pile is complete, the other men walk off. Ethan, Clay, and I stand around her body and stare. I should say something, but what words would be equal to her sacrifice, to the years of torment she endured so that Ethan and I could have a chance at this world? Should it be a surprise that this is how she died?

I kneel in the dirt and slowly lift the tarp back. There's her delicate face, the soft ridges of burned skin running up her cheek and over her chin. I place my hand there and feel how cold she's become. It lays another boulder on my heart. "I'm sorry. So sorry."

Ethan drops beside me, quietly crying. "It's not your fault." He snakes his arms around my chest. "She died because of me." His sobs rock us both.

"No," I say, wrapping my arms around him, pressing his angular body into mine. "She died for you to live. She knew the baby would kill her and she wanted the end of her life to mean something." I pull back and look into his teary eyes. "You gotta forgive yourself. Live the life she helped save."

"Then you have to stop, too." He wipes his nose on his sleeve and tosses his hair out of his eyes. "You have to stop saying sorry for her being dead. Or I won't." He swipes at the tears trailing down his face.

"Okay. We will. We go on together."

Then Ethan and I place the first stone.

***

Mage, Lavan, and the Brotherhood feed us from their food stores. Ethan, Mage, and I sit on blankets on the garage's floor and eat canned tomatoes and peaches out of jars. The plan is we eat, we pack, we leave. If the Breeders are headed this way, we need to get going as soon as possible. And I need to get to Auntie. Now more than ever I need my last adult connection to the life I knew.

I glance around the hot garage for Clay, but I haven't seen him since we buried Mama. I push up from the floor and give Ethan a pat. He looks up at me with worried eyes.

"I'm going to find Clay. Be back in a bit."

He gives me a quiet nod and then goes back to learning how to make a paper crane, his leg pressed into Mage's. As I watch them, I almost smile.

Walking out through the desert at dawn somehow soothes me. It's the life I knew, the life I've been missing. The sun is low in the east and the day critters are starting their trek. A copper-colored lizard slinks under a rock as I pass. In the distance, a hawk dives on its prey. It's nice out here. No wonder Clay came out alone.

I find him over the ridge, sitting Indian-style, his arms around his knees. He hears me coming and snaps around, his hand reaching

216

for the gun at his hip. When he sees me he relaxes, but doesn't smile. Instead he turns his eyes toward the sunrise, a sadness settling on his face. As I sit beside him, he doesn't look over. His brooding eyes crinkle slightly as if me being here pains him.

"Not up for company?" I ask, trying to sound light. I lean my shoulder into his. His body rocks at my touch, but then stiffens. His good left hand tightens over his right. His jaw is stone.

"You wanna be alone?" I ask, a coldness crusting over my heart. "Am I bothering you?"

He swallows hard, his Adam's apple bobbing. "You're not...botherin' me." He flicks a glance in my direction. "Just figured you didn't, you know, need me much."

His words are weighted. They fall around me like shards of ice. I drop my eyes. I have no words to sooth this rift. Words have ceased to help me lately.

"Yeah," Clay says, standing, brushing dust off his jeans. "Figured as much. I'll be over the ridge, huntin'." He takes a step down the gravel path.

"Stop!" I stand up, my hand out, reaching for...God knows what. "What did I do?"

His blue eyes cloud. He runs a hand through his brown hair. "What d'you mean?"

"What did I do?" I gesture at his rock-wall posture.

He crosses his arms over his chest, his brow furrowing. One boot toe digs in the dirt. "Nothing."

"Then what?" I take a nervous step forward, the gravel crunching under my boots. "After all we've been through, I thought you'd be there for me." I sniff and blink back tears. How can he pick a fight when my mama's not even cold?

He barks an incredulous laugh. "Ha. Like you'd ever *let* me be there for you. Funny, Ri. Good one." He starts down the ridge again.

I run after him, skidding in the dust. I grab his arm and haul him back. His eyes are cold when he whirls towards me. I jab a finger into his shirt. "You don't get to do that!" I shout. "You don't get to walk away."

"Why don't I?" he yells. "That's all *you* ever do." He clenches his jaw. "You push me away every chance you get!"

My heart bangs into my ribcage like a frantic animal, but my anger is fading. "What're you talking about?"

He jabs a finger back at the mall. "You. Push. Me. Away. Every time I try to help. Every time I step in." He tugs his hair until it sticks up wildly. "I get it. You're independent. You can take care of yerself. But here's the thing." He leans in, his eyes narrowing. "Everybody needs help. And if you're not gonna let me get close, then there's not much to us."

I stare at him, letting his words crest over me like an ice-cold wave. Up above, the hawk's wings cast a long shadow over the land.

"I ..." I shake my head, sudden tears welling to my eyes. "I'm not good at trusting." My words come out in harsh whispers. I look up at him. His blue eyes sparkle in the light. I can't lose him. "It's hard...to trust when I've been let down so much. You know?"

His jaw unclenches first, then his fists. Slowly, he turns toward me. His thumbs find his belt loops. He takes a deep breath. "I know I let you down when we got captured—"

"No." I touch his arm. This time he doesn't yank it away. I stare into his beautiful sun-lit face. "You didn't let me down."

He runs a hand through his brown hair. What I want to do is I step close until our bodies are inches away and thread my fingers through his hair, feel its softness between the pads of my fingers. Instead, I stand there and wait for him to break my heart.

He closes the gap between us in two steps and throws his arms around me. His smell overpowers me, that deep musk that sends my heart scampering. I press into him. My right hand grips his shirt back, my left the hair at the nape of his neck. As he leans down, the stubble on his cheek skims mine. My body ignites with wanting.

"You don't trust me," he whispers. His words flutter at my neck, sending shivers over my skin. "You think I'm gonna leave." He slips his hand under my chin and lifts my face up until I'm staring into his steel-blue eyes framed with long dark lashes.

"Riley," he breathes, his mouth moving only inches from mine. "I'm right here." His hand circles behind my neck. "I'll always be right here."

He presses his lips to mine and his mouth ignites me with a slow, smoldering fire. His hands lace through my hair as his lips part and his tongue finds mine. The muscles of his back ripple under my fingertips. Panting, I pull back from the kiss and tug his shirt over his head. He stops and looks up at me in surprise.

"What're you doin'?" he asks, his eyes flashing, his bare chest heaving.

I run a hand over his skin, amazed at the feel of it. His pecs flex instinctively beneath my fingertips. "I trust you," I whisper. I look up at him—the smooth round muscles on his chest and arms, the scar that runs down the hard muscles of his abdomen. Then I stare up into his sky blue eyes. "I trust you," I repeat. Then I draw my shirt up over my head. The evening breeze playing over the bare skin on my arms and shoulders sends shivers over my body. Slowly, I unwind the binding on my chest.

"You don't...have to," he says, watching with rapt attention. He lifts his eyes to mine, softness in his gaze. "You don't have to do this to keep me. I'm with you whether you want to or not."

I nod and continue to unwind the cloth that covers me. "I know."

I pull the last of the cloth away, and I'm bare, undone before him. His eyes go wide and a smile plays at his lips. I reach for him.

"Wait," he says. He fumbles in his pants pockets. He pulls out a small gold ring—simple, beautiful. "I want you to have this." His face is bashful, his long lashes fluttering as he takes my hand and slips the gold band on my finger. I hold it up to the light.

"Clay," I whisper. I place my hand on his cheek. "Where did you get it?"

"Mage," he says, smiling. "I asked her for one before..." He waves his hand back toward the mall. "People used to give each other rings as symbols of their commitment. Or marriage or whatever." He blushes. "Wanted to give you one a while back, but I wasn't sure how you felt."

I twirl the gold band on my finger and marvel at the silken feel on my skin. I press my lips to his with a tender kiss. "Being with you is the most right I've ever been."

He draws me to him and I'm lost to sensation—his skin on my skin, his hands on my body, his mouth, his tongue, his breath skimming the bare flesh of my collarbones. We lay together under the open sky and I let go of the fear and the pain of this place. I give myself to Clay. And it's beautiful.

CHAPTER TWENTY-NINE

Once again we're loading up a truck, yet this time there's two empty seats that will never be filled. I toss another sack of gear into the back. The Brotherhood have allowed us to fully stock ourselves from their warehouse. We've got more guns, ammo, cooking utensils, spare parts, fuel, and knickknacks than we need. Ethan even found a comic book and a T-shirt his size that reads *Red Sox* in big red letters. Clay's got a revolver on each hip, boxes of bullets, and a smile so wide you couldn't scrape it off. He finishes up a conversation with Lavan, slapping him on the back and laughing. When he walks my way, my hand reaches to the ring resting on a chain under my shirt.

"We ready?" he asks, pulling me in to kiss the top of my head. He runs a hand through my short hair. "Mage really gave you the barber shop treatment, huh?"

I touch the hair at the nape of my neck and blush, self-doubt rising like a cork. What if Clay doesn't like my haircut? But, as if he senses my insecurity, he presses his lips to my ear. "You look gorgeous."

I sigh and kiss him. Then I go find the kids.

Ethan and Mage lean against the back garage wall. Mage gave him a haircut too, so that he no longer has to toss dark locks out of his eyes. He looks good. Older. I realize he's probably had a birthday by now. Is he nine? Did I miss it? I shake my head, feeling that pang of loss that always hovers just beyond my line of sight. Mama wouldn't have missed his birthday.

"Riley," Ethan says, pulling his hand from where it rests on Mage's. A blush burns in his cheeks.

"Ethan." I nod. "Mage. Sorry to interrupt. We're all packed." Both kids' heads droop. "Ten minutes," I say to Ethan. He nods. I don't walk over and muss his hair or pull him in for a hug. He'd kill me and rightfully so.

It'll be hard for Ethan to leave Mage, but I've promised him that once we have Auntie we'll come back here. Maybe by then Lavan will have the Citadel up and running. Maybe we could stay. But then, we'd have to be free of the Breeders.

I find Clay already in the truck cab, his cowboy hat pulled low, a twig clamped between his teeth. He nods at me as I open the truck door and slide in.

"Ho there, pretty lady. Can I give ya a lift?" He throws me a wink.

I press my palm to his cheek. "You better quit that pretty lady stuff when we get back on the road."

He dips his head, his cowboy hat tilting down. "Whatever you fancy, ma'am." He smiles big. Then his smile drops into seriousness. "Lavan says we got a couple days of rough drivin' 'fore we get back to town. That's if the old girl makes it." He pats the truck's door. "And if we can find a place to refuel."

I don't say anything, just stare out toward the road and the gentle uphill climb out of the valley.

"You scared?" he asks, his hand resting on my thigh.

"Nah," I say, placing my hand on his. "We've gotten ourselves outta worse scrapes."

He smiles, flashing his straight teeth. "We sure have, pretty lady. We sure have."

I pat his hand. "I gotta do one more thing."

He nods, understanding in his eyes. "Take all the time you need."

I walk over the ridge, my heart heavy. When I see the two rock piles, brown and silent in the dawn light, my pulse picks up in my temples. I sink down beside Mama's grave as the dawn light bleeds into the sky. How can I leave her here? I look at the mound of stones and think of Mama beneath them. All that weight, as if we wanted to hold her down, to tie her soul to the earth. I want a way to lift her body into the sky. Let her float somewhere far from this earth.

My eyes lift up to the sky. A bird skims the ridge, dipping low on a gust of wind. Above, the sky is turning orange.

My eyes trail to the west where the deep purple night hasn't yet been washed out by dawn. There, in the cloudless sky, is a bright pinprick of light. A morning star? I stagger to my feet, my heart instantly beating. Could it be?

The star, like a diamond tucked in a sea of blue, winks brightly and I'm transported to that first night in the mall when Mama held my hand and told me about Arn, about feeling his love shine down from a morning star.

I stare up, tears spilling down my cheeks. "Please, Mama," I whisper. "Give me a sign. Let me know you're up there. Let me know you love me." Tears course down my cheeks in waves. I wait, my heart pounding, my chest tight. I want to feel her hands on me. I want to hear her whisper, *I love you, baby.*

There's no whisper on the wind, no hands on my body. And the star is fading with the spread of dawn.

I turn my eyes upward. The morning star, *her* morning star, seems to wink. Is it a trick of the light? The tears in my eyes? I kiss my fingertips and raise them toward the sky. I could choose to believe it is all in my imagination, that there's nothing in the sky but light, but instead I choose hope.

I choose love.

THE END

EPILOGUE

Lavan watched as the three outsiders drove away, their truck coiling a trail of dust. He'd given them more supplies than he'd wanted to spare, but then the Messiah's girl wanted them well stocked. He never could say no to Mage.

Footsteps drew him out of his thoughts. A Brother was running up with pink cheeks and wide eyes, something black clutched in his fist. Lavan turned, one hand instinctively reaching for the gun slung over his back. But then he saw the radio in the Brother's hand. Lavan closed the gap in three quick strides and reached for the black radio.

"There's a call?" The squeak in his voice betrayed the nervousness he'd hoped to hide. Lavan grabbed the radio from the Brother and felt the weight of it in his palm. He'd only heard the voices from far away a few times and each time it scared him. They'd never spoken to him before. He swallowed, not sure if he was ready.

"A call," the Brother panted. He wiped sweat off his forehead and flicked it ground-ward. "They wanted to speak to whoever was now in charge."

Something hitched in Lavan's chest. *He* was in charge now. This both terrified and excited him. His hand trembled as he leveled the radio with his mouth.

"Hello?" He hated the weakness in his voice. Clearing his throat, Lavan tried again. "Hello."

Static. Then a voice crackled forth from the void. The voice, he realized, of a woman.

"With whom am I speaking?" the woman asked. Or more demanded. Lavan's arm hairs rose.

Awkwardly he thumbed down the talk button again. "This is Lavan. Lavan LaVue." He let off the button and then hastily pressed it again. "I'm in charge." Gods, he wished he sounded like it.

A long pause. When the woman's voice returned, she sounded even less pleased. "Lavan LaVue, this is Nessa Vandewater. I'm head of research and development for the Breeders. Do you know who we are?"

Lavan swallowed hard. Gods yes he knew who they were.

Rumored to be monsters, maniac doctors who mutilated people for what they called science. The very people his followers were indebted to. The people who would come and kill them all if he stepped a toe out of line. The tremor returned to his hand. Thank goodness she couldn't see it.

"Yes," he said as evenly as he could. "I know who you…who the Breeders are. I know the Messiah worked with you. That you told him how to work the grow lights and where to find the outsiders." He pressed the radio so close to his lips they brushed against the dimpled speaker. "I want to work with you too." He didn't, not really, but for now he wanted her to think that he was on board.

"I'm glad to hear it," her voice said. He wondered at her age. She sounded ageless, like a mountain and just as sharp.

"Lavan LaVue, we can help each other. I have a shipment of medical supplies already en route. I knew you'd need them."

Lavan bristled as her message crackled over the airwaves. How could she already know what happened? Was she watching them? Unease crawled over his skin as he pressed the talk button. "Thank you."

"You're welcome," she said. "Lavan, in return I need something from you."

He knew this was coming. He flicked a glance at the Brother who'd stood all this time, listening. The boy shrugged. "What…what is it?" Lavan asked.

The silence that followed was heavy.

Finally, her voice squawked through the machine. "The outsiders." Her voice was taut now, almost…angry? "I want to know where they were headed and exactly when they left." She cleared her throat, an awful sound like metal scraping metal. "They have something that belongs to me."

Lavan shivered, but he snapped the button down as fast as he could. "They left near abouts five hours ago, headed north on the old highway. Said they were going home." Lavan wiped sweat off his upper lip. Thank the stars he wasn't those outsiders. From the tone in this woman's voice, he could tell whatever they had, they'd better be ready to part with it and quick-like.

"Home," she said. He could hear the smile in her voice. "Perfect. We'll be waiting."

If you enjoyed this story, please pick up a copy of the first novel, THE BREEDERS.

Sixteen-year-old Riley Meemick is one of the world's last free girls. When Riley was born, her mother escaped the Breeders, the group of doctors using cruel experiments to bolster the dwindling human race. Her parents do everything possible to keep her from their clutches-- moving from one desolate farm after another to escape the Breeders' long reach. The Breeders control everything-the local war lords, the remaining factories, the fuel. They have unchecked power in this lawless society. And they're hunting Riley.

When the local Sheriff abducts the adult members of her family and hands her mother over to the Breeders, Riley and her eight-year-old brother, Ethan, hiding in a shelter, are left to starve. Then Clay arrives, the handsome gunslinger who seems determined to help to make up for past sins. The problem is Clay thinks Riley is a bender—a genderless mutation, neither male nor female. As Riley's affection for Clay grows she wonders can she trust Clay with her secret and risk her freedom?

The three embark on a journey across the scarred remains of New Mexico— escaping the Riders who use human sacrifice to appease their Good Mother, various men scrambling for luck, and a deranged lone survivor of a plague. When Riley is forced into the Breeder's hospital, she learns the horrible fate of her mother—a fate she'll share unless she can find a way out.

ABOUT THE AUTHOR

Katie French imagined herself an author when her poem caught the eye of her second grade teacher. In middle school she spent her free time locked in her room, writing her first young adult novel. Though her social life suffered, her love for literature thrived. She studied English at Eastern Michigan University, where she veered from writing and earned an education degree. She spent nine years teaching high school English. Currently she is a school counselor, doing a job that is both one of the hardest things she's ever done and the most rewarding. In her free time she writes, reads great books and takes care of her two beautiful and crazy children. She is a contributor and co-creator of Underground Book Reviews, a website dedicated to erasing the boundaries between traditional and non-traditional publishing. She lives in Michigan with her husband and two children. You can find her at www.katiefrenchbooks.com, on Facebook or Twitter @katielfrench.

ACKNOWLEDGMENTS

The dreaded sequel. Visions of its fiery demise floated in my head for months as I wrote this book. What second book is ever as good as the first? Think of movies. *The Matrix Reloaded?* Terrible. *Back to the Future II?* Bizarre. How could I live up to the mounting expectations of my fans? This was the first book I wrote where people were waiting for it, begging for it even. Wouldn't I just let them down?

Well, the jury is still out in that department, but what I will say is I poured my blood, sweat, and tears into this book. I left no dusty stone unturned, no character unscathed. I hope it reminds you what you loved about *The Breeders* and then takes you to a deeper level of understand in regard to Riley's world. And if it doesn't, at least I know I tried my hardest. That's all I can offer.

Much props and virtual fist-bumps go out to my first readers, Kimberly Shursen, Amy Trueblood and Amy Biddle. A better set of writers and friends does not exist. Thanks to Kimberly for always telling it like it is. Thanks to Amy Trueblood for her editor's eye. Thanks to Amy Biddle for her amazing attention to detail. The book would never be as polished if you three hadn't had your hands on it.

Thanks goes out to my Underground Book Reviews team, Amy Biddle and Brian Braden. Along with Kimberly, you were the ones that helped me believe I could make this dream happen. Thanks to my amazing Indie author friends, Zoe Cannon, Kate Ellison, S.K. Falls, A.G. Henley, Megan Thompson. Go buy their books. You won't be sorry.

Thanks to my cover artist, Andrew Pavlik, who put up with my constantly changing mind. No matter how many fonts I threw at you. Thank you to my agent, Amanda Luedeke, who told me to go for it. Thanks for all your sage advice.

Thanks to my parents who always told me I could. To my family and friends, you hit me with love the size of a Mack truck and I am thoroughly bowled over by it. I'm so blessed to have dozens of people who have my back no matter what. How did I ever get so lucky?

To my children, I love you to the moon and back. Always. And to Ryan, this book is and every book for you, my one and only love.

If you enjoyed this book, please leave a review on Amazon or GoodReads. For updates on more of the series, visit her website at www.ww.katiefrenchbooks.com.